Charlotte and Claudia Keeping in Touch

Charlotte and Claudia Keeping in Touch

A Novel

Joan Barfoot

KEY PORTER BOOKS

Canadian Cataloguing in Publication Data

Barfoot, Joan
Charlotte and Claudia keeping in touch

ISBN 1-55013-557-0

I. Title.

PS8553.A7624C53 1994 C813'.54 C94-931234-7
PR9199.3.B37C53 1994

Key Porter Books Limited
70 The Esplanade
Toronto, Ontario
Canada M5E 1R2

The publisher gratefully acknowledges the assistance of the Canada Council and the Ontario Arts Council.

Design: Tania Craan

Printed and Bound in Canada

98 99 6 5 4 3

one

THE HEDGE WHERE CHARLOTTE IS crouching is cool, green cedar; prickly, but not impenetrable. Fortunately it's been well tended, the branches grown dense over the years, good for camouflage, if not for comfort. Charlotte remembers Andrew telling her about planting it, a painful improvement, among many, to his home. And not only the planting, but the preparations: the consideration given to type of hedge, cost, purpose, maintenance; her recollection is of the time he and his wife must have spent together, perhaps at their kitchen table, looking at evergreen advertisements, discussing budgets and possibilities.

So that would make it more than three decades old.

It's the little things that get a mistress down.

No longer a mistress, and not so much down as merely stooped, Charlotte feels, naturally, like a fool. Who wouldn't?

What if she's spotted? What on earth could she tell a curious neighbour, or the police, or Andrew himself? Just, "I wanted to see how it turned out"? How would that sound to someone who discovered her hunched in his hedge, peeking through branches at his home?

It may no longer even be his home. What if she's settling in here to watch someone else entirely, a different portrait altogether of domestic life?

But it's still the address listed for him in the phone book. She was surprised he hadn't moved in all these years. Of course, she hasn't moved, either. Would that surprise him?

Or it might be only his wife left here now, Andrew's widow. In telephone books and other public, official documents, women don't usually advertise that they're on their own.

Whoever lives here, Charlotte does wish they had let the cedars grow a bit higher as well as thick, so that she wouldn't have to hunker down this way. Even after just a few minutes, she's not too sure she'll be able to straighten up again, unfold her legs and stride away. What if she gets herself stuck here?

She must make quite a picture: a tall old woman in a green track suit, parting prickly branches to peer at a house where nothing appears to be happening.

Silly old woman. Would that be an excuse, if she were caught? Could she just say, "Well, I'm old and foolish, that's all." And then promise, to avoid hospital or nursing home, "It won't happen again. Really, it was just a whim. I was just curious. It won't happen again."

With considerable effort, she has pulled branches aside, clearing a small space and a somewhat less obstructed view for herself. The house is just as Andrew used to describe it: white clapboard, one-storey, rather stretched out. What they used to call ranch style? Charlotte remembers it has three bedrooms. One for each of the boys, one for Andrew and his wife. She

doesn't recall much of what he told her of the other rooms. The bedrooms were haunting enough.

"The man who lives here used to be my lover," she might say to a discoverer. "For years and years."

Of course what would have been the point of keeping the secret so carefully for almost a decade, only to blurt it out now, when they're both old (if he's still even alive) and only harm could come of it? She suffered at the time from discretion; silly now to make that mean nothing.

"I'll go first," he would say outside a bar or a restaurant. "Make sure there's nobody here we might know." Or, planning a rare trip together, "I think this'd be safe. We aren't likely to run into anyone."

Charlotte shakes her head. You'd think she had no brains at all. What efforts she contributed to sustaining his marriage – more than his wife could have dreamed of.

So if they're together in this house she's peering at through these difficult branches, really, they have her to thank. All these years together they will owe to Charlotte's discretion. And compassion. And, after all, a reluctance that may have equalled Andrew's to make some huge and critical, life-altering decision. She wouldn't have wanted to be responsible for so much upheaval.

He wouldn't have been happy, if that had happened.

She could never tell what exactly would have made her happy. At any rate, she rarely was, not with a full heart. You can't be full-heartedly happy when there's really no hope. You can only have moments of joy.

And now, in her old age, she has turned into a spy.

What's the right answer? That Andrew still lives here, or no longer does? Which way would she want it to have turned out?

She spent a few hours last week scouting the neighbourhood. The people next door go to work early each morning,

don't return until dinner time. This leaves her nine hours to linger in the hedge between the properties, shielded from the street. Shielded as long as other neighbours don't glimpse her, as long as Andrew and his wife don't spot her from one of their windows, as long as a stray person, like a meter reader, doesn't come plunging onto the property, stumbling into her.

Or dogs – lord, she never thought of dogs! Skunks, raccoons, curious squirrels – there must be wildlife in the suburbs. Charlotte is a kind of wildlife herself.

If she stayed here for a whole nine hours, she'd be paralysed. Every muscle in her body would have contracted, seized up, the blood would have slowed, she'd have pins and needles and cramps, and of course she'd need desperately to go to the bathroom.

She'd just have to wet herself, and topple over; go to sleep and die here.

So she really can't stay long.

Enormous events are happening in the world: wars and hunger, injustices, and movements towards freedom of one sort or another. In a very few weeks Charlotte will have her seventieth birthday, and there are still a million things to think about and do. It isn't possible to keep up with the books she wants to read, the movies she wants to see, the music she wants to listen to, the places she wants to visit and the conversations she wants to overhear or take part in, the letters she needs to write or the people she'd like to meet, the thoughts she needs to think and the events she needs to clarify in the unknown length of time she has before she gets dotty or sick or dies. And what is she doing? She's hanging around a strange neighbourhood, hoping to spot a man she hasn't seen, or really so often thought about, in almost thirty years.

It may be too late to worry about getting dotty.

She never was inside his house. Even when his wife went

away without him, and even when he asked her, Charlotte never went. She had, she admitted, somewhat peculiar standards: that she would make love with him, and laugh with him and talk and listen to him, she would touch his body and his face and his hair as if they were her own, but she would not sit on his wife's sofa, and certainly would not sleep in her bed.

Andrew didn't seem to care. "But I'd like you to see where I live," he urged. "How can you care for me if you can't picture where I am?"

Her pictures were vivid enough, without giving them real colours and shapes. She had enough trouble imagining him walking naked through his house in the mornings, stepping in and out of the shower, pouring out cereal, perhaps offering farewell embraces to its inhabitants at the door, without knowing exactly where the bathroom was or what colour it was painted. She didn't particularly want to know if the kitchen table was pine or plastic.

If it turns out that Andrew and his wife aren't home, might she break in today? Creep around to the back, find an unlatched window and step inside to tour and touch?

Oh my, she must be mad.

Anyway, there's a car in the driveway. A silver Volvo. Andrew used to laugh at cars like that. He drove a Volks; the early kind that's now a classic, then was only a sort of reverse snobbery. How else might he have changed? When he and Charlotte parted, did he give up, slide back beneath the sheets of his wife's bed, raise his boys and settle down?

Charlotte supposes that, contrary to appearances today, she is settling down herself. This is her first adventure in quite some time; her first outing into what might be a perilous circumstance.

Well, not perilous exactly. Potentially humiliating.

Potentially? It *is* humiliating, if only to herself, even if no one else sees her, catches her, questions her. There is something extraordinarily debasing about this position she's in. If she were watching a character in a television program doing this, she might look away, so as not to be peering into that woman's shame.

To say she is curious hardly covers this circumstance. The most profound curiosity couldn't account for this.

If she succeeds (and success may be merely absence of disaster) who knows what she might try next?

At least she's not bored. At least she feels bold.

She'll be fine as long as Andrew doesn't decide this is the day to trim the hedge.

Who keeps the gardens? There are large half-oval plots, defined at their edges by round, whitewashed, uniform stones; one descends, from tall plants to small, outside the bay windows of what may be the living-room, the other, in similar tall-to-small style beneath what are likely the bedrooms, on the opposite side of the solid, blue front door. And on the front lawn, at the base of a magnolia tree, a circle of blooming impatiens. It's all very tidy, very neat and enclosed. But then Andrew was not, when it came to the point, especially adventuresome. His wife may have been cautious as well. Charlotte wouldn't know. She never met the woman.

Andrew sometimes seemed to regard Charlotte as an adventure, exciting enough.

Why on earth does she care?

Well, if this position-in-the-hedge is humiliating, think what a foolish woman she'd have been to spend almost a decade dodging about in the darkness with a man with ordinary longings! With a man who perhaps considered her something of a thrill, an exotic specimen in an otherwise calm, sturdy and in the end preferable, life. It would be a sorry

thing for him to turn out to have been ordinary.

For all those years he was her lover, a man. Now he seems to be less flesh than a possible answer to a question she hasn't quite formed.

How can he bear all this quiet? No children, no cars, no voices – a few birds, that seems about all. Charlotte's used to buses and ambulances, car horns, kids yelling on their way past her house from school, a city raucousness that sometimes strikes her as lonely; but never as lonely as this. This is like being dead. She hears birds and her own breathing.

And the sound now of a door clicking open – that's how quiet it is, that across this green stretch of lawn, she can hear the front door opening. And voices.

Two young boys run outside, chasing each other across the lawn, so that Charlotte, startled, shrinks back a little although still holding the cedar branches aside, afraid to let them move, and anyway, wanting to see. One boy is a little older, bigger than the other, although neither looks to be a teenager yet. They're both wearing sneakers and blue jeans and T-shirts, one white with red indecipherable printing, the other plain blue. The smaller boy tackles the larger around the ankles, bringing him down. These cannot be Andrew's sons; the boys for whom, he used to tell her, he felt such an intense and protective love that whatever happened, he couldn't bring himself to pull their small lives down around their ears. Not those boys, no. Those boys must be grown up and gone.

But perhaps this is one of them now, stepping through the door, a tall, straight-spined middle-aged man yelling, "Cut it out. Come back here and say goodbye to your grandparents and get in the car. You'll get dirt on the seats. Just quit it right now!" He sounds impatient and irritable, but not angry. He might have sounded angry if his father had left him, years ago, back when that was a thought spoken out loud.

Isn't it interesting that Charlotte, who might have entirely altered that man's young life, is watching from the hedge as he calls to his boys, and he's as unaware of her as he must have been then. What accidents and enormous possibilities must surely hang around the edges of everyone's vision, invisible and undreamed of, but with the potential to cause chaos. Or, for that matter, to cause incalculable pleasure, who knows? And sometimes those possibilities step into the picture and sometimes they don't.

Charlotte is no longer hearing the birds, but she does hear her heartbeat. What if she had a heart attack, right here? It wouldn't matter so much if she had a heart attack right here and died, but what if she didn't die? What if she had to sit up later in a hospital bed and explain?

"Where's Dad?" she hears the straight-spined young man ask, turning back to the doorway.

One hand on the frame, one foot on the top step, wearing a smile, short-cropped grey hair and grey trousers, white blouse, something glittering around her neck, is a very small old woman. Can this be who Andrew wouldn't leave?

Well hardly. That woman, like Charlotte, like Andrew as well, was thirty years younger. Otherwise, yes, it must be the same woman, as Charlotte is the same woman, essentially, she was then, and Andrew, no doubt, the same man. Really, only hair changes greatly, and faces and bodies.

Hard to feel much stirring, except of curiosity, at this sighting, finally, of her rival.

How jealous Charlotte was of this woman! How bitter and frightened. Perhaps she should have agreed to meet her, after all. Perhaps Charlotte made her, in her mind, too powerful and large.

But then, she was powerful. She did end up with Andrew.

"He's still in the bathroom," the woman says. "He'll be out in

a minute. You sure you can't stay? We'd love to have you stay, you know."

So she's one of those clinging women; the kind who can't bear to let go. Charlotte watches a flicker of irritation appear, then vanish from the young man's face. "No, Mom, I told you, we've got to hit the road. The boys have school tomorrow. They shouldn't have been out today."

"Oh now, they're smart, a few days out of school doesn't hurt them."

"Yeah, Dad." The smaller one is laughing. Charlotte sees that when he laughs his entire face crinkles. It's not that she hasn't always understood that children can be, no doubt should be, irresistible. It made her wonder, in her work, at how many parents found their own children so resistible they could hurt them, sometimes badly.

This boy, these boys, don't look as if they get hurt. It is interesting, after all, that Charlotte's care and discretion and fear years ago must have had something to do with the smooth tenor of the lives of these boys. And of that man, and that old woman. Perhaps she should be proud.

"Then do you know when you can come again? Stay longer next time, plan to stay longer." Good lord, the woman knows nothing about letting people go free – no wonder Andrew decided it would be too complicated, hard.

Or it could be that she does know about other people's freedom, and it has terrified her.

Maybe the man in the bathroom isn't even Andrew. Maybe he's some other husband entirely, achieved after Andrew's departure with some more insistent, post-Charlotte mistress.

What a word, mistress! Conjuring up ropes and domination. Not appropriate at all to how it really was.

Charlotte's head is keeping very busy. Andrew is about to appear. She will see him any moment. And if she wanted to,

she couldn't avoid that moment. She must not move, or she'll be caught. And in any case her limbs are locked.

"There you are, Dad," the young man says, perhaps with relief. "Boys, come say goodbye. We have to hit the road."

He doesn't seem as tall as he used to. Except for a small, thin-man's belly, he still looks trim. He has a good head of hair, although it's gone white. He stands straight, like his son. She can't see his eyes. It used to be that Charlotte could look into his eyes and believe she saw precisely what was in his heart, on his mind.

He steps past his wife, down the steps. She follows him. He embraces his grandsons. He puts his hand on his son's shoulder. He is smiling. Three decades ago he embraced Charlotte. He placed those same hands on her breasts, between her legs. Under the crisp tan pants and shirt he's wearing is the body she used to touch and kiss and lick, that loomed over her and lunged up at her. She is dizzy, within the cool protective greenness of the cedar hedge, not with lust, but wonder.

The boys climb into the car (so the silver Volvo isn't Andrew's). Their father gets behind the wheel. They all roll down windows and call out goodbyes. Hands wave and the car backs out of the driveway. It begins to move slowly down the street. The boys are still shouting goodbye, and they and their father are waving. On the lawn, Andrew puts one arm around his wife's shoulders. He waves with his free hand. So does she. They look all right together. They look content. Or reconciled.

The woman turns to go back inside the house. Andrew bends to pull something, a weed, out of the half-oval garden beneath what is likely a bedroom window. He still looks lithe, for his age. He is a year older than Charlotte.

It might have been worse. He might have been dead, or decrepit. There might have been nothing to see. This was not the

ending she would have had in mind, although if she'd thought, she might have expected this.

She wonders why she didn't think. She wonders what she expected. She wonders how she feels about this little family scene she's watched.

She wonders, as Andrew heads into the house and closes the door behind him, if she's going to be able to stand straight again, with the muscles in her legs and back so tight. It is a slow process, and she doesn't get her back realigned properly until she's almost home, and later she has trouble sleeping, wakened by moments of pain; so she has plenty of time during the night to wonder what the hell she thought she was doing, and what the hell she expected to accomplish.

two

"DEAR CHARLOTTE,

"After so long you will, perhaps, be surprised to hear from me. I know it's been ages – more than a year? And I can imagine how impatiently you may read this. I imagine you thinking how selfish I am, only writing when I need something.

"Because I feel most particularly the need for a friend right now. Well, for you, really, not just anyone. Someone who knows me in her bones. I wonder, do many people still have someone in their lives (as I hope I have you, and vice versa, of course) who has known them practically forever?

"I am addicted at the moment to nostalgia. Or no, not quite that sort of fondness for one's history. More an awful desire to make sense. I seem to have become a sort of pathologist of my own soul, turning over organs and events with shiny (bloody) tools, trying to make a pattern, or give a diagnosis. Something.

"You will say, no doubt, that I am evading (or babbling), and of course it's true, I am. How crisp you've always been! I hear you telling me, as you did once, 'You know, you always turn things into an image, you never just look at a thing as itself.' I expect you were right. I guess I thought making a picture might make something more clear, or show it from a different angle, but maybe it was just a matter of obscuring the view.

"And there, you will say, she's doing it again. I can't seem to help myself.

"But let me say this my way. I'm surprised how difficult it is. I've written to other people (just with the news) and the words haven't come so hard, but this – this is unexpectedly hard.

"Because you know me so well, I suppose. And because I know how little you liked Bradley. It felt to me as if I'd failed you, marrying him, and then staying with him. Or that I'd made myself less than you hoped. You never understood, did you? But I had some feeling for him, in spite of everything.

"You are so lucky, not to have had to hold on to certain feelings through sheer *will*. In for the long haul, it's so *necessary*. But you never believed that, I think. At least it was never your choice.

"It was mine, though. It really is a choice, you know. You look at someone or something and think, 'This is what I must do. This is what I must train myself to feel, and to believe.' It can be done, some of the time, at least.

"Oh dear, it really is hard to come to the point. But then, perhaps that sort of thing *is* the point. The rest is only what is new, what's been happening.

"And that (my dear, impatient Charlotte) is that Bradley has died. We were married forty-seven years, isn't that extraordinary? I think it's a quite remarkable length of time. I remember when to be forty-seven years old seemed ancient (but that was when we were young), and now it turns out I lived forty-seven

years with a single human being! Not counting all the years before that. And now, all the years after.

"Those are the years that trouble me now, the ones ahead. And I can't seem to get to them. I can't seem to pull myself out of this swamp of history and into the next thing.

"How have you been able to do that? Part of your clarity, I suppose, declaring one thing finished, the next ready to begin. I've always been more of a coward. And yet it worked, didn't it? We must choose somehow the best ways to get along. You have done splendidly being brave and decisive, and I, I must say, have not done badly by working with what I've had, and putting off decisions until the need to make them goes away. You know, whatever you've thought over the years, he was always in my life, one way and another. I don't think I knew until recently how huge that was, his part of me. I thought of us (although this may sound foolish) as inseparable in a peculiar way. It turns out, of course, that we are not inseparable; but I do feel as if there's been some kind of amputation: some large limb or organ has gone missing, and if it wasn't exactly essential, I am somewhat crippled without it. I don't know if it will always feel that way (you read about the phantom pains of amputees, don't you? They seem to go on and on, although perhaps people simply get used to them).

"I have always thought it's important to do your best. Then at the end, whatever form the end takes, a quarrel or death, some disaster – at least then, if you believe you've done your best, there can hardly be guilt, or self-reproach. That's what I believed, and yet, you know, I could have been better. I could have done better. And there is also one terrible, enormous flaw.

"I know you'd say he could have done better also, and of course he could. In every way Bradley could have been better. But then, it was my rule, not his, to do the best possible. It

wouldn't have been reasonable to expect him to follow some rule that wasn't his.

"I find I have become frighteningly reasonable in my old age. Perhaps that makes you and me more similar than we have been, perhaps we have many things in common these days.

"The one thing I haven't really wondered since Bradley's been gone is whether I should have made some other choice. Well, there's no point in wondering that sort of thing, is there? But even if I were inclined to, I'd believe that while we may have had (well, we did have) some bitterly unhappy times, there is much to be gained from bitter unhappiness. I've become quite strong, for one thing. I'm not sure that's the best it's done for me, but I want you to know there are things about me now you could admire, and which might surprise you.

"This must seem an odd and confusing letter. I find my mind jumping all over the place these days, although I hope most people can't see that. Ordinarily, for instance, I can write quite a plain and coherent letter, and I've been doing a good deal of that, letting people know that Bradley's gone.

"Isn't that silly? Why do I say 'gone'? I hear your voice saying, 'For heaven's sake, Claudia, he's *dead*, not just gone.' Remember how we laughed at that Oscar Wilde line – Lady Bracknell was it? When someone said he'd lost a relative, and she remarked on how careless that was, losing someone as if the person were merely a mislaid parcel.

"But indeed Bradley is gone, finally and forever.

"If you find this jumbled, I'm sure you'll understand it in the spirit in which it's so hastily and badly written. I feel you can follow me, you've always been able to.

"I think, you know, that past a certain point it's too hard to make real friends. There's too much missing that they can't know (and that you can't know about them). It gets impossible to fill in enough details and blanks for them to catch up.

"Although I suppose an advantage of new friends is that you can become a new person with them. They have no way to tell.

"I wonder how you look these days? I see you – angular, I think. Distinguished. Elegant and spare, rather regal, which must be a grand way to age. Me, I've gotten plumper. (Not fat, I won't admit to fat, but plump, yes.) I've heard of people unable to eat with the grief of widowhood. I have been ravenous. I keep trying to fill myself up, but I could eat until I got sick and never feel *quite* full. I'll have to get a grip on that, or I truly will be fat. Still, for the time being I'm regarding this as a period of self-indulgence, a kind of compensation. (Not, I wouldn't want you to think, that any amount of food makes up for Bradley's absence. Really.)

"You know, a picture just flashed past my mind's eye of when we were little. I admired you so much, even then, when we were just starting school! You looked as if you were already sure of so much. And of course you were. Did I ever tell you (I must have, we must have talked about how friendships start) how utterly, blissfully thrilled I was when you asked me to be your partner when we lined up to go outside for recess, or for skipping, or for walking home from school? Truly, you know, I don't think I was so excited when I first fell in love!

"Does that sound excessive? But then, the emotions of children are always excessive. How did you see me then, when you chose me to be your friend?

"I never felt I chose you. I always believed you chose me.

"I didn't choose Bradley, either. I wouldn't have dared. But I wonder now, what did the two of you see in me, you when we were six, he years later?

"Are we old Charlotte? Are we done?

"I never see you done. I always see you headed for the next thing, whatever it is. What thing are you trying now, Charlotte?

"I have something to tell, but I can't say it in a letter. It's

huge, like a big black balloon filling me up, squeezing important bits and pieces into just tiny, leftover crannies. Do you see your insides like a picture? As if they're the geography of a desert or an ocean, or like some other planet entirely? Sometimes I do. Perhaps I learned that watching Bradley in the past few months. His body became such a mystery, changing on the outside, and with so much corruption inside, creeping and creeping. I really grew to hate that, knowing awful things were happening beyond where I could see.

"Perhaps you will say it was always like that for me, with Bradley. But those were avoidable matters, not like feeling him decay before my eyes.

"Have you ever spent time with a dying person? If so, you'll likely know what I mean. If you haven't, I don't think I can describe it. But the skin changes. It loses moisture, or mobility – something, anyway, so it's not quite alive any more. And the eyes turn inward. Not physically, I don't mean that, but as if they're not really seeing you. They're looking somewhere past you, or inside. Bradley came to look as if he was staring into his own head, at his own visions.

"Well of course people dying that way, slowly and immovably, lose muscle tone, get weak, so there's that. But oh, Charlotte, what I didn't know about, what was worst, was the smell! His breath, his body, all changing and terrible. As if he was dead before he was dead.

"But then, there were things inside him that were rotting. Did I mention it was cancer?

"Of course it was cancer. It almost always is, isn't it?

"Are you frightened of death?

"You may be surprised to hear that I'm not any more, not for a second. I am terrified, though, of dying.

"And of course I have no one to look after me, not the way I cared for Bradley. Oh, the girls would come, I wouldn't want

you to think they aren't fine, loving women, and they'd come. I'd be afraid of dying in front of one of them, though, or all of them. I'd be afraid of what I might say.

"In Bradley's illness, he often surprised me. He said some things he would have bitten off his tongue to avoid saying when he took care over words. He told me secrets he'd kept from me for years. I expect you know, or could guess, some of them.

"I wouldn't want that to happen to me. Not in front of the girls. Strangers, maybe it wouldn't matter. Why would they care?

"I imagine you've thought my life has been fairly dull, just raising my girls, running my home, trying to survive with Bradley. By and large that's true. But now there's this terrible thing, and I'm frightened of it spilling out when I'm not able to stop it. It's funny, the deeper and darker a secret is, the more it seems to need letting out, at the end. That's how it was with Bradley, anyway, that some things had been locked away inside him so tightly that as soon as he was weak, out they leaped!

"At least that's a nice way of looking at it.

"I'm so grateful you're my friend. So many years! Oh, I hope you're still my friend. That you're not away somewhere, off doing some new thing, or too busy and involved with someone else. You may think that's quite a nerve, when I've been too busy and involved with someone else to be in touch, at least for the past year. I hope you'll understand, I was nursing Bradley. For the most part, I cared for him at home. There was no time, I had no strength. I can't begin to describe how it was.

"At least I'm not so weary any more. And I sure could use my friend.

"Oh, look at that word – use! I didn't mean it that way.

"Please, if you can, write to me. I want to know you're there. I'm lonely, Charlotte, I feel all alone. Not just because Bradley's gone, but because I'm scared.

"I have to say I'm sorry about this letter. It is, I know, typical self-absorbed Claudia. Will you understand if I just say I do care how you are and what you're doing, and I hope you'll tell me everything you can about yourself these days? I would like to be your good friend again, and I'm stronger now than you can likely imagine. I have, in recent weeks, quite surprised myself, one way and another. I bet I could surprise you, too!

"Meanwhile I hope you're well, and that your life is, too.

"Love,

"Claudia"

. . . .

She would have hoped, having written this most difficult letter, addressed the envelope, searched out a stamp, set it on the bedside table, finished and waiting to be mailed tomorrow, that she could now simply turn out the lamp, lie back and rest. She does turn out the light and lie back. But sleep – why can't Claudia sleep?

Too many pictures whipping across the screen of her closed eyelids like a frantic, speeded-up movie, no plot, no dialogue, just flickering, familiar figures. So much conflict – she feels the resentment and rage of the figures aimed at her. Were so many of the people she loved so angry with her? Or is it that all this time she was furious with them?

Whatever it amounts to, the turbulence keeps her restless, night after night. She would say (and did say on the telephone tonight to Sonia, the oldest of her now middle-aged daughters), "I'm fine, except for not getting any sleep at all," but of course that isn't true. Of course she sleeps finally, although sometimes waking sharply, like a child from a nightmare, confused and on the verge of action. She has found herself flailing, reaching out to strike, or holding up her hands as if fending something off. The nightmares, as she can only assume they

must be to cause this, vanish in the instant of waking, but they must grow out of those night visions.

Sonia said, sympathetically, "Yes, it must be hard to get used to sleeping alone. But you have to get a proper rest, Mother. If you're really having trouble, see a doctor, why don't you? I know you don't like drugs, but some pills just until you're over the hump would be a good idea."

Maybe because she's the oldest, Sonia has always tended to sound definite. Or, the more negative way of looking at it, somewhat bossy. She has appeared in some of Claudia's night visions lecturing and even hectoring, mouth open and closing, finger wagging, but silent so Claudia can't hear whatever instructions she is intended to receive.

Sonia has a good heart, though, and never, in real life, wags fingers. She wants the best for Claudia and, no doubt, for her three sisters, and for their families, as well as her own, and for her neighbours, friends, community and all the earth, for that matter. If everyone would only do as she suggests, it would be a better world, of course it would. Sonia doesn't like standing back watching others make mistakes. She does like to leap in and help, and prevent.

Sandra, the daughter next in age to Sonia, is better at helping to pick up the pieces following errors of judgement committed by people who have failed to follow Sonia's advice.

But each of the four girls – women – Sharon and Susan also, has her virtues. Claudia has been very fortunate in her motherhood, give or take some volatile, if predictable, times.

She has no intention of asking any doctor for drugs. For one thing, and this may come of being of the generation she is, she suspects sleeping pills or tranquillizers are an admission of an inability to cope. People of her times have believed it necessary to face and confront. That was their strength. Or so it seems, in general, to Claudia. Obviously there have been people who

have not coped, faced or confronted, but that was seen to be their failure, their weakness and their breaking down. Claudia will not be weak, and she doesn't intend to fail herself and certainly will not break down.

More important, though, and more personal, she believes something about these night visions and nightmares: that she must try to be patient, watch and absorb them even if she can't understand them. They are, however silent, speaking to her, and she'd really better pay attention.

And if she lets them run their course (hoping, naturally, that their course will complete itself at some reasonable, non-terminal point), they'll be finished; whereas if she tries to avert them, they'll just return, catching her off guard in a more innocent, less frightening future.

It seems to Claudia that this is a time, like the months of Bradley's illness, that she simply has to survive. If she can only get from this moment to the next, from this night to tomorrow, there will be an ending; completion of some kind.

Not that, during Bradley's illness, she considered herself to be waiting for his death. Although that was obviously the completion they were headed for.

Did she ever think, as she tried to care for him, "Oh, I wish this was over, I wish he'd just *die*"? He behaved so badly, often; worse than during his healthiest, most rambunctious years. As if he were testing her, or her devotion, or his power over her. "I need a drink," he'd command, and she would bring him ginger ale. "I mean a *drink*, not this shit. Get me a rye. And pull me up, I'll choke to death drinking it lying down like this. Are you trying to kill me, woman?"

When he was angry, he called her "woman." As if she were some generic object of loathing. She thought, "Well, he's dying," but didn't examine whether she meant that excused his cruelty, or that it could hardly matter if he had a shot of rye,

or that it didn't matter what he wanted and what he called her, he wouldn't last much longer.

She didn't hate him. She did pity him, for his pain, but also because he appeared determined to leave life in such ill-humoured fashion. He insisted on testing her right to the end.

She was determined not to fail. It wasn't so much a matter of failing him, since he was going to die at some point anyway, but of failing herself: because she would be living on, judging her own results and stuck with whatever they were. She didn't want to have to live with anything undone she might have done.

Sonia suggested it was merely a matter of learning to sleep without him. Whatever was she thinking? She must know Claudia and Bradley hadn't occupied the same bed for a long time, even before he got ill; that Claudia had already had her share of sad, dry, passionless nights without a shoulder to touch, or a breath to listen to if she woke up scared.

Well, she got over that, didn't she? Even turned it into a sort of pleasure, the luxury of reading herself to sleep, or waking in the middle of the night hungry, making a sandwich, carrying it back to bed to eat propped up, lights on, scattering crumbs and clinking glasses and plates. Bradley wouldn't have liked that; he wouldn't have permitted it. This added to her pleasure.

Now, of course, there's no one here to disapprove of secret pleasures. Secrets require another human, but now she can do anything she wants, and that turns out, in Bradley's absence, to be meaningless.

Charlotte would say Bradley was hardly human anyway. Claudia giggles at the sound, inside her head, of her friend's dry, cutting voice. It was sometimes difficult to have a husband and a best friend who despised each other, it certainly caused some awkward moments, but whatever else Bradley demanded of her, and Claudia acquiesced to, she never gave up Charlotte.

"I don't want you seeing her any more," he ordered once. "You're different after you've been together, I can always tell when she's been here, and I don't like it."

"Oh, don't be silly, she's my oldest friend. Of course I'm going to see her. And anyway, what do you mean, I'm different?"

"Just what I said. You get stubborn and, frankly, it's not attractive the way you talk. You get like her instead of yourself. *You* wouldn't tell me not to be silly, *you* wouldn't tell me you're going to do something when I don't want you to. That's her, that's how you get after you've been talking to her."

Claudia didn't answer, but also never stopped seeing Charlotte. At least not until they found themselves in different cities, and it wasn't so easy to visit.

It was a little disappointing, though, that Bradley didn't know his own wife better. Apparently he didn't recognize Claudia's voice, admittedly somewhat unleashed by Charlotte, but still her own. He must have thought her awfully weak and susceptible; a mistake, if not one she found it necessary to point out to him.

How long will it take for Charlotte to get Claudia's letter? But perhaps she's away, off on one of her jaunts. Or maybe she's dead, throttled or stabbed by one of her broken-winged, broken-brained urchins. Who would think to let Claudia know? Childless Charlotte leaves behind no one who would necessarily know of Claudia.

Not like when Claudia dies. Then her daughters will take turns on the phone, calling everyone they can think of who was acquainted with her. Even at that, Claudia fears a small funeral. Outside of relatives, she means, of whom she has plenty, taking the far-flung grandchildren into account. Relatives, though, have a stake in her life; how many would be on hand just because of liking Claudia, or having been touched by her?

Still, there were a few unexpected faces at Bradley's funeral,

some unforeseen tears, and more. At least those secrets he spilled towards the end left her, if not undistressed, not terribly surprised by odd appearances at the service.

She wonders if he was out of his mind, delirious with the need to unburden himself, or if this was just another aspect of his final cruelties. She might as well assume it was both, given that she'll never know, and that it likely *was* both.

She can still hear that rasping, aching voice going on and on, feel that grasping, gaunt hand gripping her wrist, holding her so tightly she was forced to lean in, to listen to events he clearly, and sensibly, had thought it unwise for her to know while they were going on. This continued for as long as his voice would hold out, which blessedly wasn't for more than a few minutes at a time. He got so angry, hearing his words fade, turned dark with the effort to say just a few more, to cause her just a little more pain.

Did he hate her so much? In her nightmarish visions, his face can be twisted with something like hatred.

At any rate that's the way he ended up, in a whine and rasp of cruelty.

When she first met him, he was rather splendidly cruel.

Well, no, that makes him sound like a Nazi and her like an idiot. It wasn't that he was cruel then, splendidly or otherwise; but that there was a sense about him of hardness and danger. This could be, and often was misinterpreted, including by Claudia, as both comforting and adventurous. The hardness made it seem it would be safe to lean against him in perilous times. That edge that signified an acceptance and even seeking out of danger meant he would offer the unexpected to more timid souls. Claudia found this an excitingly safe prospect, and naturally fell in love.

Even more naturally considering he was lean and older, handsome in that mid-century way that is now unfashionable.

But even now Claudia's body can be tugged by the view on the street of a lean dark-haired man, if he is moving as if he knows himself and is confident in what he knows. Bradley strode, and when he was still, he stood straight and close to the object of his attention. With Claudia, courting, he would look down with his brown, grave eyes intent, and she felt assessed and was flattered that, having assessed, he decided to approve of her. "You're a lovely woman, Claudia," he told her in his then rich and serious voice. "A good woman, I believe." And so she was, in those days.

So she still is.

She remains startled by how much and how sharply she sometimes misses him. If ever, during the past long year, there drifted through her mind the wispy, fleeting idea that she'd be relieved to have it over (to have, to be blunt, *him* over), it was true in its way, but in only a relatively small and quite specific way. It's true she doesn't miss turning him, or trying to quiet his pain, or hurrying up and down stairs, attending to his wants, demands, for this or that, and certainly she doesn't miss watching him change, so that each day came to mean a shrinking or some alteration in his colour. She doesn't miss, as she tried to describe to Charlotte in the letter, the way he came to smell, the evident and terrible decay. She doesn't miss the grating sounds of his efforts to breathe.

It seems she does miss the fact that there was a smell, and there were sounds, and certainly there were things to do, efforts to be made, routines to follow. She would never want to return him to life if it meant he had to suffer again all that unrelievable pain; but she does miss his existence. His presence was at least a purpose, and one, however it became altered and distorted, that was familiar. Forty-seven years! A lifetime of consciousness of another human in the house, however that human behaved from day to day.

Even pain was something, even misery. And whatever Charlotte may have thought (and she needn't think Claudia wasn't aware of her views, that tight-lipped sucking in of air, it was the same as if she'd gone ahead and spoken) – whatever Charlotte or anyone else may have thought, all those years were by no means entirely difficult. If Bradley created a certain amount of grief, he also was the source, for Claudia, of moments of such joy and relief and, yes, perhaps love, at any rate desire, that pain became, for the moment, unreal in her heart, and she could almost have thought none of it had happened and it was all her own creation. Because how could the same man contain so much?

But he did, of course. Now, from the distance of his death, from the coolness of this perspective and from some fresh knowledge of herself, she can quite see the extremes.

The nice choice would be to recall only the joy, and let the rest die with him. There's no purpose in brooding, and if she couldn't understand at the time, it's unlikely there's any amount of going over and over events that will make them clear now.

How odd, to be with a man for forty-seven years and be left still unanswered at the end.

It would be cheating, though, wouldn't it, to fix a false image, to design some benign picture for comfort? She may not be as rigorous as Charlotte, but equally, she's not a cheat.

What did Bradley believe about an afterlife? The basic heaven and hell, she supposes, but he was hardly a theologian, and was anyway impatient with questions that couldn't be answered. "Why worry about it?" he'd ask, so that Claudia learned to keep some thoughts to herself, or at least from him. "I do not see the point of wasting time on things you can't do anything about, even if there was an answer you could figure out, which there isn't." A man of action in his way, her Bradley,

although she couldn't help thinking he was the one who missed the point.

Charlotte, on the other hand, was apt to say, "The most interesting events are the ones in your own head. All those questions and unknowns. The rest's just plot, it just gives some grounding and a focus."

Claudia didn't entirely agree with that, either. Her children and Bradley, for instance, were far more than mere plot, they were meaning, too; but Charlotte, lacking children and mate, wouldn't have realized that. Charlotte likely spoke what was true enough for her, but made the statement too sweeping, applying it far too broadly.

There are ways in which Claudia's husband and her friend were not dissimilar. Which, Claudia supposes, may say more about her than them.

They met on a beach, she and Bradley. And Charlotte as well, for that matter. Charlotte had suggested the outing. "Let's go watch men in bathing suits." She grinned. Perhaps Charlotte was merely ahead of her time. Certainly she fit more comfortably into subsequent decades than Claudia, who has never felt at ease with developments that have included loud demands and raucous jokes.

At any rate, off the two of them went to the beach, Charlotte driving her father's grey Hudson, and for all Charlotte's intentions, it was Claudia who found the man. Who was found by the man.

They were lying on beach towels, each, daringly, in the bold two-piece bathing suits of the time (hardly bold at all considering what's worn now, even by Claudia's daughters, who are well past the unlined, unmarked tautness of lithe youth). Their eyes were closed, and there was a lull in their conversation. Claudia remembers herself almost falling asleep in the heat of the sun, with the rhythm of small waves on the shore a few yards away.

She felt a shadow fall over her, a cloud passing over the sun. But a voice made the cloud a man, and her eyes flashed open, so that she was looking up through her dark glasses at a figure, only a figure, no features, framed by the light. "Excuse me, I hope I'm not disturbing you," he said. "I wonder if you know what time it is? I forgot to take off my watch in the water and it seems to have stopped."

It was Charlotte who sat up lazily, groped in her beach bag and drew out her watch, told him the time. As if, briefly naïve, she thought that was what he really wanted.

Claudia, unreasonably (or irrationally) dazzled, merely stared up, not stirring until the voice said, "Would you ladies mind if I joined you?" And suddenly he was seated cross-legged at the bottom of Claudia's beach towel, and deep brown eyes were regarding the two of them in friendly, apparently frank and guileless fashion.

Claudia remembers thinking, "Oh, no, now I'm going to be the third." She thought someone so attractive, even handsome, would lean towards the intense and vivid Charlotte. Claudia was almost used to that, although it was hard at moments like this, when they were miles from home, and Charlotte had the car. Now the rest of Claudia's day would be at the mercy of what this man and Charlotte decided to do.

And it was hard, after all, it was only natural that it was hard, to be the one not chosen. Not that Charlotte wasn't careful to take Claudia into account, she was always included; but could hardly help feeling herself trailing behind, like an unwanted little sister.

That afternoon, though, it began not to feel that way. It felt as if, when they talked, it was the three of them talking; and maybe even more attention was paid to her quiet self. Charlotte seemed more than usually sharp-tongued, even argumentative, although Claudia can't recall now much of what they

spoke about. A stranger like him might not have heard that extra edge in Charlotte's voice, but he couldn't have missed the fact that she kept contradicting him.

Claudia was more content to listen and confirm.

Was it, she wondered even at the time, that Charlotte could feel that his attraction was directed more to Claudia than to herself? Did that annoy her, make her proud, make her want to taunt him first, to show she didn't care?

Whatever, it made them prickly with each other right off the bat, and that never improved.

Or perhaps Charlotte really did see through him. But what did she see? He wasn't evil, he was just a man.

He'd been a soldier, and he talked about the war and where he'd been, he'd even been to Germany towards the end. He seemed brave and glamorous and sophisticated to Claudia, who hadn't been anywhere. Who didn't actually want to be anywhere, given that so much of the world suffered violence and illness and poverty and hunger. Who would deliberately seek out suffering, even a view of other people's that one was not required to share?

Bradley never showed much inclination to travel, either, after that one wartime outing. He also seemed content with what he had come home to.

He and Charlotte argued about the war; tactics, rather than the intent of it. Even Charlotte couldn't have made a case for peace, even at her most contrary. Everyone knew Hitler had to be stopped. There might have been some disagreement over the ex-ally Stalin at the time.

After a while Charlotte fell silent and the three of them strolled over the sand, far from their beach towels, then back. Claudia doesn't know what words he said, exactly, but she remembers his deep and soothing voice speaking on and on, a melodic soliloquy.

"My God," Charlotte said later, "he never shut up, did he? I couldn't believe one man would have so much to say about himself, could you? And never once asked about us."

That wasn't true. Claudia remembers telling him she'd worked in a hardware store during the war and now hoped to be a teacher. She wouldn't have said so if he hadn't asked.

Charlotte was almost finished university by then, just a year to go. Even through that change, they'd stayed friends. Charlotte spoke in those days of what a great deal there was to be done. She had some inclination to save. Claudia considered herself the more gentle and tender-hearted one, perhaps, but it was Charlotte who tried to save the lives of wounded birds or who stopped on the street to talk to the troubled or the crippled. The people most other people stepped uneasily around.

Anyway, that was how they all met. Bradley'd hitchhiked to the beach (soldiers, ex-soldiers, it seemed, had no hesitation about doing that sort of thing), so they gave him a ride back to town. Who suggested that? Charlotte wouldn't likely have; perhaps Bradley asked.

"May I call you?" he asked Claudia as they dropped him at his boarding-house. She thought how bold (in a good way) that was, to invite her in front of her friend. Because what if she'd said no? How humiliating that would have to be for him.

Of course she didn't say no, why would she have? And how could she have? And then he didn't call for days and nights, and she was quite astonishingly hurt.

She hadn't foreseen a future, exactly; only that something might happen. She hadn't thought she was bored, until her boredom was punctured by hope.

Then just as she was abandoning hope and restoring herself first to resignation, next to a renewed alertness to other prospects, he did call, did ask her to a movie, did then arrive on the doorstep of the house where she lived with her parents,

and spoke with them politely before, in what she thought a quite masterful way, sweeping her out the door and down the walk, along the street and to the movie, where they watched something to which she paid no attention at all, and which she can now not remember.

How was he masterful? A certain force of will; a hand on her elbow, guiding her as gently, but clearly, as a man might steer a well-trained horse, just with his knees and a small gesture with reins. He seemed to know what they were doing, anyway, and after the movie guided her in much the same way to a restaurant, where he ordered for them both, without asking.

She felt so taken care of, and so safe!

She thinks now that every virtue must be also a sin of sorts; that every loving gesture and word contains its opposite, as well: the gesture of hatred, the bullying word. Leadership can also be dictatorship. Protectiveness can smother.

Her failure to understand that may just have been a failure to realize love's compromising definitions: that it contains as much sorrow and misunderstanding and pain as it does pleasure and joy and tenderness. So that for many years she was often startled, both by joy and by pain, and by both Bradley and herself. There must have been calm, there must have been long periods without turmoil and upheaval, and perhaps those will come to be the times she remembers, once she has made her way beyond whatever space it is through which she is now travelling. But at the moment she recalls the peaks and the plunges, the dramas and extremes, the places and events and passions from which, she supposes, those figures of the night emerge.

She hears Charlotte speaking to her, as she has often done at times when she's needed a cool, brisk voice. "At least you weren't bored. At least you had passion, whatever forms it took. You got to learn a lot more than you would have ever done in peace." Yes, but there must be better things to learn,

about yourself, about the world, than that you are capable of screaming and attack; or that the person to whom you are most closely and inevitably and irrevocably attached is capable of the most vicious and deliberate brutality.

Remember the sweet moments, too, Claudia reminds herself. She must frequently remind herself not to travel too far in a single direction. She needs also to recall him holding her, face in her hair, her arms tight around his ribs as they rocked each other, standing, sometimes weeping, the two of them saying, in turns, "I'm sorry, I'm sorry, I didn't mean . . ." Whatever it was they didn't mean. She supposes they were sorry for misunderstanding, right from the start, each other's natures.

She must have expected perfection: an encompassing answer. Hardly fair. Hardly reasonable. Such a terrible burden for him, no wonder he tried to shake free of it sometimes. So at the base and root of all their troubles was this flawed and thoughtless assumption of hers; so, really, everything that went wrong was her fault, she could see that.

She forgot to ask, now wishes she could, what he'd expected of her, what he'd seen. "You were so sweet," he used to say. "So pretty and quiet and gentle." But that's not what she means. What she means is, who did he think she was?

And who exactly, what sort of woman would have done for him, made him happy in all the ways he wanted to be happy? Someone merely sweet, pretty, quiet and gentle? Who exactly could be those things only, and not other, less attractive, more demanding things as well?

Only someone who set out to drown herself, determined to hold herself under until there was no sign of life left.

And then he would have complained of being bored. That she, being drowned and dead, was as a result insufficiently stimulating. As Bradley did anyway, on occasion, accuse Claudia of simplicity and narrowness of interest, because, it seemed,

of her intense interest in himself and in their family. "You need to get out more," he would urge. But by then, how could she? Where exactly was she supposed to go, what radically fascinating hobbies and excursions was she supposed to undertake, with babies and toddlers and children and adolescents, finally four, on her heels, in her head, on her hands?

Her work was hard enough. Her passions for her children, which seemed pure, and for him, which were mixed, were exhausting and consuming enough. She could see she might seem tedious, compared with certain outside glamours and fields of expertise, but what was she supposed to do about it? She scarcely had time to read a newspaper, to keep up with bare event.

If he wanted someone else so badly, why did he make her what she was, why did he set her up this way?

But then he'd curl his body into hers some nights, wrap legs and arms around her and speak to her of love: what an anchor she was, how he could not imagine going on without her, how he could not tell what might have become of him without her. It is possible to suffer a great deal, in return for moments like that. The great, grand luxury of feeling cherished made up for a lot.

Maybe all couples have such radical swings, such violent curves, over years, it's hard to know. Even now, people still don't often reveal to each other the true slicings that get carved in their hearts.

It was only six months, of movies and dinners and hand-holding walks in the dark, of kisses, furtive at first and then passionate, groping, before he took her hands one night, as they sat on a park bench, watching the darkness and stars, and suggested they marry. "I have never met," she remembers him saying, "anyone better than you."

But what if he had? And what if someday he did meet somebody better, however unlikely he considered it? She never

thought to ask. She was astonished by how much joy she could feel, and understood what it meant when people, books, spoke of hearts that overflowed. Hers did indeed feel filled with some liquid, greater and thicker than water, not frightening or brutal like blood, but something sweet that threatened to spill out and swamp her and possibly the two of them. Gratitude. She was so grateful to be loved, cherished, protected, *noticed*, by this hard and handsome man. She was grateful to be chosen. She was grateful to be settled. She was grateful to be taken care of, future assured, all that and this great passionate love, as well.

Because when his hands, or his lips, were on her breasts, or travelling down her hips or along her spine, all those places on her body that he moved so gently, with such restraint that she felt his body trembling – at those moments she wanted him. She wanted to be so close to him, and so entirely attached, that they would be inseparable, even when they were apart. She wanted to feel all of his body on and in all of her body. She thought these longings might be unsuitable, abnormal, and spoke of them, and even then with shyness and hesitation, only to Charlotte.

Who said, carelessly, "Oh, that's just lust. Imagine what you have to look forward to! Oh, you are lucky, you'll have a grand time, I expect."

Charlotte was no longer a virgin. Sometimes Claudia stared at her as if she were a stranger, because her body had been naked with a man, and they'd done things together that were still a secret to Claudia. Charlotte said that, with her, matters had improved with practice; as if she were merely learning to play a new instrument, like the piano or trombone. But then, leaning closer to Claudia, eyes glittering, she also spoke of pleasure. "I can't tell you," she said, "how beautiful a man's body can be. Or how you can fit together sometimes so you

feel like the ocean, rolling and rolling. I don't know why it's such a secret, and I really can't see what it has to do with marriage, either." Because in those days, with some soiled exceptions such as Charlotte, it did have to do with marriage.

Claudia thought of the end of her longings, the rolling culmination Charlotte spoke of, as a reward for her patience. She thought, "I can't wait," but was delighted to, since that could only add to the pleasure when it happened.

Which she didn't picture clearly. She didn't try to imagine the event itself, or what would lead to it or follow it. It would be something like a mountain peak, standing out by itself and well worth the effort.

She was vaguely startled, at her wedding, by the sight of Charlotte weeping. It seemed to be from something more than sentiment; but of course there wasn't time, nor was there a suitable place, really, to ask. The whole day, not just Charlotte, was somewhat vague to Claudia. She'd expected it to be sharp and clear, every moment sculpted into her memory so that she would always be able to recall it perfectly, but that's not how it turned out. It was misty then, and remains misty now, as fleeting as those figures in her night visions, if not malevolent.

She must ask Charlotte why she cried that day.

On Claudia's worst days with Bradley, she was never as alone as this. Every creak and crackle of the house, every car horn or dog bark outside, is a knife in her solitude. These small, sharp flickings at her flesh – is that what she will now have to live with?

She can imagine God, knowing all her sins and secrets, deciding how best she should be punished: this warm-hearted, domestic, sweet and hopeful, not-unintelligent woman who has on occasion shrieked and wept, and who tried, however inadequately, to love the best she could.

Claudia can't speak the reason, even to herself, within her

own thoughts, but she knows exactly why God might set aside quite a special punishment for her. And what a clever God, to realize that the worst she could suffer is this: this lying-awake, middle-of-the-night, middle-of-the-day, every-minute, every-second loneliness.

She hears her own voice moan, horrifying in the darkness. If she could weep, which she can't seem to at the moment, it would not be for a dead husband, but for her own despair.

three

ONCE UPON A TIME THERE WAS A girl named Sleeping Beauty, who only had to be beautiful and good and fall asleep in order to be wakened a century later by a kiss from a prince. Once upon a time there was another girl, named Cinderella, who worked very hard and without complaint for cruel relations and was rewarded, like Sleeping Beauty, with a prince.

Were they sisters, or is that just what used to happen to good girls?

That's where those stories ended: with a pair of princes and a happily-ever-after. Even when she was young, Charlotte was dissatisfied. The stories felt to her as if they must be really just beginning.

"Then what happened?" was her question. Her mother, who of her parents was the bedtime storyteller, looked at her

as if she didn't understand. As, no doubt, she didn't.

"I said. They lived happily ever after. That's how it ends."

But take Sleeping Beauty, for example. If she'd slept for a century, think how much older she'd have been than the prince by the time he wakened her! Wouldn't she be awfully wrinkled and grizzled, especially compared with his young smoothness? The story didn't really explain that; and nor did Charlotte's mother. She said, "Well, I guess she was in the kind of sleep where she didn't change."

Maybe she didn't, but if you slept for a hundred years, the world would be very confusing when you woke up, wouldn't it? Other things would have changed. Sleeping Beauty's parents would have died. There'd be different kinds of food, and different ways of doing things. The trees would be a whole lot bigger. People she knew would have moved someplace else. Wouldn't the prince wonder about all the things she didn't know? Mightn't he think, "Well, she's beautiful, but awfully stupid when it comes to the point." And he might find it hard to believe her tale of sleeping for a century.

Charlotte supposes she never got from stories what she was intended to. She has failed to believe. She has never been faithful, has never had faith.

Often she's had hope, though. She has even been, she suspects, quite stupidly hopeful from time to time.

What on earth was she hoping for, lurking at Andrew's?

She has a small, tingling longing to return to that cool, green, prickly, heart-hurting place. She hasn't decided whether or not to give in to this urge, and can't tell if indulging it would make any difference.

She was scared at the time of being caught, she can remember that, although evidently not vividly enough. But venturing out there in the first place was an effort to make a difference to fear: to do something outrageous, to feel like herself again.

This unaccustomed fear of fear – here's how it began: in a quiet, sneaking-up way, in a perfectly ordinary place.

Every three weeks Charlotte goes to the supermarket. She makes a long and careful list; pulls her car into the parking lot; takes her list from her purse; steers a cart through crowds, along wide aisles, picking out necessities. All this takes some time and effort, because she is slower than she used to be, and also somewhat poorer, so she has to keep an eye on bargains and exercise restraint. She can't afford to be dazzled by too many displays, or tempted by too many treats.

Until two weeks ago, this was an ordinary, irritating chore. That day, though, something hinting of terror rolled over her, leaving her shaken and amazed.

She was in the long check-out line, waiting her turn to shift her groceries from the cart to the conveyor belt, watch them all rung through and finally pay for them. There were three people ahead of her, two with full carts. A young woman was wrestling with a child over candies on display. Two more carts were lined up behind her; the place was very crowded, very bright and, it seemed to her, exceptionally noisy.

She found herself thinking not merely, "What a waste of time, why aren't we moving?" but also, "How long will I have to stay on my feet? Can I manage?" She had a terrible desire to sit down, right there on the floor if that was the only place.

She was frightened she might *have* to sit down. What an embarrassment that would be, people staring and flustered and annoyed, and even worse, pitying.

Her legs were heavy, her head light. She felt dazed; enclosed by, wrapped in bright hazy sound, voices and music, clickings and rumblings. It wasn't her body that was weak; something else. She thought, "So this is how it happens": that she was suddenly, in this moment, old and frightened, and this light-headedness was fearful age itself.

She shook her head, dipped it, tried to concentrate on reading labels. Anything.

Her vision cleared, the noise returned to normal; but she understood that something critical had altered.

She has seen fears creep up on other people, not only the old, until they've left themselves just the smallest piece of corner in which they may feel safe.

She continued to wait in the line, took deep breaths, calmly counted out her money, took back change, had the bags loaded into her car and quite competently drove home. Where she stood inside the door, looking around, seeing how dangerous the great warm love of home could be. She understood there were some things she'd better do, although she couldn't yet tell what they'd be. But she knew she couldn't afford to doubt herself. And was startled by the mere possibility of doubting herself, after all these years.

Doubts can bind limbs, cripple actions, throttle lives.

Eventually, and in a complicated sort of way, that moment in the supermarket did lead her to that other moment in the cool green cedar hedge outside Andrew's suburban home.

Each lover she had began with a small moment, an inadvertent touch of skin, a meeting of eyes, a well-placed, well-spoken word or phrase that caught attention. It is quite wrong, as it turns out, to think, as she did in those days, that she would be content, when she was old, with memories. Memories are just that; and not comparable at all to real skin, real hair beneath the fingers, the pressure of real mouths, real bodies. Memories are utterly inadequate; but certainly better than nothing, better than having missed it all.

She is grateful, at least, to have had her most joyous, passionate years before the time real horror entered sex. It must be entirely different now from the days when one could look, attract and act without much heed to consequences.

Oh, there were some consequences; but none she couldn't deal with. None that actually killed her.

It's funny that she can recall pain and despair more vividly than the touch of skin and hair and bodies. She can call up anguish in a second, but joy – that's harder to grasp.

And what was it about Andrew that has brought him particularly back to mind, so that she has behaved in this peculiar way and has an impulse to do so again? Perhaps he mattered; just as she used to tell him. "It's odd," she used to say. "To find out you matter so much. I'm a bit old to be learning what matters and what doesn't."

"You mean the others didn't?"

A tricky question. She might, by agreeing, make herself sound not merely promiscuous but a fool. And even though he was lying in her bed, facing her, elbow propped on the mattress, chin in his hand, grinning, she understood that he was serious.

"I must have thought so," she told him. "But they all seem to have vanished."

"Maybe I will, too. When you find someone else."

"I don't think so." She believed that was both serious and true, and decades later, in just the last few days, has discovered she was right.

He was, too, of course. She did find other men and also other pleasures. He didn't take her life away with him. But still.

Perhaps he caught her at the right hingeing moment, as she began to swing from pleasure and experiment and a certain heedlessness of future towards a more serious scrutiny of how she would be, and of shortening time.

Or perhaps he taught her that.

She met him at the courthouse. She was to testify in a case of child abuse – which one? One, anyway, in which she can remember the desperation with which she wanted to get and

keep the child away from its pathetic mother and her brutal boyfriend. These were not uncommon cases, and Charlotte by then had some years of experience with them, but those tattered, beaten children never lost their capacity to make her weep and make her want to punish. And even then, before the subject became much studied, she knew those small, tormented children were all too likely to become the grown-up batterers and torturers she railed and testified against. While they were children, they were pitiable and sometimes salvageable; as adults, if they fell into that perpetuating trap, they belonged behind bars.

She was waiting her turn to testify, pacing and sipping a coffee from the court-house cafeteria. A man came around a corner, head bent towards a client, listening to his story and leaning in to counsel him. He crashed into her. Her coffee spilled on his trousers. "Oh shit," he said.

She went to the women's washroom for dampened paper towels, took them out to him. He apologized for swearing, and for bumping into her. He said it was his fault, which was true enough. "No, I should have been watching better," she said. "I wasn't paying attention." He probably thought that was true. She thought his dark voice was extraordinarily appealing; and then that it probably was very useful for convincing juries.

She was called to testify, her name rolling down the corridor. When she finished, he was waiting outside the courtroom. He must have waited for the entire hour she spent on the stand. She was touched.

They went for coffee. He asked her about the case in which she was involved. She talked and talked, angry and impassioned, because there is always so much that can't be said in court. He was a lawyer, so he understood. "How can you stand caring so much?" he asked. "Don't you wear out?"

"Someday, maybe, but not yet. If that happens, if I don't care

any more someday, I think it'll be time to quit." Perhaps they should both have paid closer attention to those words.

She forgot, carried away, to ask him about the case on which he'd been so intent when they crashed into each other. Later, when she was home and reviewing her day (which after all had gone well – the child was indeed given into the custody of her agency, the first hurdle successfully completed), it occurred to her that she knew almost nothing about him.

But it hardly mattered. She'd seen his ring, understood he was married, knew they'd met literally by accident, then had shared a companionable hour in a coffee shop.

Of course, why had he waited so long outside the courtroom for her to finish testifying?

He phoned her at her office the next day, invited her for a drink after work. She didn't say no. Well, why should she?

Something happened and it took up almost the entire decade of her thirties.

Once – more than once – he told her, "You're so different. So bright and brave and sure of yourself. I can be myself with you, and I think it must be because you won't lean. You don't need me to be somebody, you take care of yourself."

She thought there was something wrong about that, but couldn't quite find words to explain. Yes, she liked to believe she was bright and brave and independent and could look after herself, of course, and it was good he felt free with her. So all that was true enough; just incomplete.

(Fatally incomplete; by the end of their time together she had plenty of words to tell him there were things she'd needed, and price tags he seemed unaware of to choices he made; that if she had needed nothing from him, why would she have bothered to be with him, or he with her, in this arduous circumstance? She never wanted to marry him, but that had nothing to do with what she did need and hope for.

But by the time she had the words for all that, it was too late.)

Putting forth a case for the other woman, the mistress, the lover, the slut, is about as easy as making sympathetic the troubles of the rich. Yes, they may suffer, but who cares? Do they not bring their problems on themselves? Are they not themselves responsible for their pain? Which is insubstantial, after all, compared with the pain of legitimate women, wives; or that of the poor and powerless.

So neither mistresses nor the rich often go looking for sympathy. They keep their troubles to themselves. Or among themselves. Charlotte has never had any shortage of women acquaintances with experience of married men.

Old, close, deep friends, though, are different. How could she have kept this from Claudia? But what a leap, a gamble! This was the sort of thing that risked their friendship, if Claudia, some years married to the ghastly Bradley by then, felt strongly enough. And of course Claudia's friendship was tested. She looked troubled and sad. Charlotte watched her anxiously. "Oh dear," Claudia said finally, and reached out to put her hand on Charlotte's. "I hope you aren't hurt. I hope it works out, whatever that means. Whatever you want. I hope you get what you want." Charlotte could have wept. How good Claudia was!

Especially good, knowing what she did about Bradley by then. It would have been quite reasonable for her to rage at Charlotte: to tell her she was wrong, was doing wrong, could be creating dramas and tragedies she couldn't foresee. That she should give Andrew up before it was too late. Do the right thing, respect his marriage and promises. "Think of his wife!" she might have cried.

Well, but by then he'd made promises of sorts to Charlotte, too.

How confusing and torn his life must have been! And now

he is an old man, embracing his grandsons and stooping to pull weeds from his gardens. And putting an arm, casually and easily, around the shoulders of his wife. How did he get from then to now?

Perhaps the same way Charlotte has – from moment to moment, day to day, event to event, until here she is, old as well, with a long and not-uninteresting history and a future that is necessarily much shorter than the past, and as interesting as she causes it to be.

His house, his home – all those nights he rose from Charlotte's bed, the one she still sleeps in, saying, "I'm sorry, I have to go home now." How sorry could he have been when he still, always, called it home? He never mistook Charlotte's house for his own.

It's difficult, now, with a picture of it in her head, to see what its attractions could have been. It's pleasant enough, but hardly compelling; so its importance must have been in what it contained, not the place itself, the people in it, not its own dull design. In her mind, at the time, Charlotte made it large, unique, a reflection of the ways she saw Andrew himself. Rather the way she saw his wife, more formidable than, as it turns out, she looks. Perhaps in her mind she made Andrew larger, also, than he warranted. Would he have become smaller if she'd lurked then outside his home, scouting her rivals?

Like Andrew, Charlotte loved her home; and now that affection may be the most comforting, enduring, constant one she has. Perhaps that's how it is for him, as well. And is that pathetic? Pitiable? Sad?

She has lived in this small house for more than thirty years. It contains light and air and a great deal of her history. Walking through its front door, she can still feel herself embraced by her life. The kitchen has a wall of glass, and there are big old-fashioned, farm-style windows in the living-room and dining-

room, an avalanche of sunshine on good days, and a spectacular view of storms. How safe she is here!

She is touched, sometimes sharply, by the grace of shapes, eyes drawn from the plum-and-white-striped cotton-covered sofa to the vivid iris print hung, uncentred, over it, to the bronzed floor lamp with the plum-coloured shade and to the small table stacked with magazines and books, littered in a deliberate way with a tall pale candle in bronze holder and a clutter of unmatching small figures of glass and pottery and wood.

In the kitchen, plants hang in the windows and bright pots from ceiling hooks, and upstairs in her bedroom there are stark cool white bedside lamps, more books and that bed, scene of many pleasures, covered with the lightest of pale yellow duvets. Charlotte has always had a fondness for simplicity; perhaps because events may get so complicated.

But less so, recently. Now that she's old, she supposes that signs of settling down, such as fear, should not come as a surprise.

It's not that she's been accustomed to dangerous or daring adventures; has never been a mountain climber or skydiver or explorer, has never had a moment when she has thought, "If I do this, I may die." She doesn't count as daring those times in her work when she had to take a child from its murderous parents, or, overtaken by pity and hope, invited some angry adolescent into her home for a meal. Those were dangerous moments, no doubt, but she didn't think at the time, "If I do this, I may die."

It never occurred to her, embracing Andrew, that his wife, if she learned of this, might object in some fatal fashion.

Now, with a fresh alertness to fear, she can look back at some of those moments and shiver at the risks she took.

Now, she must admit that when she goes downtown, she looks at some of the young, with their odd patchy clothes and

odd patchy hair and very peculiar make-up, female and male, and feels, if not afraid, at least nervous. She supposes they have come to seem too far away, and foreign – her failure, hardly theirs.

There are no doubt several good reasons to give up, and failures of curiosity and desire must be right near the top of the list. On the other hand, how much *should* surprise a woman her age? One shouldn't be too constantly taken aback.

She doubts, after all, that those young people on the streets downtown who look so odd are any more dangerous or peculiar than many who passed, relatively placidly, through her life. Or she through theirs. How many of them remember her? Do, for instance, Lissa and Tim? For that matter, how many of them does she recall very precisely? (Other than Lissa and Tim.) She does hope she didn't expect gratitude. She hopes she didn't offer the odd meal, an ear, a little acknowledgement of their existence, with expectations of a return, in the form of letters, or visits, or grateful telephone calls. Dreadful to be the sort of do-gooder who yearns to bask in her own benevolence, yearns for the card that says, "I want you to know what those few hours you spent with me meant. They changed my life. I became a good human, thanks to you." She would like that to be true, of course; she just wouldn't want to be the kind of person who behaved somewhat decently in order to achieve gratitude.

She has never cared for cheap sentiment.

Andrew was always more sentimental than she. Sometimes, at movies or birthdays, he even wept, extraordinary for a man, and one of the reasons she believed him a particularly precious soul. He may have wept, though, for not measuring up; for not being all the Andrews he was called on to be by one person or another. In the end, however, he does not find himself alone, apparently.

But then, how much did she really see, peering through that hedge? Perhaps just the taken-for-granted gestures of people who live together. That happens, too. She may be assuming too much.

It wasn't impossibly uncomfortable, after all, in the cedar. And it begins to seem less outrageous.

Although it remains a bit of a mystery why she has selected Andrew for this adventure. It may be true that, because of duration if nothing else, he returns more vividly to mind than many others. (Not *that* many, after all; but many more than, say, Claudia, stuck with just one all those years.) And he may have been more heart-breaking (or heart-altering) than others. But surely if the object is to gauge impacts and effects, it would be more useful to look up some of those bad, sad adolescents and track them down and lurk outside their homes. Because she was never a fool, after all; she never counted on any man, even Andrew, for purpose. So why him, now?

Perhaps it doesn't especially matter. Certainly she's not interested in his flesh, or even, any longer, his soul. So maybe this mad hedge quest is only aimed at what he represents, an answer to a question concerning only herself.

Would that be a sad ending?

She hears the clatter of the mailbox lid at the front door. Her heart does lift at the prospect of word from the outside world.

A pizza coupon. A flyer from a student painting company. The gas bill. And a letter.

Not, after all, from some grateful former adolescent.

It's ages since she and Claudia have been in touch; a year, at least. Charlotte remembers writing the last letter, and waiting for an answer. It's been a long time coming. And then beyond that, how long since they've seen each other? A good five years, anyway, and then just for a weekend, a sleepover like the old days, giggling and confiding into the night. Not long enough to

catch up on two lengthy lives whose circumstances could hardly have been more different, but still, they were friends; had confided their first periods to each other and then, years later, their last; observed each other's breasts' first growth and then their early saggings; walked home from school together with their arms around each other; laughed helplessly for no reason in particular, and celebrated triumphs, and wept together for losses of one sort and another.

This calls for some ceremony, a celebratory Scotch at least. A long letter from the oldest of old friends shouldn't be read standing in a hallway, it should be read slowly, and cherished.

Charlotte has drained her glass before she even reaches the hard nugget cushioned in all these pages. She is taking the first sip from her second Scotch as she reads, "Bradley has died." And puts down the letter, although holding on to the drink.

Bradley has died. Poor Claudia. Although it's true that in Charlotte's view Claudia long ago muddled up whatever distinctions there are to be made between character and love, and set out to love a man of poor character.

But then, what does Charlotte know about forty-seven years of trying to get along, or the discipline of sustaining emotion? Although she does know something about men of poor character.

The tanned and lean older man stood silhouetted by sunshine, at the edge of their beach towels, and asked the time. Charlotte's eyes opened, she sat up slowly, reached in her beach bag for her watch and told him. His beauty, when she could see him properly, took her breath away. Perfect features, perfect bones. Both she and Claudia sat up and paid attention.

At some point, though, even Sleeping Beauty, Cinderella and their respective princes must have had to open their mouths. Find subjects in common. Even small talk at the breakfast table might have been a challenge; because what

could they have known about each other, besides the attractions of the waking kiss, the glass slipper, the simple princeliness of those men? When they spoke, might not the spells be broken? What if they turned out to be dull, as it sounds real princes often are?

Beautiful Bradley spoke, introducing himself, and his voice was beautiful, too.What a pity Claudia was still, even in her early twenties, so inexperienced. Of course one of her chief charms, always, has been her willingness to believe. She, for instance, would never have wondered what happened later to those young women with their princes. "Happily ever after" would have satisfied her entirely as an answer, an ending.

And that *is* charming. And in its way tough. In its way, that attitude permits survival. Perhaps that answer also satisfied Sleeping Beauty and Cinderella; they were glad enough to have reached where they were, and wouldn't want to make waves.

Charlotte thought as soon as Bradley opened his mouth that he was both boring and arrogant. He really did believe he was important. Because he'd been overseas and now had something to boast of? Had he come home thinking he could live off the glory of his war forever?

Charlotte thought, as the three of them walked far along the sand by the edge of the water and then back to where they'd begun, and Bradley talked and talked about himself, where he'd been, what he'd done – she thought what a shame he was so beautiful, but then opened his mouth.

"Full of himself" was how she put it to herself, and later to Claudia, before she realized that what she saw, or at any rate heard, was by no means what Claudia had seen and heard.

In a way, of course, they must both have been right. The marriage lasted forty-seven years and ended only with death. So whatever drew Claudia in the first place must have been as true as whatever repelled Charlotte.

One thing that was true, which Claudia has never known, is that Bradley called Charlotte first. Should she have told Claudia then?

This is one of those questions that linger, even haunt: if, when Claudia was rapturous from his call, their dates, eventually their engagement – if at any time Charlotte had said, "You know, he phoned me the day after we met at the beach, he asked me out but I said no," would that have saved Claudia? She might have been hurt, but would it have saved her? Charlotte, by an error of omission, out of mistaken kindness, may have been responsible for a terrible turn in the life of her friend.

Or not. Claudia might not have cared so much. And she has, after all, been content in some ways. She has four daughters, which must be counted a gain in the end.

"I thought you were interesting," he'd said when he called, then hurried on, "and beautiful, too, of course." As if she'd be insulted to be considered merely intelligent; that's how unacute, unthinking he was. "But I liked talking to you. I thought maybe we could talk some more."

She couldn't imagine he'd enjoyed their beach conversation any more than she had. He'd spoken of battles and manoeuvres, military events, and she had corrected dates and geography. They had sparred over the significance of various trenches and hills, offensive and defensive movements. She thought she'd made her view of him quite clear.

Very likely he called to convert her. He would want to seduce, salve his pride, then abandon. Even then, she thinks, she saw Bradley clearly. Rather clever for such a young woman; or perhaps it was that Bradley was rather transparent.

Although not to Claudia, who solemnly watched him, and solemnly listened and solemnly believed.

Something else Charlotte has never told Claudia: some

years after he and Claudia were married, Bradley called her again. "Just for a drink or two," he said. "I know we've never been close, but I'd like us to be. I still think you're a real interesting woman. And attractive. I wish you'd give us a chance." Whatever possessed him? What made him dream?

Betrayal seemed to come so easily to him – perhaps he thought it came as lightly to everyone. Except to Claudia, of course. He wouldn't have dreamed of Claudia betraying him. And he was right (although he might have counted as betrayal all the tales of him that Claudia confided. Men often do seem sensitive to women's conversations).

Perhaps, as Charlotte suspects she has done at times herself, Bradley relied on Claudia's gentle virtue as compensation for his various wickednesses.

Was he wicked? Perhaps not. Perhaps just a common man. Imagine forty-seven years with a common man – imagine forty-seven years with any man at all.

And of course having caused Claudia so much grief when he was alive, Bradley would hardly loosen his grip posthumously on her capacity for suffering.

Gentle Claudia, and her determined iron will. Charlotte remembers Bradley saying impatiently one night at dinner at their place, back when they also lived in this city, "How could you be so stupid, Claudia?" It was something that can't have been important or Charlotte would remember what it was. Charlotte would have tossed a drink at him, or walked out of the room and out of his house. Claudia looked embarrassed, looked down, said, "I'm sorry." If that's what she means by will, Charlotte is quite happy not to be so strong.

Cancer. Well, she does hope he didn't suffer. It sounds as though he must have, though, taking more than a year to die. Charlotte would bet he made sure Claudia was suffering right along with him. Why did she have to do the nursing? They

could surely have hired people, or he could have gone to hospital. Charlotte can just hear him saying, "No, Claudia, I don't want anyone but you, I don't want anyone else to see me like this, or to do all these things. I trust you, but nobody else."

How many times during their marriage did he say those words in other contexts? "I don't want anyone but you," or, "I trust you." As if all his misadventures were merely frivolous and quite separate from the truly wanted, deeply trusted Claudia.

But Claudia had terrible moments. In Bradley's absence, when he wasn't looking into her eyes, speaking in his sincerest tones, Claudia had her doubts, oh yes. Sometimes she telephoned Charlotte and wept.

Does she remember, or does his death cause the sort of benevolent amnesia Charlotte has observed in other widows?

Even in Charlotte's experience, though, love isn't logical. Even she can't account for all her attractions. But she is sure she would have heard what Bradley's words were really saying, when he said, "I don't want anyone but you," or, "I trust you." He had to be lying to someone, could hardly be telling the truth in all directions, so however you looked at it, he was a liar.

Still, whether Bradley and his words were real or not, Claudia certainly was. Is.

They've had one rule of friendship, Charlotte and Claudia: they've never advised. If they had, Charlotte supposes they might have prevented some of each other's mistakes; but more likely they would no longer be friends. What they've said to each other instead is, "You must do what seems best. However things go, I'll be here if you need me."

Tolerance does not, however, apply to partners, who may well be judged harshly (if silently) for the pain they cause. Or, for that matter, be judged generously for the delight they provide. Which may be even more difficult: to be neither jealous nor resentful, but to rejoice.

It has been difficult, getting used to the absence of men. To miss love, and even lust, was hard enough; still more difficult has been mourning companionship, and the loss of the opposing minds of men. Charlotte misses trying to explain what, to a friend like Claudia, hasn't required explanation at all. Andrew (and others) looked at her with such incomprehension, across the chasm of language, custom, culture; whereas Claudia (and others) knew the codes perfectly. Charlotte did enjoy the challenge of men, along with the comfort of women.

She also wouldn't mind being touched. A little love would be nice.

How much harder then for Claudia, with one man, however bullying and dense and treacherous, for forty-seven years, to become accustomed to his absence. If Bradley himself cannot be mourned, Charlotte can at least summon considerable grief for Claudia.

Yes, Charlotte does remember the Claudia of more than six decades ago: the little girl who hung back, whose eyes watched the floor, or the ground, or her own feet, who didn't speak unless someone spoke to her, and who rarely laughed out loud. Perhaps the small Charlotte saw in that scared, pudgy, freckled, quiet little girl quite a different sort of power than her own.

Claudia says Charlotte might be surprised by her strength? But why would she be?

Charlotte came close to disgracing herself at the wedding. She and Claudia were, what, twenty-two? Bradley was an ancient twenty-nine. Charlotte couldn't stop weeping – how embarrassing! Why, she outdid even the mother of the bride when it came to tears, and her shoulders shook with the effort not to sob out loud. What was the cause of this? If she could tell that, perhaps she could stop; but she couldn't tell.

Later, at the reception in the old church basement hall, she

saw some people regarding her curiously. She also overheard a cousin of Claudia's asking another, "What was the matter with her? Do you think she's queer for Claudia?" Charlotte flushed, but couldn't bring herself to challenge them or protest. She felt lost in a funny way; or as if something huge was lost to her. Well, she must have thought Claudia was lost to her. And that this marriage could only harm her friend.

And look, she was right, because see what happened? Forty-seven years later and here's Bradley dead, Claudia abandoned. Charlotte must have known from the beginning that, one way or another, the son of a bitch was going to abandon her friend.

She pours herself a third Scotch, tipsy now, in the middle of the day, to congratulate herself for such acute correctness. Even if it did take almost five decades to prove her right.

But what, now, is this great secret Claudia writes of? What could be so evil she can't tell Charlotte? Their loyalties are deep and unswerving. Charlotte can't imagine anything so terrible that Claudia should feel afraid. In front of her daughters, perhaps, or other friends, or neighbours; even in front of Bradley, if he weren't dead. But never, surely, with Charlotte.

Good heavens, the terrible secrets Claudia knows about her!

She will, right this minute, make a pot of coffee, sober up and write to Claudia, even though it'll mean lying awake tonight. She used to be able to drink gallons of coffee and drop right off to sleep, but not in recent years. Still, if she lies awake and ends up sleeping in tomorrow, so what? It isn't as if she has a full schedule of life to be lived. She can afford a little morning time in bed.

Bed isn't exactly what it used to be; more functional than fun, these days.

Perhaps tomorrow she'll go back to Andrew's, see what she can see.

She thinks that, in Claudia's view, she has been a woman going freely through her romantic, sexual life, picking and discarding, making choices and abandoning them. And yes, if Charlotte half-closed her eyes and regarded her history mistily and somewhat out of focus, she could see it that way, too. It's true she has had the advantage of variety. She hasn't stuck herself, like Claudia, with a single mistake.

Claudia misses Bradley? She mourns him? Well, so she says.

Perhaps when Andrew dies, his wife will also miss and mourn him; but what will she do with her rage? Her fury at his absences and betrayals? Because unless she has been far more adamantly deaf, dumb, blind and stupid than Claudia, she must know something of Andrew's secrets.

Has he crept back to his house and his wife, spending days puttering in the garden, reading in his easy chair, watching television, nagging at her, disorienting her with his constancy?

The sons on whose behalf he so often excused himself from Charlotte's presence are obviously long grown; so there he is, alone in that house with only the woman he wouldn't leave.

At the time, for that decade of her thirties, Charlotte considered Andrew's wife to be, of the two of them, the more fortunate; because presumably she didn't know about Charlotte, whereas of course Charlotte was only too aware of her.

In Andrew's wife's position, Charlotte would certainly have wanted to know. She would have wanted the knowledge required to make certain judgements for herself, decide how best to spend her years. But Andrew said he couldn't bear to cause so much disruption. And pain, of course. At the time, Charlotte managed to interpret this as an aspect of his tenderness.

Charlotte wonders if, perhaps, Claudia might not be similar to Andrew's wife; and has Andrew's wife had a friend like Charlotte, outraged on her behalf?

It's not merely the combination of Scotch and strong coffee

that causes Charlotte to laugh out loud, alone in her living-room – only a person with no sense of humour at all could fail to be amused by irony.

This is probably not something she should mention in a letter to Claudia, although if they were both sitting here, she can imagine them falling about together in helpless amusement for quite a few minutes.

four

AT LEAST IT WAS GOOD THAT WHEN that woman knocked on Claudia's door so many years ago, Claudia already had some experience of shock and grief under her belt. Otherwise who knows what she might have done?

But by then she had some ideas about her marriage. And she was no child any more, no innocent, believing bride. By then, she was in her thirties, and a mother, and a practical woman; a surviving woman. She'd learned a lot.

By then she and Bradley had already gone once through their ritual of sorrow and abasement, so her skin was somewhat toughened. And she had decided it was best, after all, to be safe and a wife. Bradley always came home. There were choices, of course, but how bleak they were, at the time. A woman in her thirties, with four young daughters (although there were only two the first time she found out – perhaps if she'd stopped it

there, it would have been easier to start again. But then she would not have had Sharon, or Susan. And after all, when there are already two, how much difference could another two make?). She had her house. She had her children. She was safe in several important ways. She thought it only mature to understand that there were bargains to be made, not something she could have known when she was much younger, starting out. Young girls believe in everything. By the time they're really grown up (or perhaps this is what constitutes becoming grown up) they realize there are some things they will simply end up settling for. This was Claudia's experience, anyway, and even Charlotte agreed, in her way. She said, at more or less that time, "I'm learning to make do. I know I can't have Andrew, really, so I try to be pleased with what I do have."

Claudia didn't know (because Charlotte didn't) how Andrew prevented his wife from learning about his semi-life with Charlotte. It must have taken some fancy footwork. And that must have been footwork of which clumsy Bradley was incapable.

That first time she learned, it was because of an inept lie. He told her he'd met an old friend, and they'd gone drinking and talking and lost track of time, and he'd ended up staying overnight at the old friend's place because he was too tired and drunk to drive. (Or to phone her, and she sat up on the sofa waiting for him, worrying, until she fell asleep right there, and was impatient with her two little girls in the morning because she was exhausted and still worried.) He came home in the morning rumpled and smelly and sheepish, but said, "At least I didn't kill myself trying to drive. Or wipe out somebody else. Or get stopped by the cops. It's only sensible."

Probably it sounded sensible to him, and Claudia was agreeable enough. But then some weeks later he invited that same friend and his wife to a Saturday night dinner, and Claudia

mentioned the little adventure, just as a joke, to make conversation, and the friend looked blank, said, "But we haven't been out on the town for years," then caught on too late and fumbled his words, and shortly afterward he and his wife left. Claudia noticed that his wife did not say goodbye to Bradley, but did touch Claudia lightly on the arm. "If you ever feel like a coffee, please give me a call," she said. "I know how tied down you can get with small children." Claudia heard the husband whisper to Bradley, "Sorry, I was a bit slow there. You should have warned me. I hope it's okay."

It wasn't okay. The moment the door closed behind them, Claudia found her arm swinging, stiff from the shoulder, to strike him. Her small fist hit his arm, was absorbed by his jacket. She failed, of course, to hurt him, but did get his attention. "What was that for?" How quick he was at becoming indignant, preparing her to be at fault. "What's the matter with you?"

She hated it, that she found herself crying. She wanted to hurt him but he gripped her wrists (much as he did towards the end, as he was dying) and she was helpless. In every way, she saw bitterly, she was helpless.

"You bastard." Even in that moment she whispered, a vicious, furious whisper but still quiet, so as not to wake the children – what would they think, to find their parents battling and struggling in the front hall, swaying against each other in her efforts to get free and injure, his to hold her?

"What?" That injured innocence.

"You liar. You son of a bitch. You cheat. I work to make a home and raise our children, and you *betray* me." Her rage gave her words, a woman of kindness, even meekness, come undone.

So he saw he couldn't carry it off. Perhaps he was frightened. Certainly he looked very surprised. "Oh, Claudie," he said,

dropping his head, but keeping his grip on her wrists. As if he were ashamed now, but still in control, and still afraid of her blows. He called her Claudie sometimes, in moments of fondness or passion, and this time, their first time, in a moment of contrition. "Oh, Claudie, I'm sorry. Truly, believe me, it was nothing. I love you. I wouldn't hurt you for the world. It was just – stupid. Nothing. And it won't happen again, I promise. I didn't know it would hurt you so much." His eyes, now meeting hers, seemed filled with true pain. Sorrow for causing her damage, denting her world. Bringing something unclean into it. Was there also, though, a glint of assessment? Was he gauging if she'd fall for it?

Ah, she fell for it; because what would it mean if she didn't? Already she was weary of the drama, so how could she sustain the undramatic results of refusing to believe, declining to forgive, turning her whole life upside down. And the lives of her two little daughters, still sleeping upstairs.

She let him fold his arms around her and rock her, back and forth, the two of them still standing in the front hall, until she stopped weeping and was still. He kept stroking her hair as if she were a small, much-loved pet.

Later they sat on the living-room sofa, facing each other, calmer. "Tell me why?" she asked. "I don't understand why you'd do such a thing." It was a struggle to avoid pictures of precisely what constituted "such a thing." Pictures of bodies and glamorous, more appealing women. Women who weren't mothers, and had time and money to make themselves glamorous and appealing. Women who didn't have to struggle to get themselves out of bed in the mornings to face drudging days.

Women who had the illicit thrill of taking strange spoken-for men to their beds at night.

Women like Charlotte? Charlotte didn't speak of it that way.

She spoke of it as difficult and painful, involving a kind of loss and sacrifice, although certainly a loss and sacrifice quite opposite to Claudia's experience at the moment.

"I don't know." He shrugged. "But it's nothing to do with you, please believe me. It's just, I think men are different."

"What do you mean, men are different?" Hardly forgiving, but beginning to be curious; a glimpse here of a foreign culture, malehood. The world to which her husband devastatingly belonged.

"I don't know. I guess that it doesn't make so much difference to us. It doesn't mean anything. It's just something that's maybe interesting, but it doesn't have anything to do with . . . I mean, I *love* you. That's why I go out and work so hard, because of you and the girls. You're what matters, nobody else."

How puzzling. How unnerving, to be living with someone who says sex doesn't matter, making love can be nothing. A matter of what – "Something," as he put it, "that's maybe interesting"?

"How many?"

"How many what?" That face of innocence again. Buying time.

"Women, Bradley. How many women?"

"Oh look, what difference does it make?" In fact, she could see his point – what difference did it make, one or a dozen? "None of it meant anything, I told you, that's the point."

"But how could you lie to me?"

"Would you rather I didn't? I love you too much to want to hurt you. I never wanted you to be hurt."

Well, she can see how stupid that was. And how stupid she was, too. Not to believe him (how could she possibly believe him?) but to have accepted.

"Do they have something I don't? What do you want I don't have?" So already, in such a short time, she was taking on

blame. Somehow, this must be her fault, her shortcoming. Well naturally – look at Bradley's beauty! So tempting, women must find him. They must reach out to him; after all, Claudia herself did.

"Nothing. Nothing at all. You're the best, Claudie, let me tell you, you're the best."

Apparently he'd know. Having sampled so widely.

It was something, anyway: being the best. And she was the one with the house, with the children, the one he came home to. Usually came home to.

That was their bargain. It was the first time she made it, but by no means the last. It's a little late now to wonder if she was wrong.

So anyway, that's why she was already a little toughened by the time that woman knocked on the door, the day Claudia began to really comprehend the nature of her choices and her future.

The woman was so striking, Claudia thought at first she must be selling cosmetics; if so, she was at the wrong house – Claudia had no spare money for make-up, and for that matter, little time, either, to spend highlighting cheekbones, outlining lips. She'd been interrupted with the laundry, putting sheets through the old wringer washer hauled out of its closet twice a week and into the kitchen, a steaming, unwelcome, necessary part of her work. She was in no mood to linger.

"Yes?" She couldn't have sounded very welcoming. She pushed back damp hair off her forehead, wiped her hands on her apron. She must have looked – pathetic. A drudge.

"Mrs. Mossman? Mrs. Bradley Mossman?"

"Yes. Can I help you?"

The woman didn't drop her eyes. Brazen, was the word Claudia thought of later. "I think we should have a talk," she said. "Can I come in?"

"Why?" Did Claudia have some inkling then? At least she no longer imagined this woman was selling cosmetics.

"Because there are some things you ought to know about that I don't think you do. And when you do, I'm sure you'll want to do the right thing."

The right thing! What would a woman like that have known about the right thing?

"What's it concerning, please?" Oh, Claudia, however hot and at whatever disadvantage, could put a chill in her tone.

"I'm sorry, didn't I say? About Bradley. Your husband. We need to talk about Bradley."

Sharon was playing in the backyard. Sonia and Sandra were in school. Susan hadn't been born yet; had yet to be conceived. Claudia lifted her eyebrows. "And what does my husband have to do with you?"

"That's what we need to talk about. I'd rather not do it out here, if you don't mind, and I'm sure you'd rather not, either."

Not an ill-educated woman. Well-spoken and cool. Slim, blonde, in a pale green linen dress, high white heels, smooth nylon stockings, precisely and discreetly made up, with shoulder-length hair in the popular style then, a page-boy. Claudia's hair, too naturally curly, would never restrain itself that way. It wasn't fair, to have had no warning.

"I can't imagine what you think you have to do with us, but all right, come in. As you can see, I'm quite busy. I can only spare a few minutes." She wasn't about to offer coffee, or anything else. She gestured towards the living-room, and wished it was tidy. Too many children's belongings scattered about; but that might be a good thing? "Sit down. I'll be with you in a moment."

In the kitchen she stopped the washer, leaving the sheets soaking. She ran cold water into the sink and splashed her face. She pulled a comb from her purse and ran it through her

heat-crinkled hair. She looked despairingly into the mirror over the kitchen sink. She was pale. She never got quite enough sleep, had dark bags under her eyes. She could powder her nose and add lipstick, and she could change from her sweat-stained housedress into something more formal, but she would still not match that cool and narrow woman in her living-room. With all the time and notice in the world, she couldn't achieve that look of self-possession.

Nevertheless.

She straightened. Strode to the living-room, sat in her chair, opposite Bradley's, leaned back, crossed her legs. She did have good legs, she knew that; and could see the other woman glancing at them too. The other woman had chosen the sofa. She must have had to move aside a few things. There was laundry at one end, waiting to be done. Claudia was pleased to see Bradley's shorts – that would tell the woman something.

What, that this was the poor weary woman who did his wash?

"Now then," she said briskly. "As I told you, I'm busy, so perhaps you could get to the point, whatever it is, so I can get on with things here."

"Mrs. Mossman." The woman leaned forward, looking earnest. "Bradley won't tell you this. That's why I'm here, because he doesn't want to hurt you and he keeps putting it off. But you should know we're in love. He and I. We want to be together all the time, so he needs to be free. He wants to be with me. I've been telling him I was sure you'd understand, if he'd just talk to you about it. I mean, I know you've got children and I want to assure you they'd be provided for. And so would you, of course. I know you'd want to get a job as soon as you could, and you'd likely get married again, you're still young enough, but Bradley would certainly support you till then. Maybe not in this house, you wouldn't likely need a place like

this, but he wouldn't let you suffer, that's for sure. Only, he needs to be free. We want to be together. Do you see?"

The woman was actually regarding Claudia as if she did expect her to see. Astonishing!

Claudia suspected herself of gaping. That wouldn't do. "This is my house," she reminded herself. Her hands gripped the arms of her chair. She thought, "This is my furniture. I have three daughters, and two of them will be running into this house soon from school, and the other may come in any time from the backyard. *My* backyard. In a few hours Bradley will likely come home. He'll be expecting a dinner I've made. Or he may be late again. Or not show up. He may be with this woman. Is it possibly true, what she says? But he's *my* husband."

She had never before had so many thoughts of ownership. She'd had no real idea, until now, how much she possessed.

The trick now was to be self-possessed.

"Who the hell *are* you?" she asked.

The woman looked startled. "Good heavens, I'm sorry, did I forget to introduce myself?" Hardly the greatest of her errors of etiquette, Claudia thought. And was proud of herself, for achieving wryness, at least. "I'm Sophia Clarke."

How cold Claudia felt. "Well, Miss Clarke – it is Miss Clarke, I assume? There's no husband confusing these very clear waters, I trust?"

"No, you're right, I'm single."

"How fortunate. Well then, Miss Clarke, I'm afraid I must be brief, but as I said, I'm busy. I'd suggest some other time, since we do seem to have things in common, but I doubt there'd be much purpose."

The woman was regarding her in a puzzled, waiting way.

"So let me say, simply, that I'm afraid you've made a mistake. Oh," raising her hand against the other woman's attempt to interrupt, "not that I doubt much of what you say. I'm sure you

and Bradley have enjoyed some happy times together. But I think you may have misjudged the depth of his intentions." Where were these formal words coming from? Claudia was quite enjoying herself in a way; at least, as long as she kept talking, she didn't have to think about the cliff she was walking towards. Something terrible was going to happen; but not quite yet, not as long as she still had words.

"Look around, Miss Clarke. This is Bradley's home. Two of his daughters will be coming home for lunch from school, and the other's outside playing. They're all quite fond of him, and he of them. And of course there's me, as well. We all exist. And we exist here together. As I said, I don't doubt much of what you say, but if you think you can cause any of this to cease to exist, I'm afraid you've been misled.

"Now, I'm not saying Bradley is the perfect husband. If you can imagine yourself in my place, you'll see right away that he's hardly ideal. On the other hand, there are worse men and I expect you've known some of them, too. At any rate, this is Bradley's home, and it's my home, it's our home together, and I'm not inclined to move out. How old are you, anyway?"

"Twenty-six."

"Really. Well, I'm older. Obviously. I'm thirty-four. Did you know Bradley's over forty?"

"Yes, of course. We have no secrets. Anyway, I don't care how old he is."

"I'm sure that's true, and of course he's still quite attractive. It's the next ten years that will make a difference. They do, with men, between forty and fifty, that's when they age. But if you love him, that's unlikely to trouble you. I am surprised, though, that you're as old as you say and apparently know so little about how people go along together. I understand you're in the midst of a romance, and that does, I expect, tend to obscure the vision somewhat. But I hope you can see that I'm in

the middle of a marriage, which is something quite different, and I'm not inclined to give your misty passions priority over my interests or my children's. So, no, Miss Clarke, I won't be leaving this house, or hunting for work, or moving into an apartment or even looking for a second husband. I won't be leaving Bradley, and I don't think, whatever your impressions, that he'll be leaving me. I don't think he'll be very pleased with you, you know. I rather think he's going to be annoyed you came here, and I expect he'll be letting you know that.

"Meanwhile," and she stood, "I have a load of washing to finish and lunch to make for my children. Perhaps that will sound dull to you, but it's what I do. Now forgive me for being inhospitable, but it's time for you to get back to whatever you do. Whatever sort of job you have, you'd better hang onto it."

She gestured towards the door, and the woman, looking, to Claudia's pleasure, confused, rose also. "But," she began, and Claudia lifted her hand in a gesture of silence.

"No, you've said what you came here to say, and I've expressed my own point of view, so I think our discussion should be left where it is. I apologize for not offering refreshments, or suggesting we get better acquainted sometime when we're both less pressed, but I doubt there'd be any point. I don't suppose we'll encounter each other again."

"I don't think you realize," the woman began again, and again Claudia stopped her.

"I realize quite well. You shouldn't worry so much about the state of my knowledge. If I were you, I'd be more concerned with where you go from here. I mean from this moment, not this house. That would be my concern, if I were you. Especially if you really are fond of my husband. If you are, you'll be occupied in getting over him, because believe me, you have no future with him. Whereas I, for better or for worse, do. And now," opening the front door, standing aside to herd the other woman onto the

step, "while I can't say it's been a pleasure, or that I'm glad you dropped by, I hope I've been able to make things clear for you. So you can get on with your life. Goodbye, Miss Clarke."

She shut the door; and finally, with no longer a witness or a listener, began to tremble. She bent over, arms wrapped around her stomach as if she had a terrible pain. Which she did, in a way. She wanted to howl and howl. Instead she ran to the bathroom and threw up in the toilet.

By the time the girls got home for lunch, the sheets were hung on the clothesline and Claudia, while pale and still shaky, was back in possession of her smooth mother-face. She listened to them without hearing, and hugged them hard when it was time for them to leave again.

She put Sharon down for her afternoon nap.

And then what? A whole blank afternoon, for contemplating betrayal and lies. Was she angry? There didn't seem to be a word, beyond despair. She was so tired; so immensely, irretrievably, irredeemably tired.

That woman, that Sophia Clarke, she was lovely. And young. No cares about her. A careless young woman, and also stupid, to have come here. But not the point, after all.

The point was Bradley. Who'd made promises and failed to keep them. "Never again," he had pledged. Had she believed him?

"Never again," he'd said, and they'd turned gently to each other and made another child.

What if she'd never known, that first time or now? It might have been all right, to have known somewhere, but not to have had to face it.

That determined young face.

And what if Sophia Clarke was right? Claudia'd made herself sound certain, but what if Bradley did want rid of Claudia and his daughters and this house and all his responsibilities, so

he could start again with a slim, graceful, unbattered young woman?

What if Claudia's husband really was such an uncaring, frivolous fool? What if she really had made such an error in judgement, and Charlotte had been right, from the beginning?

Charlotte didn't criticize him so often, once she saw Claudia was serious about him. But was this why she wept at the wedding? Did she foresee this?

Oh, then why didn't she say? She should have spoken up.

Although, Claudia had to admit, she wouldn't have listened. She was as entranced by Bradley as that unfortunate young Sophia Clarke seemed to be.

What would Charlotte say? Not "I told you so," anyway.

She wondered what Charlotte thought of Andrew's wife. Charlotte certainly wouldn't dream of showing up on the woman's doorstep, she had far too much pride for that; but did she consider his wife's actual life? Her getting up in the morning, the routines and efforts of her days, her lying down at night?

That would surely be hardest to bear: knowing that Andrew and his wife did, finally, lie down together. Just as Claudia and Bradley did.

And would do again tonight. How could she?

Strange, though: thinking of Bradley and that woman, then Bradley and herself, was – interesting. Rather exciting. She thought that must be disgusting, but there it was.

And it was still true that when Bradley came through the door, not so late tonight, she was stirred. Angry and also weary of thinking and feeling, appalled by herself and by him, nevertheless she looked at him, just starting to grey, and with deepening wrinkles around his eyes and mouth, a small stooping to his shoulders these days – nevertheless she looked at him and thought she could, if the girls weren't there and this day hadn't been the way it was, have taken his hand and led him to their

bed.Which she had never done in their life together. Reaching out was what a man did. She wasn't sure women should even demonstrate desire. He might think less of her. She doubted he thought very highly of Sophia Clarke.

"I had a visitor today." There was an edge to her ordinarily soft voice.

"Yeah?" He was eating. Apparently he failed to hear the edge.

"Actually, a friend of yours, not mine. But of course you weren't here, so it was up to me to entertain."

She seemed to have more of his interest now. "Who?"

"A young woman. Quite attractive, really, in a way. Sophia Clarke, she said her name was. She was only here for, oh, I'd say twenty minutes, but we were able to get fairly well acquainted, for so short a time."

How pale he became! And then flushed. She watched him, dispassionate now, and wondered if he was going to keel over with a stroke. If he did, she'd have to hustle the girls upstairs fast, so they wouldn't see their father suffering. Then she'd call the doctor. He would likely call an ambulance. There'd be sirens and noise and a good, painful, stab-to-the-heart punishment for bad Bradley.

A neighbour could stay with the girls. Claudia would ride along with Bradley in the back of the ambulance, holding his hand and staring down at him. He would be helpless. Breathless and terrified, he would look up at her and understand how thoroughly and entirely he was in her hands. How much he owed her. The power she had over him, of life and death.

Of course, he appeared to have a short memory. No doubt once the crisis was over, he would forget. Crisis didn't seem to get them anywhere.

Still, here they were, in another one. "Have you girls finished your first course?" she asked. "Because it's so nice out,

you could take your desserts into the backyard, if you like. It's a shame to be indoors on such a nice evening."

"Okay," Sonia said. "Are you coming too?" Bradley started to rise, but Claudia gestured at him to sit down again. How adept she was becoming at controlling people with mere movements of the hand!

"No, your father and I will finish our dinners here. You girls go and play."

She had nothing prepared to say. Thousands of words had passed through her head during the long afternoon, but none designed to be spoken aloud, to him. Still, she had managed with Sophia Clarke, for whom she had been even less prepared.

"So," she said, moving her plate to the side, setting her elbows on the table, hands folded together under her chin, regarding him coolly, "our guest this morning was telling me the two of you are in love. So sweet – I was touched. And what else touched me was, she said you want to live with her, but you haven't mentioned it because you didn't want to hurt me. That was very considerate of you, Bradley." He was looking down, into his coffee. His shoulders looked more stooped than when he'd first come through the door tonight. She thought his hands trembled slightly. Claudia herself had done her trembling earlier, and felt relatively steady.

"Still, she seemed to feel that meant she had to tell me; and of course that's understandable, in a way. It's so much easier, I'm sure, to give unpleasant news to someone you don't know." She paused: his turn to speak.

"She shouldn't have come," he muttered. She waited, but that appeared to be all he had to say. He glanced at her briefly, though, and she hoped he saw what she intended him to see: a bright disinterest.

"No doubt she shouldn't have, although of course that's

between the two of you. Still, I never feel information is wasted, or useless. You know, when I'm at home so much, I don't have your opportunities for meeting different people. Having different experiences. At the very least, a conversation with a stranger can be stimulating. Especially interesting in this case, since it had to do with me. That's really the most interesting kind, isn't it, the sort that has to do with oneself?"

Again, she paused. Pretty soon it would be too difficult to hold her hands still, or her voice steady. Really, she wanted to reach out and batter his bent head.

He looked up. "Sarcasm doesn't become you, Claudia. It doesn't sound like you." He sounded reproachful, as if she were failing him, demonstrating a flaw in her character! She could almost admire this ability of his to turn the occasions of his own sins onto her.

"Perhaps not," she agreed. "But of course you have to expect there'll be things you don't know about me, just as apparently there are things I haven't been aware of about you. My capacity for sarcasm – I don't know how it stacks up against your wanting to move out and live with someone else. Or that you lie and don't keep promises. Is it silly of me to think that maybe sarcasm is small potatoes compared with that? Given that neither of us is perfect, which seems pretty obvious, do we have equivalent imperfections, do you think?"

"Oh look, Claudia, what do you want? What am I supposed to say?" Good question; the one that could make her weep, could shatter that image of bright disinterest, crack her façade into slivers. How did he know how to do this?

Well, what did she want him to say? Probably what he'd already said once before: that he loved her, and their children, and their home. That no one else meant anything to him. That Sophia Clarke had misunderstood, or was a liar, or crazy. That he barely knew the woman. Or that he knew her, but was very,

very sorry. That it would never happen again, truly. Honestly. This time, she could believe him.

That was the best she could expect of him, and none of it would wipe out knowing he had been with Sophia Clarke. That while the woman might well have exaggerated, or misunderstood, or for that matter might have been, like Claudia, a victim of his awful lies – nevertheless, he had without any doubt been with her. At least when it happened before, Claudia had no image of whoever was involved. This time, whatever else, that face, and that body, would always be in Claudia's mind.

"Look, what can I say, Claudia?" Now he, too, was leaning forward, elbows on the table, sincerity glowing – how easy, how pleasant, to believe whatever he said! How Claudia would like to believe. "I can't deny I know her. All right, I had a little fling. But Christ," and he flung up his hands, "I don't know why she'd have thought it was serious. I swear to you, Claudia, I never, ever suggested I wanted to live with her. I couldn't leave you, you know that. I can't believe she came here and told you a thing like that – she must be crazy. I'm sorry she upset you, I never meant anything like that to happen. She's got to be nuts."

So, Claudia understood, this was no longer the fault of herself and her sarcasm and flaws, but entirely the fault of a crazed blonde stranger, and Bradley was merely misunderstood, not responsible at all.

"I'm hardly the one," she said, "to defend the woman. I would have thought you might, knowing her so much better, but that's your business and hers, not mine. But really! It's up to her how she behaves, and if she wants to have affairs, well, she'll have to live with it. That has nothing to do with you, though, or with me. You have your own responsibilities. In this house, you're the one accountable for your own behaviour."

He seized on the word. "Accountable? So I have to account to

you for everything I do? I don't have any kind of *life* that doesn't have to do with you? Do you want me to come home every night and tell you about every second of every day? Account for myself? Like you're my banker? You want me in a vault?" The answer right then was, she would prefer him in a coffin.

"Really, Bradley, how stupid do you think I am? You think I'd fall for that? Let me tell you something." Her voice was shaking now, but at least it seemed to be from anger. "If you want your so-called freedom, take it and get out. If you don't, you have to grow up. Keep promises, make the kinds of trade-offs grown-ups do. If you want this home and this family, you'll have to give up some other things. It's quite simple, it's only the sort of choice we all make: this for that. Not so difficult, once you get the hang of it."

His eyes narrowed. "Is that a threat?"

"It's advice, Bradley, and an ordinary fact of life. And at least it's a clear decision, this or that. Most of the choices the rest of us make are less obvious. So you're lucky yours is clear. That should make it easier."

What if she'd gone too far? What if he thought, "I never really considered living with Sophia Clarke, but it's bound to be better than this. Who knew Claudia could be so hard? Thank God there's still time to get out. I better walk through that door while I can." What would she do if he did? What if he did stand, go upstairs and pack a bag, come down and kiss the girls and walk out the door? How would she sleep? How would she get up in the morning? How could so much change in a day? And how could anyone be prepared for so much change in a day? Was it necessary to live every day as if everything known, seen, touched and heard could be maimed or vanished by nightfall?

He stood. She got the most terrible pain in her chest, just below her breasts. But he walked around behind her, put his

hands on her shoulders, bent to lay his cheek on the top of her head. "I'm sorry, Claudie."

So he was a coward.

But so, it turned out in those last few seconds, was she.

Quite a family.

Stuck, anyway. She could see that whatever happened now, they were stuck with each other. He'd made his choice, such as it was, and she'd made hers, and the rest would just be a matter of making the best of it. Learning to live with it. She felt quite old.

"I'm sorry, Claudie," he repeated. Now his hands were moving on her shoulders, down her arms, tentatively, lightly across her breasts. When she didn't brush him away, he'd have known.

"I'll try to be better, honestly. You deserve someone better. You're a good woman, Claudie. I love you. I never meant to hurt you so bad." She sighed, and gave up.

And the girls came back in, and Claudia cleared the table and washed the dishes, and there was a good deal of noise from the living-room where Bradley, it seemed, was able to settle down to read the newspaper with the girls' racket going on around him, and then she put them to bed, and read them one story each, fetched them each a glass of water, turned off their bedroom lights, warned them to get to sleep right away.

She was so weary, she went to bed herself then, keeping far on her side of the mattress. Bradley was still downstairs. She wondered if he was telephoning Sophia Clarke, and if so what he was saying. She wondered if he'd wait, instead, until he could see her. She expected he'd be angry, and would probably shout at the woman and blame her for his troubles. That might end it, or might not. They might, like Bradley and Claudia herself, wind up in a sort of reconciliation. It would depend on whether Sophia Clarke was as willing as Claudia to make these adjustments.

She hoped her own daughters would grow up braver than she. It would be hard for them, though, given such a poor

example. Would it be better for them in the end if she threw their father out? Would they think, later, "Our mother really had gumption"? Not likely. They would miss him. No doubt they would blame her. They would grow up, probably, to be the sort of women who hung on to men, no matter what.

Of course that day ended trust; but it didn't end the marriage. It might not be what she'd had in mind, it was certainly no young girl's dream, but it had its advantages. It was, at worst, a workable economic partnership, a practical way to raise children. Since their rages and upheavals had to do with huge events, betrayals, they rarely quarrelled about smaller matters, and so their union turned out to be, in a peculiar way, more placid in the long run than the marriages of many others.

Also, pleasure was still possible. She can almost feel him now, all these years later: can feel herself longing for skin. He was very skilful. Even knowing how he must have learned those skills, she continued to enjoy them for some time.

And now, at more than twice the age she was when Sophia Clarke knocked on her door, she appears to have no more idea than she did at thirty-four what she'll do without him.

She wonders what happened to Sophia Clarke?

Perhaps he went on with her, after all. For a time, anyway, until there were others. She'll be in her sixties now. It's not impossible, at this distance, for Claudia to wish her to have done well. She wonders if, looking back, Sophia Clarke sees herself at all the way Charlotte may: as a woman who has had adventures, perhaps has done some bad, betraying things, but in the end is not a bad, betraying person, by her own, quite personal lights.

She wishes Charlotte would get in touch. It would be interesting, with the perspective of years and a kind of attached dispassion, to talk about this kind of thing with somebody who likely knows.

five

ONE DAY WHEN CHARLOTTE WAS still in university and relatively aimless, her eye was caught by a photograph of a battered child on the cover of a magazine. The child had a blackened eye, a flattened nose, bruised swollen lips. Its eyes stared passionlessly off the page. She was stopped by those eyes. Their flatness seemed to demand attention – at least that she buy the magazine. Reading it, she learned something for the first time about tortured children. Is it stupid to choose a life on the basis of a picture in a magazine?

Sheltered and cherished herself (a sign of being cherished that she even went to university, at a time when not so many girls were allowed those dreams and decisions), she'd never seen such a thing before; had never imagined.

Charlotte, who didn't long for children of her own, longed

for that child; desired to hold it in her arms; raged to keep it beyond the reach of its tormentors. She couldn't account for the power of the photograph; then thought it maybe didn't matter: that there might be simply messages in the universe that demanded attention. There were answers out there, if you kept alert.

It made her aware of the kind of cosmic magic that also accounted, with luck, for love.

She realized that the photograph that resulted in her life (and which, much folded and worn, is still tucked into the dresser drawer where she keeps important papers) might not even have been a real one, of a real beaten child. It might have been merely a model, brutalized by clever cosmetics. But real or not, it was true. She became a social worker. She got work with a children's agency. Whatever else she came to doubt or question, she has not lost faith with that photograph.

She did, however, learn in the course of her career that little was as simple or as clear as the picture. Some things were: a dead child, and there were several of those over the years, broken-boned, with organs crushed and shattered, little bodies, and sullen, frightened grown-ups; children with the burns of stove elements engraved in their buttocks, or those of cigarettes on chests and backs and thighs; slow, brain-damaged children, held under bathwater until their oxygen died, emerging dull-eyed and permanently anaesthetized – all those were clear enough.

Other lines were more difficult to discern: distraught, overburdened mothers simply snapping; tense, struggling fathers lashing out, uncontrolled for the moment, then filled with regret. But it would happen again and again. Outraged or irritated neighbours might call Charlotte's agency, and there she would be, knocking on strange doors, terrified of her own possible misjudgements. Parents might turn on her, children

might be loyal to them, a whole bruised family might cling together and insist, "We love each other. We don't mean to cause this hurt, but sometimes it just happens. But we love each other, and anyway, it's not your business."

Parents might weep, from guilt or fear or true regret, and say, "I promise you, it won't happen again. It was a terrible thing, and I won't let it happen again." Of course it would happen again. But children, seeing their parents weep, and frightened also of this stranger in their kitchen, and of their own unknown futures, wrapped arms around the necks of guilty parents and clung and wept as well, so that Charlotte often felt herself becoming the cause of their terror and pain. What was she to do? If she made a mistake, she might find herself returning to claim only a small dead body. Or she might find herself condemning a child to separation and longing, a new and different sort of brutality.

Whatever happened, it was beyond her powers to heal. She could never make things right. It was hard, getting used to being unable to fix. Having put faith in her own will, it was a shock to learn how easily her will could be thwarted, by parental pleas, by rules that prevented action and by frightened, damaged children themselves.

There was a woman, only in her late twenties, the same age as Charlotte then but looking a decade older and many decades more weary, who looked at her blankly, as Charlotte talked and talked. "Look," Charlotte said, "it's against the law to whip your kids with a skipping rope." Their toy had turned into a weapon, so that the three children had great red welts around their legs, their hips, across their backs. "You could lose them for doing this to them."

The woman frowned, puzzled and innocent. "But I got whipped. Anyway, what am I supposed to do when they won't mind? I can't make them mind."

And Charlotte, looking into that woman's tired eyes, told her, "We have to find some other way. Whipping is wrong and if you keep on, we'll have to take your children away from you for their own safety. You'll find yourself in court." She paused, hearing the hardness of her voice, feeling her own desire to punish, took a breath, went on. "You have to learn to keep a lid on your temper. You're the grown-up, it's up to you to control yourself. Children don't always know how, and you have to show them. Whether it happened to you isn't the point now; the point is, it's not allowed. We won't allow it." The woman's eyes narrowed. It rather looked as if she hated Charlotte.

It wasn't, perhaps, very different from the way her eyes might have narrowed with hate as her parents whipped her, or the way her children's eyes narrowed with hate as she whipped them. On and on it went; and it seemed that now, Charlotte was also joining this ring of pain with some barely controlled desire of her own. Was she any better, then?

What would she do in this woman's position, with three helter-skelter kids underfoot and a husband who brought home almost no money? Who knew how this young woman had expected her life to be? – not like this, anyway. No one would hope for this.

"Look," Charlotte said, leaning forward over the table. "What you owe your children goes beyond basic food and shelter and warmth. You do that, I can see, but if you bring children into the world, you also owe them love and protection. That's your job. So maybe you could try to think of love as if it was food; give them a hug the way you give them lunch, just automatically. Give them a kiss when they do something right instead of whipping them when they do something wrong. Get yourself out of the habit of hurting them; because hurting them hurts you, too, I can see that. Children have so much love to give, you surely don't want to lose that."

"My kids love me," the woman said sullenly. And so, they said, they did.

Charlotte felt surrounded by misery some days, but not in misery herself. Frustration and sorrow, she believed at the time, could hardly constitute true despair. It took Andrew to teach her differently (among other lessons), but she hadn't met him yet.

She wondered how Claudia managed. At the time, Claudia had only two children, but she and Bradley just scraped by, and she was home all day with the girls, and didn't she just want to scream sometimes? "Sometimes I spank them," Claudia said. "But never hard, and never when I'm really angry." She listened with horror to Charlotte's tales. "It's hard to believe people can be so wicked," she said. "Especially parents. How can they? Children are such a miracle!" Claudia did regard her daughters as miracles, and doted on them. Charlotte wondered how that felt, to be a doting mother.

So by the time Charlotte met Andrew, crashing into him in a court-house corridor, she was somewhat experienced in the shortcomings and tragedies of others, as well as with some flaws and sorrows of her own. But she would have to say, looking back, that she was only on the brink of learning what it meant to be truly refused her desires.

She spent her thirties learning that.

And other more joyful things, too, of course.

It was remarkable, after all, to have stumbled into a man who cheered her independence (however useful he also found it) and her intelligence, as well as her bones and breasts. Perhaps over ten years she forgot how remarkable that was, so that her appreciation lapsed somewhat. Her sharpness had seemed (and would again in the future) often to frighten men; except for Andrew (except when her sharpness was aimed in his direction, and then he didn't much like it either).

A man who appreciated both her brain and her body and whose brain and body she could appreciate, as well; whose work she could respect, and who respected hers; with whom she could talk about practically anything, working through events with him, and ideas, arguing amiably about ways of seeing so that the scope of their views grew wider and broader and deeper – all this was what seemed to her a miracle: this rare combination of respect and (reasonable) truthfulness and, really, delicious lust. The times they had!

He said, "You must have known some pretty stupid guys. Or harmful ones." He said he wanted to offer trust, companionship and love; a refuge from her disbelief and wariness. He said what he wanted with her was also refuge. From duty, she supposed. From obligations and necessities.

It was a romantic view. She thought men tended, in general, to be terribly romantic. In her own unsentimental view, she found this sweet but incomplete, and a substantial luxury. Romanticism pretty well ruled out ambiguities; so that he didn't care to see that as well as being a refuge for her, he also demonstrated her disbelief and wariness. And that she could not always be a refuge for him. Their circumstances required her to be alert, all the time, to the inevitable departure. It wasn't possible simply to *rest* with a man who took so many other people into account.

Claudia said, of herself, "You learn to live with some things. You weigh them against each other and decide." Charlotte thought that was what she was doing, also, and more or less successfully.

How different was Bradley from Andrew? Charlotte and Andrew spent almost a decade together (as much as they could be together, given the constrictions) before that moment when she looked at him and thought, "I'm so tired."

This was not particularly his fault. "But nothing's changed,

nothing's different," he cried. "I thought we were doing okay. I thought we'd found our own way to manage. I've tried so hard, Charlotte! How could you think I could do any more?"

She had also tried hard. Could not do more.

Nothing had changed, nothing was different. How could this go on?

Hundreds and thousands of times over the years he said, "I love you." And then, "I should go home now." Eventually she simply couldn't bear to hear it one more time. It was hardly her fault, or even Andrew's, that he didn't foresee that.

How astonishing that thirty years later there is still this bitterness hovering at the tip of her emotions. Whatever is the point? Do other old women have these little rages that leave them trembling, looking back?

Does Claudia?

At least, unlike Bradley, Andrew didn't turn on her, he didn't try to make their failure her fault. She can no longer see, but can recall seeing, his face filled with grief. And also, it must be said, anger. She remembers him saying, "Are you sure?" And, "Oh, Charlotte, I do love you. Are you sure? I'll miss you so badly."

And has he missed her? Does the old man behind that blue-painted wooden door out in the suburbs still ever regret her? Does he ever wish he'd made another choice?

Does Claudia? Did Bradley, ever?

To Charlotte, visiting her friend and her husband, it seemed obvious that Bradley's petulant, self-regarding and punishing angers were a kind of abuse. And how did he dare? She thought that at least he was afraid of her. She thought that at least he was probably muted, in her presence. She wondered if that made Claudia's life more difficult later, when Charlotte was gone.

As far as she knows, Bradley never struck Claudia; and she's

sure that she'd know. He had other means of torment, though.

How could Claudia bear him to touch her? Yet she went on, having her babies, her daughters. The death of love, for Charlotte, is so immediately the death of desire. She imagines it must be a dreadful thing, to make love without some kind of trust, or some kind of respect.

Claudia said it was not impossible at all, and laughed in that secret-pleasure way some women have for some private circumstances. She used to say that if she wasn't too sharply or recently reminded of Bradley's failings, she found it oddly easy to enjoy his body. The idea made Charlotte shiver.

All that was a good many years ago now, for both of them.

Perhaps between the two of them, Claudia and Charlotte, they've managed to create one single, whole, full life. Maybe Claudia actually relished, the way she could Bradley's body, Charlotte's excursions into what must have looked like wickedness; and maybe Claudia gave Charlotte a relationship, however remote, with solidity and normalcy; at least of the sort promoted by certain kinds of magazines.

Maybe Claudia looked at Charlotte and thought, "Well, if that's the sort of hands Bradley's in, it may not be so bad. At least it's not insulting."

Aside from being a husband, a father, a man spoken for, who had made quite serious promises he found himself able to break, Andrew wasn't a bit like Bradley. He was interested in Charlotte and in her life and her work. He asked questions, and then spoke as easily about himself as he expected her to talk about herself. It seemed fair. He seemed unusual. He was unusual. That must be why she remembers him so vividly.

He would have been the same way with his family, his wife and his two sons. Charlotte was bitterly jealous, but could see how funny that was.

The other funny thing must be getting into circumstances

even knowing that they'll likely end, and even guessing how. Wouldn't Charlotte have assumed she'd know better?

No. And yes. She knew better.

But it was like the fairy tales: there were far more questions than the answers offered in the stories. The grown-up Charlotte couldn't always make sense of the rules. She didn't see that it was possible to promise love would last, for instance, so what sense or sanctity was there necessarily in marriage? (She could, of course, make out its practical benefits, as an efficient organization that smoothed certain difficulties involving survival.)

But love (by which she did not mean romance) was astonishing, whatever form it took. Because it was rare and therefore precious, who would turn away from its comradeship and laughter and loyalty and trust, affection and pleasure (and pain)? That may have been what people were supposed to do if love appeared in inappropriate or awkward circumstances; but it seemed absurd to her.

On the other hand, she understood that this absurdity which seemed so obvious would be disagreeable to the world at large; so that disobeying the rules would require secrecy, discretion and a grave discordance between interior and external lives.

That seemed simple enough, if not easy.

She knew some other things, as well. She had learned that when it comes to love, however it appears, the end is revealed in the beginning. In the face and voice and words of the loved one on the first day are contained the face and voice and words of the loved one on the last. Only on the last, the face may be twisted, the voice edged, the words as intense, only aimed at a different passion, intended to hurt.

Charlotte knew all this so well by the time she met Andrew that she could watch him sleeping (on one of those rare mornings, his family out of town, that he permitted himself to stay

over) and decipher in his peaceful features the bitterness of ending. She listened to soft breath and understood it could, and no doubt would, turn harsh one day. She looked at the closed, crumpled-skin eyelids with their long pale lashes and saw behind them dark blue eyes that could become capable of loathing.

Although, as it turned out, she was somewhat wrong.

Do men, waking early beside sleeping women, scrutinize them also and wonder about the mysteries behind eyelids and lips? Do they wonder what words, in which tones, are waiting to be spoken? Hurled? Do they realize there are things that won't be permanently borne?

Perhaps not. Perhaps good women, wives, teach them otherwise. There are women who seem to have the gifts of constancy and faith. Or, as Claudia suggests, simply determination and will: to make something last.

Those women must encourage that romanticism in their men, then. Which isn't very fair or realistic, and causes these problems for honest mistresses.

Oh my.

And still another funny thing is this desire to peer into his life now, see how it looks and sounds from the vantage point of his hedge. Or the shrubbery beneath his bedroom window.

Could she be getting that bold?

Perhaps not, but she is increasingly inclined to go back.

Claudia might say Charlotte has never had to cultivate the grit of will, the pure determination to go on, that Claudia herself required to live with Bradley for those forty-seven years; and of course she's right. But a decade isn't nothing; ten years also require some adjustments; bendings and alterations to both desire and will.

And more than mere bendings and alterations: true terrible events, as well.

There is, of course, no point in regrets, and it isn't regret, only a question, to wonder how it might have been to have a child.

Charlotte has only heard about, never felt, the longing for children that apparently consumes some women. She has wondered if it's a true longing, or merely a learned desire. If it is true, then to be missing it would make her freakish, she supposed, missing some normal component of womanhood. And if she were freakish that way, she might be in others, also.

Would that account for a certain incapacity for guilt? Did not most women absorb guilt like water, like food? Did they not breathe it in from the air, transforming it into a basic element? So one might gather, from how badly they seemed to feel about even the smallest things, and how warmly they seemed to welcome blame.

If a man beat a woman, she might tell Charlotte, "It was my fault, I should know better when he's in that mood." If he beat her children, she might say, "It was my fault, I should have made sure they were out of his way, I should have made them be quiet, I should have made sure he had nothing to get angry about." Women were always blaming themselves, and it made Charlotte herself want to shake them.

It seemed Charlotte lacked crucial requirements for becoming a mother herself: desire and guilt.

Impulses were hardly the same. Those she did have on occasion, but their source was less desire than curiosity, or hope. Now and then she might think, "How interesting, to have this man's child," or that man's. The questions would be, "What would the child be like, and what would I be like?" And the man, of course, how might he be with a child in his life? But she never felt it with such urgency, force or determination that it came to anything.

Quite the opposite, in fact. Because when it did come to

something, all the urgency, force and determination were in the other direction: what on earth would she do with a child? Andrew already had his sons. She couldn't bear it, couldn't do it and so, at some risk to herself, she didn't bear or do it.

How she envies women who came of age with birth-control pills, however perilous they turned out to be. And then later still had better access to abortion. Charlotte had, at the time, to rely on less certain preventions, and then, that once, on a dangerous, difficult, painful, expensive and shoddy operation – who are the fools who think this is simple? At best it is not simple. At best it's still a horror.

But then it was also blood in a back room, searing pain, and terror, alone later, of bleeding to death. And grief, of course – who says there isn't grief?

It was interesting to see Andrew's face when she told him. She'd known it would be, one way or another. "I'm pregnant," she said bluntly, because there was no gentle, easy way of going about this. "We weren't careful enough." She saw he was trying; that he was making, considering his own circumstances, quite an effort. If she hadn't been so absorbed in herself, she would have felt touched. Even as it was, she understood he was exceptional. She knew of other men, not even married ones who were already fathers, in this situation.

But all his goodness couldn't prevent horror, then despair, then fear, from flickering unmistakably across his features before he got them under control. "What do you think we should do?" he asked then. "What do you want to do?" His voice was even, and neither it nor his expression gave any further sign. It was correct, of course, his response, but how lonely she felt, for a moment. Had she hoped for something else?

She has always been cautious with her hopes. She has always understood it's unwise to spiral from a small picture, a vague desire, into great possibilities or sweeping perspectives.

So she hadn't permitted herself to examine very closely the possible scripts they might follow.

In this situation there could be no satisfactory script or happy outcome.

It was already clear what she would need to do. Only, maybe it would have been nice if he'd looked surprised rather than frightened, delighted rather than despairing. Or just if he'd put his arms around her with an offer of mutual comfort. Instead he quite properly asked, "Tell me what you want to do."

She supposed he trusted her not to say, "You'll have to leave your family and marry me." Or anything like that. They trusted each other to behave well.

"An abortion, I think," she said. Speaking the words out loud, even having known she would be saying them, did make her weep, and that did result in his arms around her. He wept, as well. She knew, though, that the pictures he was seeing were not of her. She understood he was seeing his living sons. Perhaps he was also hearing the other occasions on which he'd heard the words "I'm pregnant" and there'd been no hesitation. No doubt like her he was sorrowful now, but it was a different sorrow.

Bound to be, of course. She was neither an unreasonable nor an irrational woman.

"Oh God," he said. Then, "Do you know how?"

"I can find out." As of course she could, knowing so many different kinds of people.

"I'm so sorry, Char." He was rocking her. "I don't know how it could have happened. I thought we were careful. But I'm so sorry. I hate it, that you have to go through this."

She loved him, of course. "It's all right," she said, and stroked his hair.

He drove her to the place she found. He paid the money, waited for her, drove her home. He sat with her, and made her

tea, until she couldn't bear his distress at her distress, and couldn't contain her own and made him leave. "Call me," he said, "if you need anything at all. If anything at all feels wrong, I don't care what time it is or if you need to call me at home, promise me you won't hesitate for a second."

She promised.

"I'll be back tonight anyway," he said. "To check that you're okay."

Those hours alone were terrible and long. She believed she might die, from the pain and from being alone. She bled and bled. It felt as if she were being stabbed. She would not call him, or anyone. She was grateful for his grief and concern, but didn't have strength for anything beyond her own wounds. She couldn't comfort or reassure him, if he saw her like this, curled up, crying out, bloody; and he couldn't help. This hurt so much, he couldn't have begun to divert her.

If she died, he would find her. It would be awkward and difficult, but he would do something. If she died, she wouldn't care, anyway. She fell asleep finally, and when she woke up he was back and holding her hand, shaking it slightly, clearly frightened. "Oh, Char," he whispered. "I'm so sorry. I thought I was losing you. I was just about to call for help. Is it terrible?"

Not any more. She was just exhausted, in every way. She couldn't even get clear to herself what it meant when he said, "I thought I was losing you." It could have been grief, she supposed, or selfishness or only fear. They held hands for a while, without words, until she fell asleep again.

She was fine again in a couple of days. She was a strong woman. It seemed to be some time, however, before he was able to regard her as restored. He treated her delicately, and humbly, for several weeks.

She supposed this was almost as intimate an experience as having a child together. She expected it was somewhat similar

to the way he would have treated his wife, after she bore their sons. Did he see parallels and similarities? She imagined that in his position she might try to streamline events and emotions to keep them as manageable as possible.

Perhaps he was simply guilty, in either case: for having caused so much turmoil and pain, in childbirth or in child prevention. Enduring this event together, however, or as much as it was possible to endure such a singular event together, had a welding effect. They were joined in very serious, unfrivolous ways. Much as, Charlotte imagined, he and his wife were joined, by momentous events, in very serious, unfrivolous ways.

For herself alone, she was relieved. Certainly she did not want a child, could not have managed with a child, had no desire whatever for the various kinds of disruption a child would have meant. She felt her body was her own again, pain-free and uninvaded.

Also she did not believe she would have been a good mother. It seemed, from what she had observed, a very risky undertaking for everyone involved.

But she did not forget, and has not forgotten. There has never been an August tenth since that August tenth when Charlotte was thirty-two and lay on a table in that back room under the hands of a stranger, bleeding and in pain, when she hasn't remembered. For a long time now, the memory has been more or less detached from Andrew, but now it seems to have reconnected. She can see him again, bending worriedly over her, stroking her hand.

Before she left that back room that day, she was shown the form of the foetus. There wasn't much to see. She turned her head away. Later she wondered why someone who made his living that way found it necessary to try to punish a person who had hired him, who helped keep him in work. When she

got her strength back, she became angry, and wished she'd thought of something to say at the time.

She wondered how it was disposed of; although it hardly mattered. As with other matters, as with Andrew himself, she has found it quite possible to remember and be sad, but not for an instant to regret.

She told Claudia, of course – what a burdensome friend she has been to such a nice woman, patient wife, devoted mother! Really, Charlotte has been or done just about all the things Claudia must despise.

"He was tremendous," Charlotte said of Andrew. "It must be awful, going through something like that alone. I feel so lucky." Claudia might well look puzzled at Charlotte's concept of luck, but it was true: he had stuck with her, and cared, through an extraordinary and dreadful event. And then was extremely careful to prevent it from occurring again.

She never thought of asking him what course he might have wanted her to take. It occurs to her now that it was astonishing she didn't ask; and remarkable he didn't say. He might well have liked to be a father again.

Not that that would have likely altered anything.

Does he ever remember on an August tenth what day it is, what happened all those years ago? They might by now have had a middle-aged child. A boy; the foetus was male, she was told.

One way and another, by the end of Andrew, by the end of her thirties, she could hardly remember herself from before. Her work was much the same, and the children, and her concentration on them and the things that happened to them and that she tried to change for them, but she couldn't recall how she had actually been, before she was thirty and collided with Andrew. How spoiled she must have been before, how indulged and undisciplined. She felt as if she went through a furnace during those ten years, and became steel.

She thought by the time she turned forty that she could almost understand saints: great sacrifices willingly made, even lives abandoned, in the name of, for the gain of, in the hope of, for the faith in, love.

Charlotte's rather stern grandmother would no doubt have called that blasphemous. But Charlotte could see aspects of her experience as a sort of secular sainthood: sacrifices made for an unfrivolous, not-romantic, hard and difficult love.

Well, what was her great sacrifice?

Saying goodbye to him night after night. Picturing him embracing his wife, playing games with his sons, teaching them to be good men, being a good man himself. Barbecuing on Saturday nights and going out to movies, dinners, visiting with friends. The whole structure of marriage, happy or not; the system and the expectations. He rarely spoke of whether he was happily married. Apparently he was at least contentedly married. Charlotte said goodbye to him night after night.

Someone in, say, Claudia's position, could hardly regard Charlotte's experience as either saintly or sacrificial.

No doubt Andrew also made sacrifices. "It's not easy for me, either," he told her on occasion. For one thing, he had to steadfastly lie about where he'd been, so many nights out of ten years. She supposed he said he was working, but perhaps that was only her own lack of creativity. Perhaps, accustomed to devising defences for clients, he was more adept at alibis.

So it's not that she was making all the sacrifices, or giving all the love. It's only that he wanted everything and could have it, and that Charlotte also wanted everything, but had to be satisfied with fractions.

She may have been strong by the end and accustomed to some forms of abandonment, but to be abandoned by her own caring and by love – that was terrible. When she thought, "No more. I don't care any more," and found her heart quite empty

when she looked at him, that was a kind of death.

Is that what Claudia's travelling through now in her widowhood – that void, that vacancy, that deep black empty pit where some great feeling used to be?

She remembers watching Andrew drive away for the last time. Her chest felt filled and closed, cemented over. She felt as if she couldn't breathe. She crept to her bed and huddled there, curled up in misery, too dry to weep. She wondered where her life was now. She couldn't make out any future. She even wondered if she shouldn't call him back; because anything was better than the chasm into which she was staring.

But if she did that, it would only happen again. Whereas if she kept staring into the darkness now, she might see her way through.

She felt transformed, transfigured into the clear white purity of pain. She tried to compare this grief to others: refugees saying final farewells to family members they loved, mothers cradling starved, dead children, even the twisted sorrow of the terrible families broken up by Charlotte herself. None of this mattered. Trying to quantify grief did not make it vanish, or even diminish.

She was surprised to find herself waking up; surprised to have been asleep. She could breathe again, although she could certainly not make out a future. She was immensely lonely. She felt as if her own voice, inside her own head, must be the only voice left in the world that she could hear.

She sat up finally, reached for the phone and dialled Claudia. She started to sob at the sound of Claudia's voice, couldn't stop, couldn't speak and had to hang up. "Oh, Charlotte," Claudia cried when she tried again, "I thought somebody'd *died*. I was just picking up the phone to call you back. I was thinking of coming right over."

She was very kind. She said, "Oh, Char, I'm so sorry you've

been hurt." Her greatest kindness was in not saying, "I don't know what you expected." Nor did she say, "I can't imagine why you'd expect me, of all people, to sympathize." Did she want to? Did she have to bite her tongue?

She said, "Listen Charlotte, pack a bag and grab a cab and come stay here for a few days. You can lie around in bed, or out in the sun, and we'll drink tea in the mornings and hit the gin in the afternoons and you'll just be *away*. I know it's hard. It might help to get out of your own place."

"What about the girls?" All four, by then. "And Bradley?"

"The girls can look after themselves. So can he, for that matter. Do come over, Charlotte. Pack a bag and come right now."

And so she did. She called in sick to work, and for the next few days they drank tea and talked in the mornings, drank gin and talked in the afternoons. Paid some attention to Claudia's family in the evenings, in a hazy, benevolent sort of way. They behaved like careless, hopeful girls again. Charlotte even made some jokes about Andrew, making them giggle. Claudia's daughters laughed at the two of them. Bradley moved around them fairly silently, pausing now and then to criticize Claudia for undone chores, but not pushing, not very hard. Perhaps he saw that Charlotte was in a somewhat dangerous mood.

After a week, Charlotte went back to her own home. It hurt to go through the front door. Everything contained something of Andrew, it seemed, some word or action attached to every piece of furniture, each wall and every vase and book. She wondered, for a while, if she would have to sell the house and move.

She wondered if he'd called while she was gone. Perhaps, worried, he'd even come over, letting himself in with his key, finding the place empty, sniffing the stifling air of a closed-up house in hot weather. Either he wondered, or he took her at her word and vanished. She did miss him. She didn't know what to do with the hours he'd filled, and her body was restless

and lost with its own loneliness. She began the process of putting him out of her mind.

She went on, of course. She phoned Claudia to say, "I just wanted to thank you, for taking such good care of me."

"Are you all right?"

"I'm better. I will be all right. Thanks to you."

Because who knows what drastic thing she might have done, without Claudia?

She'd bought this house for herself during that decade with Andrew, wanting a private place to belong, no mere apartment. Of course she didn't sell it. Andrew is still here, and so are others. It feels cosy. All those years surround her, including the rages and betrayals and various passions – all of that has soaked into the floors and walls.

She wonders what losses and pleasures have soaked into the floors and walls of Andrew's home. She wonders, if she got quite close and shut her eyes and breathed in very deeply, if she could catch the scent of how his life has gone.

Oh dear. Really. Here she is, sitting with her old friend's letter still in her hand, thinking only, or mainly, of herself. And of further, possibly disastrous, adventures. Really, coffee hasn't made her much less addled, after all that Scotch.

She could phone Claudia right now and do what Claudia once did for her. She could say, "Hop on a train in the morning, as soon as you can, and come here. We'll lie in the sun (because what harm could it do to our skin at this stage?) and talk and drink and eat and nap. You can bake out grief, and sleep it away. Come as soon as you can."

Except she can imagine Claudia, after such a time of strain, being caught unprepared by telephone calls, feeling pressured by one person and another, incapable of instant judgements, becoming resentful and harried. It would likely be better to write.

How to account for their friendship? All these years of words and silence, food and help, fondness, affection and loyalty? Certainly it must have to do with more than longevity: a comradeship begun in childhood, merely growing old. Maybe it's that while they may have been, still are, quite different women, with quite different lives, they also have some things in common: stubbornness, pride, a terrible desire for perfection.

Perhaps those bonds of character have also been their separate downfalls. Their flaws have helped to hold them, but have also caused much chaos.

What if Claudia, instead of stubbornly staying with Bradley, had struck out on her own? Hard to imagine. Claudia has always been in partnership with someone: Charlotte through their childhood, Bradley ever since. And she had her children. Now, though, what does she have? One way or another, she winds up alone.

As does Charlotte.

Their perfectionism: obviously turned to different ends, and certainly with different results. Did it mean that Claudia was reasonably free of guilt when the end came with Bradley? That, as for Charlotte, events are survivable because she knows she did her best, gave her most, spoke as clearly as she could and is sure she could not have done, given or spoken any more? In Charlotte's own experience, some people, especially men, have misinterpreted, and were bewildered when the end came. But by then Charlotte was hard. Because why didn't they see, why had they not paid better attention?

Claudia did her best with Bradley, and at the end, surely that would lessen grief; or put it in a different light.

Unfortunately, Bradley would probably be unaware. He seemed to see it as simply Claudia's job to do her best. He would have known about the death of love only from his own point of view, from those times he killed it himself.

Love dies just like people, or other animals, or plants. Sometimes it does so in a moment: a tipping instant when it becomes profound disinterest. The opposing threat to love, in Charlotte's experience, isn't hatred, it's the death of care.

She can hardly write that in her letter. What can she say?

"Dear Claudia," she begins.

"I'm so sorry. I just got your letter today, and was so pleased to see it that I poured a Scotch to celebrate hearing from you, and then I read it and had a couple more drinks and thought about us, and how sad you sounded, and now I'm a bit wobbly from drink and can't think what to say, exactly, except I'm sorry, and I wish I'd known. I would have come and helped, if you'd wanted. I'm no nurse, and I don't suppose Bradley would have liked me to be one for him anyway, but I could have made tea for you and me at midnight, and toast in the morning, and maybe rubbed your shoulders when you were weary. Maybe you wanted to be on your own, though.

"But how are you now? Reading your letter was like hearing your voice – how like yourself you sound! Now I'm sitting here drinking coffee all by myself and wishing you were with me. Would you come? Would you like to get away? I promise if you did, we could talk, or I would leave you alone if that's what you wanted.

"I have trouble realizing we're old. People are dying. It's strange. I'm finding it strange, anyway. I don't know what your secret is, but I have one or two, as well. Maybe we could sit up late again, like we used to, and tell each other our secrets?

"Yes, I remember when we met – what babies we were! And then a whole lifetime of events and upsets and pleasures. Comparing breasts, I keep remembering us doing that when we were young. (Mine have quite a discouraging sag, by the way – how are yours? Come visit, so we can compare again.)

"I get scared sometimes, and I'm finding that fear has some

peculiar results. How about you? Maybe it's the shortage of future. And the unknown timing, of course. It feels unfair to have last moments hanging over one's head.

"Forgive me if that was tasteless – just whistling in the dark, I suppose. All I started out to say was, I'm your friend, whatever you need a friend to be right now, and I would love to see you.

"Then maybe after we'd talked about our lives and all our circumstances, we could discuss the ways it's quite nice being old, too, because after all, there are some. It's only, I keep waiting to be wise, do you?

"Oh Claudia, do come, it would be so good.

"All my love,

"Charlotte"

six

CLAUDIA ISN'T SURE AT ALL THAT she's ready to face the girls, but here they come anyway, converging on her for the weekend, starting tomorrow. Sonia the organizer called last night to let her know they had it all arranged.

Do they think she has nothing to do? Do they assume that, without their father, she has no life, that they can just land in on her with virtually no warning?

"So I'll be picking up Sharon, and Sandra's taking the train, and Susan will be coming in her own car – we should all get there about noon, I expect. Susan says she can only stay till Sunday morning, she has to get back, but the rest of us are clear till after Sunday dinner, if we have it early. Is that okay?"

A little late to ask. "Of course. I'll look forward to it, dear."

"It's only, we thought you might need some cheering up. Are you sleeping any better?"

"Oh yes. I'm doing fine. I hope you haven't been worrying. Is that why you're coming?"

"Not at all!" By her emphasis, Sonia demonstrated the lie. Unlike her father, or Susan for that matter, Sonia's not very good at skirting truth. "We just decided we wanted to see you. Spend a little time, even if it's not for long. It's hard for us all to get away at the same time."

Of course it can be done, they managed for their father's funeral; but emergencies are different. This is rather touching. Can she spend a weekend, though, with these women she's raised, and maintain an innocent face? Except they expect her innocence. Like Bradley, they assume her virtue. She would have to behave in some extraordinarily outlandish way for them to think otherwise, and even if she did, they'd likely put it down to grief.

It might be interesting to behave outlandishly. To begin, with them, to slip towards whatever she will be next. Already she is no longer a wife; and while she will always be their mother, they've all been adults for a good many years and perhaps should be met on a more level footing now. She's been thinking so much of herself she has maybe paid too little attention to the effects on them of their father's death; he must have meant something to them, after all.

She wonders what. She wonders what they thought of him, and how they felt about him, and if they have also been changing and assessing since his death. She wonders what they knew, and know. She wonders if it might be possible to speak some matters out loud now; if that might, in his permanent absence, be safe enough.

Although she is still their mother, and it is still up to her to protect them, if they need protection. But if someone broke the silence, what might they all say? Perhaps years' worth of untold secrets, five women, including herself, who spent so long

together in the same house, keeping an eye on one man.

At least she won't have to pretend to miss him, because she does. Or at any rate, she still misses the space he used to occupy: all those hours, all those thoughts. That *awareness* of him all those years, and especially the last year.

It will be joyous to have sounds in the house again, for a couple of days. "Are any of the children coming?" she asked Sonia on the phone.

"No, just us. It's our very own weekend together."

Perhaps they need that anyway. Maybe she provides an excuse for them to get away, just briefly, from their very busy lives. Except for Susan, who has to hurry back for reasons she will no doubt not reveal. She keeps herself to herself, does Susan; Claudia wonders if any of the other sisters know much about her. Certainly Claudia never has. But of the four, Susan and Sonia have been the least trouble: Sonia because she's a planner, an organizer, a practical woman; Susan for less identifiable reasons that seem to mean she takes care of herself. Even as a child she didn't ask for help. If she fell off her bike, she bathed and bandaged her own knees. When her first period came, she went out and got her own napkins, then later switched on her own accord to tampons. Of the four girls, Susan has made her mother feel most inessential. Perhaps she thought her mother had little to offer in the way of comfort or advice. Although she didn't go to her father, either.

A blessing, how they turned out: all of them fine girls.

Hardly girls. Susan just turned thirty-six. Sonia's forty-four. It's a rare woman who does that sort of thing any more, producing four children in the space of eight years. Claudia recalls their childhoods as a noisy, occasionally feuding, but basically untroubled time. She can also recall her own exhaustion, impatience, bad temper and days, even weeks, when she could barely drag herself out of bed in the mornings, she was so

utterly discouraged. She might love them (did, of course), but where was the future? She felt, sometimes, snared: by Bradley, daughters, interminable, unbreakable routines. What happened to the young woman who worked in a hardware store and had a vague ambition to be a teacher? Was she so dazzled by love, or by hands on her breasts, down her spine, nuzzling warmly between her legs?

Oh yes, yes, she was. And all the rest of it, too, all those things she'd assumed marriage meant: safety, and an infinity of affection.

But if her image had turned out to lack both accuracy and subtlety, she still couldn't give it up. If exhaustion and discouragement were a price, she could learn to take that into account. Because for one thing, look at Charlotte, who kept gambling, abandoning one thing in favour of the next, which might be better, or might not, and what did she have? After ten years of marriage, Claudia had this busy, preoccupying and, yes, loving family, give or take times when love was apparently elsewhere. And in those same ten years what did Charlotte gain? She had a history. A set of romantic and unromantic memories. A difficult, troubling profession. And then Andrew.

"He's not the first one who's been married," Charlotte told her. "But he's the first who's really felt important."

Then what did the others feel like? Unimportant? Mere passers of time? What on earth did she expect Claudia, a wife, to say? It leaped to her tongue to call Charlotte names. Homewrecker sprang to mind. Tramp. Wicked doer of evil deeds whose effects could be devastating, disastrous. Claudia foresaw heartbreak all around, created by this frivolous, dangerous woman. Who was also her friend. Who was different from, say, someone like Sophia Clarke. Charlotte brought courage and light-heartedness and hard-headedness to Claudia. Perhaps

she did the same for men. Maybe, because she had those gifts, she didn't need to follow the rules. Maybe she was special. Or maybe Claudia loved her too much to know.

"Be careful," Claudia tried to tell her. "Don't get hurt. But if you do, I'll be there for you. I hope it works out." Whatever that meant, to either of them.

Charlotte did seem serious about him. A friend would naturally worry about someone in such a troublesome situation. And what would happen if Charlotte were badly hurt? She might get scared, wary, might no longer be able to be the other half of Claudia's life.

Claudia was startled: was that what she thought Charlotte was? And if so, did that mean Claudia thought she herself was missing half her life?

Well, she had to laugh. When would she have a spare moment for more? Half a life, if that's what she had, kept her quite busy enough.

She met Andrew several times. He seemed kind to Charlotte, and intelligent about her. He laughed easily. They had their troubles, some of which Claudia heard about. It did seem hard. Imagine having a man who got up every night to go home, and to some other woman! To face the existence of love elsewhere. Claudia wondered how bad a friend it made her, that she found a small secret pleasure in knowing Andrew left Charlotte every night, and went home. She wondered if Charlotte, looking at Claudia, ever thought of Andrew's wife, and if so, whether she envied or pitied her.

What would have happened if Claudia had ever packed up Bradley's clothes, tossed them out and tossed him out? A whole different life. A far less comfortable life, no doubt. Hard to imagine. And she has survived. So have her girls. Who are concerned for her, and coming to see her tomorrow. Bradley is gone, but she and her girls go on; which may be a fine revenge.

Can he watch her? Hear her thoughts? Has he a vantage point from which he can observe her carrying on without him? Is he gratified by how much, after all, she misses him? Or offended that she has not collapsed? Is he surprised by the bitterness with which she reflects on him? Imagine him listening in, necessarily silent, unable to control. Oh, he must be livid! He must be wild at learning, finally, when he can't do anything about it, how clearly she did see, and who she really was. It must make him furious to understand the silent bargain she made with him, so that in her way, she may have used him more than he used her.

But did he use her? That would mean, surely, that he actually calculated her value to him and weighed it out against whatever other pleasures were available. She doubts that's so. She saw no signs that he was anything but a man who was no doubt fond of her, and no doubt fond also, if less so, of some others, and who enjoyed without much thought whatever presented itself.

One thing about marriage, it's filled with details. There are a great many things known only to the two involved; not necessarily secrets, just unmentioned, taken-for-granted events, things known. Who can beat that for intimacy?

They had their daughters, one after the other, and the house got fuller and noisier and her attention necessarily turned more towards them, and really, all he had from her for many years was a home when he wanted it and her body when they felt like it. And the occasional rage. So he may well be surprised, looking on now from wherever he finds himself, to learn that the generally gentle, motherly woman he lived with for so long was far more brutally calculating than he would have dreamed, himself, of being. She's the one who added up the benefits and costs.

She's very hungry. It's true, as she wrote to Charlotte, that

she's hungry almost all the time. She eats: sandwiches made from thick slices of bread, spread lavishly with butter and heaped with roast beef, ham or freshly fried-up bacon with eggs or tomatoes or both; also cakes, baked and bought, drenched with icing and calories; and potato chips, cookies, boxes of crackers. Her hands seek out food aimlessly, almost unconsciously, as evenings wear by to the sound of the TV.

Even now she still finds herself turning down the volume to make sure Bradley isn't calling. How odd the silence is; and how odd to be able to sit here, not be leaping up to serve him, turn him, deliver him from pain.

None of this bears thinking about.

So many secrets, for so many years; but how many weren't secrets at all? The girls are hardly stupid, and there were, if nothing else, the horrors of the funeral. They will have discussed all that among themselves. She hopes they don't want to go on about it with her.

Perhaps they intend to bring up her future: get her organized in some suitably widowed way. Claudia was startled by how little Bradley left, and has had to make adjustments. She has the house, of course, paid off years ago. As long as she can maintain the taxes and utilities and the occasional repair, it's cheaper to keep it than to sell and pay rent on an apartment.

An apartment sounds unappealing anyway. She can't imagine being unable to step out onto her own porch, onto her own lawn, into her own garden. The day may come, but not yet.

And he left some insurance, and his pension from the post office. (Was that how he met women, selling them stamps, weighing their parcels?) Also a small amount in a savings account. He can't really be blamed for much of this. It wasn't cheap, raising four girls. They had difficult times, he and Claudia; they had to work hard and make do. Although he also had his luxuries.

Those women couldn't have sought him for his money, anyway. The war hero (as he told it) became a postal worker. No wonder he wanted glamour, no wonder he liked to sit in bars and talk and laugh, meet new people. And they weren't always women, either; he had his buddies. In fact it occurs to Claudia that he may not have liked women much, although he obviously wanted them. Never having experienced any excitement like war, she of course had a greater capacity for contentment. But oh, she had such expectations at the start. She thought, from the way he spoke, that he might become someone great – not necessarily a famous general or politician or artist, she had no specific vision, but something that would manifest itself somehow. He seemed confident of this also, if equally vague.

How disappointed was he by what turned into an ordinary life? Even his defections were ordinary. And this house is ordinary, and so are his daughters, extraordinary only in the eyes of Claudia. And Claudia herself – what could be more ordinary than a reasonably kind, relatively placid, fairly dutiful wife? Perhaps he looked around sometimes and could hardly bear it.

And is he, right now, nodding approval at her compassion, understanding? Is he thinking it wasn't such a lie or betrayal, when after all she does sympathize with his point of view?

If so, he fails to see how unimportant his point of view now is to her.

Each time she learned of one of his adventures, or suspected, or was sure but couldn't prove it, she lost a little more of her passion for protest, a little more of the strength for striking him, or weeping. But she still enjoyed the feel of him in bed. She wonders what pleasures he found in her. Funny not to know. They didn't talk about that kind of thing; perhaps couples do more easily, now. She can believe, from what she reads and hears, that people can be fairly clinical about bodies these days: touch this, do that, oh that's what I like – well, Bradley

never said. Nor did she, although he seemed to know. She, familiar only with his body, may have been ignorant of quite a number of his pleasures. Which he then found elsewhere.

Now she will almost certainly never see another penis stretching towards her with longing, with lust. This is such a thing to be mourned that she puts it aside.

She hopes her daughters have enjoyed themselves. She supposes most mothers don't know that sort of thing, even these days. And it's not even possible to speculate – private lives can be such a surprise, so well hidden. Claudia's own acting skills, although put to other uses, are not exactly unrefined.

How about Sonia, has she had a good time with her husband of, what is it now, almost twenty-five years? Or Sandra, divorced, with a twelve-year-old son, does she have intimate friends? Sharon is also divorced but has lived for the past six years with a man, which presumably implies a voluntariness, and therefore pleasure. They say they won't marry, but have cheerfully and deliberately had a child, a daughter, now four. The most mysterious is Susan – who knows about her? What is known reminds Claudia of Charlotte. Susan has two children, and Claudia has no idea who their fathers are. Apparently Susan no longer sees the men. All this has been quite bewildering to Claudia (and, interestingly, some of it gave great outrage and offence to Bradley), but all four seem to do well enough, in their different ways. Certainly Claudia has given up trying to guide. They're grown-up women and have had to choose for themselves.

What would Claudia have chosen, if she'd thought she could? Her own mother used to say, on various occasions, "You made your bed, now you must lie in it." Perhaps that used to be true, but now people can make their beds, lie in them for as long as seems right and then hop back out, try something different.

But then, bold people have always been able to do that. Look at Charlotte.

Just, it sounded like such chaos! Between the dramas of Charlotte's lovers and the tragedies of her small, battered clients, it sounded unbearable. How did she ever rest, with so much going on? At least Claudia, who also got little rest for many years, could count on patterns, which were soothing in their way. Every day for Charlotte, it seemed, began with potential for surprise or random horror in any aspect of her life.

Sometimes Claudia found herself telling her girls how lucky they were. To be fed and clothed and, mainly, loved – all that was a great gift compared with the children Charlotte worked with. Hearts could break over beaten babies, assaulted children, raped adolescents. Who could do such things? It made Claudia grip her daughters hard, hoping nothing could touch them.

Now they've been gone so long they feel almost like strangers. How much does she know about them any more? She is almost reluctant to have them visit; does she have the strength to stand up straight, reassure them and, most of all, not betray herself to them?

What would they think? How would they judge her?

She wishes she could talk to Charlotte. She can imagine Charlotte saying, "What do you mean, you're worried? You're their mother, they love you, for heaven's sake."

But Charlotte doesn't know.

"Look, Claudia," Charlotte would say. She might sound almost impatient. "If there was anybody they weren't going to forgive, don't you think it'd be Bradley? Even if they didn't know any of the other stuff, they saw the way he treated you, they heard the way he spoke. Don't underestimate them, you'd be surprised how much kids pick up. And of course your girls aren't kids, they're women, and not stupid ones."

All this is very reassuring, crisp words in Charlotte's voice. Of course they're Claudia's own reassuring words, transposed into Charlotte's voice, but they may help keep Claudia standing straight, giving nothing away. She has always protected her daughters, or tried to, and now she has knowledge from which they really must be protected. For their own good as well as, selfishly, for hers.

She has been brave and bland before. If she managed when Sophia Clarke turned up, she can surely carry off a weekend with her much-loved, sometimes troubled, essentially decent daughters. But how hungry she is, again! She builds another sandwich. Perhaps she should hide food around the house for their visit. It could be embarrassing to keep heading to the kitchen, gobbling and wolfing whatever's around. She could stash cookies in her closet, cracker boxes in her purse, plates of pasta underneath her bed.

What is she so afraid of? How dreadful would it be, if they learned everything? Well. She really couldn't bear to have them look at her with horror.

Having thought of that, tonight's visions and nightmares naturally involve her daughters, standing together, accusing and frozen. Their expressions say they despise her. She wakes up to sunshine, body sweating, head aching; begins the day frightened.

But of course reality is different. They arrive with arms filled with food, flowers and luggage, hungry and each with her own fresh news. They do bring noise and laughter into her quiet house, they make her smile. Much of their conversation for the first few hours is about their children, Claudia's grandchildren. She forgets to listen properly, captured instead by the sounds of their words. Her daughters' voices swoop and soar around her. With her eyes closed, their voices sound like music.

She knows she ought to be listening, ought to be keen for

word of those small humans who would not exist if it weren't for her. And Bradley, of course. The two of them produced these women, the mothers of those children, and she ought to be more curious about what their efforts have come to, so far. It's interesting to think of her own and Bradley's lives continuing in this way, generation after generation into the future, each new small being containing some small part of them. And will that include any of their pleasure, or their pain?

The girls sit her down in the kitchen and set out to cook, ordering her to be still and let herself be waited on. They make a kind of picnic, of salads and cold meats and rolls, to be followed by ice cream and chocolate, and carry it all to the living-room, to eat on their laps. Claudia is the only one in a chair, not on the floor. Sharon suggested they change into their nightgowns for dinner. "Because this is kind of a pyjama party," she said. "Just girls together."

Claudia has many photographs in her mind of the past, scenes from here and there, silhouettes and motions and faces, and she thinks this will become another one, this grouping of her daughters on this Saturday night, some weeks after their father's death. Long after the battles and jealousies and small tempests of growing up, they seem more or less fond of one another, relaxed and pleased to be together.

Perhaps it doesn't even matter whether Claudia is here.

They are lovely, her girls, in varying ways: Sonia, with her crisp, short hair, her body gaining weight at the hips, becoming a matron already; Sandra lanky like her father, sharp cheekbones becoming more prominent with each year, adding character; Sharon, dark-haired and pudgy, just as she was as a child; and Susan, the mystery child, long hair, some of it greying now, drifting around her face, hiding it, arms clasped around her knees, her little body looking too frail to be as bold as perhaps she asks it to be. Claudia thinks again that Susan's

life may be braver and more difficult than the lives of the others, but that may be only because she can barely picture it. She looks at this group of laughing, still-young women, and feels her heart fill with love and gratitude. Pride, too. She did well with them.

Did Bradley do well with them? Did he think he had much to do with them? Do they? No doubt absence is as powerful an influence as presence.

"Did you ever think," she hears herself interrupting, "I was weak? Do you think I was a bad example?"

"What?" ask two voices together, and all four faces, abruptly sober and puzzled, are looking at her.

Well, now she's started something, hasn't she? That just popped out; and now she isn't sure what she wanted to know anyway, and wishes she'd kept silent.

"What do you mean, Mother?" Sonia asks. "What kind of bad example?"

"Weak?" says Sharon. "How do you mean, weak?"

"Sorry." Claudia waves her hand vaguely, "I shouldn't have spoken. I'm not sure what I meant. I was just listening and thinking I'm proud of you, and it occurred to me how different all your lives are from mine, and I wondered if it might be partly because you set out to be different kinds of women." She waves her hand again, this time impatiently. "No, wait, that sounds as if I think I did wrong somehow, or I want you to tell me I did fine, and it's not that. Sorry, it was just something wandering through my brain. Forget it."

She regrets interrupting their music, their four contented, visiting voices. Now that moment, that photograph she knew she would remember, has been displaced by a straightening of spines and keen, curious faces.

Susan, head lifted, hair now tucked behind her ears so she can see clearly, laughs. "Heavens, Mother, we all *love* talking

about ourselves." (This from the one of whom that is least true.) "How we got to be who we are, childhoods, my God, and what parents did and didn't do. But no, I don't think you were weak or a bad example, I think you did the very best you could. As far as I can see, a lot of the difference between you and us is just that we grew up in a different world. We had different choices."

Do they think she was merely a slave to her times? That would make her a woman lacking will, would it not? Lacking courage to step beyond the life presented to her? Is Susan, smiling up at her, in fact patronizing her ageing mother who did her best, but what chance did she have?

And is Claudia so angry, then, to have such thoughts?

She doesn't seem to know herself, or them, very well at all.

Too many secrets, for too long. Perhaps it's time for them (most of them) to end.

And as Charlotte would say, they aren't stupid. Most of Claudia's secrets probably aren't secret at all.

"I agree," Sonia says slowly. "You were a very good mother. I think we've always known you did your best. You stuck it out, and I admired that. It was a good example."

"Yeah," Sandra says. "I don't know why you'd think you were weak. I thought you were brave."

"Although," Sharon adds, "one thing is, you had to make trade-offs, that was kind of obvious. So I've felt guilty sometimes about what you must have given up because of us. Weren't there times you felt trapped?"

How odd: in all the years of their lives, has none of them ever enquired before how their mother felt? Claudia is touched by this interest, this curiosity. And slightly horrified by the resentment she also feels, that no one has asked before, and now, really, only because she raised the subject in the first place.

"Yes," she answers bluntly, and is satisfied by their shock.

They couldn't have expected that. Still, is she inclined in some way to hurt them now? And if so, why?

She hopes it's not Bradley's death that has freed her to be cruel. Or that, prevented from hurting the guilty him, she now turns to hurting the innocent them. "But not trapped by you, exactly, more sometimes by circumstance. There's never been a minute I haven't been happy you exist. Well, you know what I mean, you're all mothers." But only two of them have stuck with their children's fathers, and what must that mean? That, as Susan said, times are simply different, she supposes. That she may well seem to have been a prisoner of hers.

She finds herself curious about their times; and about these women themselves, these daughters who once crowded her life. Here they are, in this darkening room; and in this intimacy, some previous weights and restraints are fading. These are creatures who are utterly familiar and entirely strange. Does any of them feel this, too? And do they also find it freeing?

She feels odd, and light-headed.

"Don't you find it hard, raising your children on your own?" she asks the two who are doing that. "Don't you get tired, or scared? Is it worth it?"

"Personally," and Sandra stretches, "I'm exhausted. That's why it's so great to be here, even just for a while. What do I know about raising a boy? And there he is, twelve years old and I'm terrified of the next few years. Yeah, sometimes I wish Nick was still around, because at least he'd know about boys. But," she grins, "I cook myself up a big plate of pasta, and then I have a carbohydrates nap and by the time I wake up I've seen the light again. However I screw up with Nicky, I'm pretty sure it won't be as bad as having him use Nick as an example."

Nick had an affair, Sandra found out and next thing everyone knew they were getting divorced. Claudia said at the time, "But are you sure? It was just once, after all, wasn't it?"

"So he says. But once is enough." As if she didn't need to weigh consequences at all. Where did she learn that? Was it so simple, so clear?

Claudia wishes now that she'd asked. She sees there would have been something important to learn.

"The thing to me is," Sharon says, "I can't bear to feel tied. I felt so *obligated*, being married. I guess that's stupid, I could feel obligated to Chris, I suppose, because we've been together longer than my marriage lasted. And we have Sarah, even. But it does make a difference, not having that piece of paper. I think it makes us pay attention better, it keeps me sharp. Chris says so, too. But," she shrugs, "different ways work for different people. It's not that I'd recommend it, it's just me."

"That seems so strange to me." This is, of course, Sonia. "My piece of paper makes me feel safe. We made promises, and we expect to keep them."

"But what if one of you didn't?" Sandra sounds sharp.

"I don't know, I really don't. I can't imagine what I'd do." Claudia would like to suggest Sonia think about it, at least.

"That's sweet, Sonia." Susan is smiling at her oldest sister. "It cheers me up, somebody having that kind of faith."

"You don't?" Claudia asks.

Susan shrugs. "It depends. But then, if it depends, it can't exactly be faith. I have faith, I guess, but then something happens, and then I have it again, and something else happens. It seems to be a circumstantial kind of faith." She grins, mocking herself. And how typical of Susan, the elliptical, non-specific sort of answer that tells them nothing at all about her circumstances. She seems to move through her life in rhythms rather than events, although of course that cannot be.

Perhaps her sisters know more precisely what she's talking about. Claudia does not. She is about to ask, when Susan goes on. "Anyway," she says, "all that makes men too important.

You know?" Her sisters look unsure. "I mean, whatever they do, we have lives. Men, well, they do what they do, but I can't depend on whatever that is."

"Do you ever wonder if you like men?" Sharon sounds abstracted, merely asking, but Claudia tenses. She's rather gotten out of the habit, since Bradley's death, of being prepared for major revelations.

But isn't this nice? How – *sisterly* – they sound. Have they always talked this way with each other? And now have they forgotten she's here, or are they just absorbing her into their sisterliness?

How funny, and rather awful, that she's seen them in relation to herself (and Bradley) but not as a small social world of their own. She's never been part of this sort of conversation before, but they seem so accustomed, they've obviously had a whole life of words together.

"You mean," Susan asks, "would women be better?"

"Yeah. Or, you know, just what I said: do we *like* men?"

"It's true," Sandra says, "on the whole I like women better. Only I've never been attracted. That way, I mean. On the other hand, I can't say I don't like men. There's some I do, and I don't mean anything to do with bed, either."

"I suppose," says Sharon, "it's kind of a shame to like women better but not want to sleep with them, and then to sleep with men sometimes it turns out we don't particularly like. Odd, really, when you think about it."

"I don't see why." Sonia sounds offended. Claudia wonders if it's somehow her fault that Sonia sets herself such acceptable, safe limits, even with words. "Anyway, you're all talking as if you've slept with dozens of men and I know that can't be true. And really, being attracted to a man is just a force of nature, isn't it? For reproduction, if nothing else."

"Good lord, Sonia, how about fun?" Susan blurts. "I don't

think there's anything much lovelier than a good fuck. I expect it's just another kind of taste, preferring women."

No one, as far as Claudia knows, has ever said that word in this house before. But obviously many words have been spoken here, outside her hearing.

Did Bradley talk dirty to his women, revel in obscenity? And whyever would she wonder such a thing? Sonia has sucked in her breath, said, sharply, "Susan!," glancing anxiously at their mother, and even Susan looks a bit worried. But Claudia shrugs and smiles, and considers: if she could take pleasure in Bradley's body, but in so little else about him, shouldn't that be precisely the word? More important at the moment, though, is that having it said aloud here has altered the chemistry, so that they feel like five women of various ages and experience, not quite a mother and her daughters.

It's nice, not necessarily seeing herself always as their mother. A little frightening, taking her own bold step in that direction, but it's her turn. "You know," she says, "before I got married, Charlotte used to tell me how much I had to look forward to. She was more experienced, you see. I thought your father was very sexy, when I met him. Well, I don't suppose I thought of it exactly in those words, but he was certainly powerfully appealing."

"And?" Susan asks. "Was it as good as Charlotte said?"

Claudia grins at her, grateful for the help. (But, "Susan!," Sonia says sharply, again.)

"Oh yes, I must say, I almost always enjoyed that part of it." She feels tears hovering in her eyes; not from sorrow, she hopes they understand, but because it's so unfamiliar and close, speaking to them as real, trustworthy people. As if they were friends, as if they were Charlotte, even. "It's strange, you know, to think of it never happening again. It's hard getting used to endings."

"You must miss him." Claudia thinks Sonia is presuming a good deal, as she often does. She might do better to make a habit of asking, instead of stating.

"It's more a matter of missing other things, really. It has to do with being old, I guess, getting used to the idea that some things simply won't happen again. It's not like when you're young, and you never think about something being the last time."

"But don't you miss Dad?" This time Sonia does ask.

"I miss various things, of course," Claudia answers carefully. Because after all, she is still their mother. "You get used to routines and sounds, that sort of thing. Even when he was ill, we had routines. Maybe especially when he was ill. But to be truthful, it maybe hasn't been long enough to sort out exactly what I miss. Whether it's some things about him, or some things we did, or just some things I was used to. So many years – it's not so easy to separate all that."

"Is it important? To separate one part from another, I mean?" Sandra asks. "Like, I don't miss Nick, and I don't miss anything about him." She pauses. "At least I don't think I do. But to me it's a package, and I'm shot of the whole thing."

"That's likely good then, dear." Claudia smiles. "Maybe it'll be a whole package for me, too, when I figure it out. But forty-seven years, that's a long, complicated time. I have to go on, and I don't quite know how yet, so I need to know more about my life. That sounds foolish. As if I never gave it a thought before. But I have to think in new ways now, that's all I mean."

This doesn't seem to have occurred to them. They're all looking at her with some surprise; as if they've expected her to remain as she always has been (or as they have always assumed her to be – and how, exactly, is that?). There's a silence for a few moments, and then Sandra asks, "Did you like him?"

"Your father?" However is she going to answer? Once again

they are mother and daughters, no longer just women together. Because even grown-up children surely need some comforting beliefs about their parents, if that's possible at all.

"Yeah. I mean, besides anything else, did you like him just as somebody to share a house with? A human being?"

"I don't know, really. I suppose that's one of the things I'm having to sort out. It certainly wasn't something I thought about before we got married. I expect these days people think about each other more, but I was young and romantic, and I considered I loved him, and that was what it was all about. I thought he was glamorous and handsome, and I was flattered he found me attractive. You likely think that's pathetic. I suppose I do myself, now." Again Claudia feels tears in her eyes, recalling her young and hopeful self. What would she tell that girl now, how would she warn her? And would the girl listen, or would she maintain, as Claudia suspects, that her life, then captured by strong arms and desire, could not possibly contain disasters?

"I don't know how you stood it." This is Sharon, in an unexpectedly sharp and bitter tone.

Oh dear. "Stood what?" Perhaps it isn't fair and breaks the new rules they seem to have been developing today; but what do they know? She tried so hard to save them from their parents' periodic turmoil.

And what would it mean if she'd failed? Years of secrecy, wasted? When they might have been close?

Perhaps, though, she kept secrets not so much to protect them, but because she couldn't bear to have them looking at her with pity. It might have been just her pride that kept them ignorant.

Or did not, after all, keep them ignorant.

"Him. The way he messed around. I don't know how you stayed with him. I could hardly stand to look at him, after I

found out for myself. I remember I stopped speaking to him for a while, but I couldn't really tell if he noticed."

Oh my. "When was this?"

"I was fourteen or so, I guess. I saw him in a car with somebody. But I knew before then, really. I remember when I was little, waking up and hearing the two of you whispering at the bottom of the stairs, and you were really angry. It wasn't nice whispering. And I heard him shove you, I heard you thump against the wall as if he'd pushed you. A couple of sounds like that."

"Why didn't you say something? Why didn't you ask?"

"Oh, I couldn't do that!" Sharon sounds shocked.

"But why?"

"Well, you never said anything. And I didn't want to upset you. I guess I thought you didn't want us to know, or you'd have said something, so you'd be upset if you knew we did know."

Claudia hears herself laughing. "Oh dear, what silly people we were. And you know what? Those banging sounds – I bet they were me pushing him, not the other way around. A few times, I really went after him." She sobers. "But you're right, I always hoped you didn't know. I wanted you all to be happy. I really believed children shouldn't be troubled by grown-up difficulties." Their own children, Claudia's grandchildren, must be only too acutely aware of the difficulties grown-ups can devise for themselves and each other. Perhaps she did wrong. Perhaps her grandchildren will be better prepared, more realistic.

Still, the usefulness of realism may be overrated. Was Sharon, at fourteen, prepared to see her father with a woman in a car? What were they doing? Something not innocent.

"So you all knew?"

"Sure." Sandra's hands reach out, palms upward. "It's not

that big a house, one or the other of us heard things. Or saw things, like Sharon. We figured stuff out. It's one of the things," and she smiles, "I try to keep in mind about Nicky: he's bound to know things, whether I tell him or not. Kids aren't dumb."

"Should I have talked to you, then?"

They look at each other; somewhat covertly, as they must often have done, sharing various sorts of knowledge she was unaware of. "I don't know," Sharon says finally. "Maybe not. What could you have said? Anyway, if we had questions, they should have been for him, not you. I guess I'd have liked to know why."

"Not that he'd have told us," Sandra suggests. "Or could have. Nick couldn't explain himself, at least not any way that made sense to me. I think it's because we ask for reasons, and they don't seem to have any. You must have asked, Mother. What did Daddy say?"

Daddy? How fond.

Or how miniature: a little man, diminutive in their hearts.

"Nothing, you're right, there never were reasons that made sense to me. It's not as if love was involved. Or if it was, he denied it. I used to wonder if it was worse that he seemed to wander off out of nothing more than curiosity. If it mightn't at least have felt worth the grief if he'd admitted it *meant* something. But then, at least this way he always came back."

It is extraordinarily hard to discuss this. She never has, really; except with Charlotte. And of course Bradley himself.

"But why did you *want* him back? Why did you let him?" Susan sounds angry. Are they angry with her, then?

"Oh God, I don't know." Abruptly, Claudia is weary. She'd like to go to bed. Pull up the covers and sleep. And she's so hungry! "How would I have supported you all, for one thing? And I thought families stayed together, I thought that was important."

"So it was because of us?" How horrified Susan looks. And rightly, too.

"No, I'm sorry, that's not what I meant. It was me. My image of how things should be. And you know, I can't say about liking him, but I did find him attractive." She doesn't think she could, even now, confess to her daughters her longings for his body, for his hands, how skilful and warm, despite everything else, acts of love (or whatever) remained. She shivers, remembering. How is she going to get through the rest of her life without hands? Without her body being touched? Even for the past few years, and then through his illness, even knowing he would die soon, she didn't quite understand all that was finished for her.

Ah, who knows? Perhaps Charlotte could find her a man to play with. Charlotte's always been generous with what she has.

"Mother!" Sharon's laughing. "You're grinning! Whatever are you thinking about?"

They all giggle, and Claudia smiles, also. "Well, you know. Fun. In spite of everything, men." Even Sonia is smiling a little. "Of course, you realize I had no other experience. Maybe he was awful, how would I have known?" She can't believe she's saying these things, but oh, it's lovely to laugh.

"He's the only man you ever slept with?"

How can Sandra ask? "Of course. When would I have even met anyone else, much less done something about it? Or wanted to, for that matter. Did you think that would even occur to me?"

"Of course not, Mother," Sonia says briskly. "They're just kidding. This isn't nice, you know," turning to her sisters. "It's not very funny."

"Well, Sonia," Sandra says, her tone sharp again, "if you haven't had to figure out how to make jokes about real serious things, all I can say is, you've been lucky."

"Some things still aren't funny." Sonia is still stiff.

"Oh bullshit," snaps Susan. "Sandra's right, you've got to laugh. I remember us roaring after Daddy's funeral, don't you?"

"That's true." Sonia unbends somewhat. "But not at him."

"No, but because of him. And because we were upset, and it got so weird. Look at us, for God's sake: our lives, and then here's Mother, just one man under her belt in almost seventy years, and he screwed around – isn't that funny? Couldn't you just kill yourself laughing?"And despite the bitter edge in Susan's voice, they do get the giggles, just like children, even Sonia and even Claudia, tears rolling, arms clutched around ribs. Claudia doesn't suppose any of them could say exactly what's funny; except the usual indefinable cosmic comedy.

"Remember the funeral? That woman at the back howling and screaming?" Sandra asks, and the laughter, including Claudia's, is renewed. If they can laugh at that, they're right – everything is possible.

"That black veil thing she had on?" Sharon gasps. They are bent over now, howling themselves. "Tearing at herself and yelling Daddy's name? My God!" But this goes too far. Claudia can hear and see too clearly, suddenly, and all their laughter stops.

"Did you ever know who she was, Mother?" Susan asks.

"Didn't catch her name, I'm afraid." Claudia tries to keep her voice light, although she can hear it is also brittle. "I thought afterward, though, poor thing, maybe she really cared, and there he was dying where she couldn't see him, and me trudging up and down stairs every day looking after him – oh my," and she's made it funny again, and off they go into giggles.

But of course at the time it wasn't funny at all. It was horrifying, and embarrassing. "I did think how appalled your father would have been. He hated public displays. I suppose he must often have wondered where some drama might break out next, his whole life must have felt booby-trapped that way."

But truly, poor woman. She obviously had cared for Bradley, obviously grieved for him. She and Claudia might, under other, better circumstances, have confided their experiences. Claudia might even have liked her. "We could look her up in the guest book, I suppose. She might have signed it." Perhaps she'll do that someday. Make some calls. Host a reunion. It might be interesting to see if Bradley's women shared some qualities. What exactly appealed to him? Perhaps he had specific standards, at least specific inclinations.

"Do you still have the guest book?"

"Oh yes. And the cards from the floral arrangements, that kind of thing. I put it all in a box in the basement, heaven knows why." Well, what do people do with funeral debris? It seems wrong to throw it out – flippant in the face of death. But hardly things to get out to brood over, pore over.

"Did she send flowers?"

"The mystery woman? I don't think so."

The girls may laugh now, but they were angry then. When the service ended, they surrounded Claudia like troops, their faces hard and furious in her defence. Susan, hair flying with the speed of her stride, hurled herself towards the still-weeping woman. Perhaps she thought she was speaking quietly, being discreet, but through the sounds of other people's voices, Claudia heard her say, "Shut the fuck up. Get the fuck out of here." She sounded ferocious. Claudia was proud of her; proud of them all. No one mentioned it.

They believed her an innocent widow, their mother.

Claudia thought then she would always be angry with Bradley: that because of the way he had lived, the things he had done, she could not even rest at his funeral, but had, even then, to come up with excessive dignity and courage. After a good night's sleep, though – and the night of the funeral, she did sleep well, falling into blackness, blankness, with relief –

her anger seemed trivial. Certainly not something she would care to go on living with.

It hasn't come up until now. She could, despite laughter, feel terribly angry again.

She stands. "It's been a lovely evening, it's such a treat having you all here. But it's way past my bedtime. I'm tired. Do you mind cleaning up?" They look guilty, all four of them: for having distressed her? She smiles. "My ribs hurt, you know. I haven't laughed so hard in years. That was grand."

"You're okay?" Sharon asks.

"More than okay. Really. And you know what?" She pauses, looking for words. "I like you. I not only love you all, I like you, too."

Tears? Apparently. She supposes she hasn't been a mother who's said things like that easily or often. "Good night, then."

"Good night, Mum. You know," Sharon says, "this is the best time I can ever remember having in this house."

"It was great," Susan adds. "I'm glad we came." Which means something, from her.

Claudia leans over to kiss each of them on the cheek, and feels their arms reaching up around her, as they did when they were children.

Except there are still secrets, and would they still embrace her, if they knew?

seven

THAT WAS CLOSE. IS SHE TRYING TO get caught, or what?

Charlotte is still trembling a little. She doesn't quite have control back over her legs, or her hands; she'll just sit here then for a few minutes, behind the wheel of her car, until she can drive properly again. Hoping no one notices her, now that she's so narrowly made her escape.

Stupid; stupid and reckless. What on earth was she thinking?

She parked where she did before, around the corner and down the block from Andrew's. She thought she had the makings of a plan now: to work her way, visit by visit, through the day, eventually maybe even returning late at night, dressed in black like a burglar, spying out the end-of-day, feet-up moments when guards might be most down and truest words might be spoken. Oh, she had it all worked out.

What happened to the fear of getting caught? What happened to her visions of having to account for herself: to neighbours, to police; to Andrew or Elizabeth?

Gone right out of her head, apparently. As if she'd begun to see all this as normal. As if she wouldn't have a thing to explain; would be able, discovered, merely to stare innocently, naïvely, at authority and say, "What do you mean, what am I doing?" As if she were doing nothing peculiar at all.

She must have forgotten that, while she might have established this venture so firmly in her mind's eye that it had begun to seem almost ordinary, almost routine, to anyone else it would still come as a shock. She must have forgotten how horrified she would be, herself, to be stared at by Andrew. For him to know, especially.

Now she remembers. Can she drive safely yet? She does want to go home. She would like to lie down for a while. Then, when she's calm, maybe tomorrow, she could try again, more carefully.

Oh, good lord, can she really be thinking such a thing? Perhaps she needs help. How would she know if she were losing her mind?

She'd know when she started doing crazy things like this.

This is far worse than that panic in the supermarket; which, as she recalls, she set out to cure with this very adventure. She wanted to restore boldness but seems to have gone too far: into foolhardiness. Like some pathetic shoplifter, she has become obvious in her forays. She might as well cry out, "Look at me! Look at me!"

So today has been a good lesson. She is lucky.

And, feeling lucky, she starts the car and eases away from the curb, heading back home.

A good reminder, this, that nothing should be taken for granted. In particular, events don't always go smoothly, as ex-

pected and hoped. Surprises continually lurk, however carefully plans may be made.

And she had been careful, surely; even to getting new and unobtrusive clothes for hedge-wearing. The first time, she'd worn her dark green track suit: comfortable, loose, versatile, soft, an appropriate camouflaging colour – the very thing for a less-than-flexible body with odd bags and sags; and with the added benefit of being reasonably indiscernible among the branches.

But, she came to feel, less than dignified; unceremonial for what was after all an occasion, however peculiar.

She needed a costume comfortable and flexible, but also reflecting an important event, with nothing of the skulking or furtive about it, so that if she were noticed, she would be able to stand away from the hedge (if she were able to stand straight at all) and look as well turned out and normal as, say, a woman out shopping.

Or as well turned out and normal as Andrew's wife the other morning, waving goodbye to her son and her grandsons, Andrew's hand resting lightly on her shoulder.

Equally, of course, it would be foolish to flaunt. Vivid colours wouldn't do. She didn't *want* to be caught.

She considered her wardrobe: she had clothes appropriate for dinner, the theatre, the supermarket, the backyard, her front porch; but not a thing for Andrew's hedge.

Really, she did have to laugh.

How did she used to dress for Andrew? Smartly, as she recalled. In dresses and suits and lingerie and nightgowns meant to appeal not just to the eye, but to the hands, with weaves and textures and shapes that draped here and fitted there, demonstrating grace and bones.

Not just for Andrew; that's also how she dressed before and after him, how for that matter she mainly dresses now, with the

exception of a track suit on occasion. But at the time she was also aware of her own disadvantages. Not for mistresses, who must keep up their guard, the luxury of worn and faded flannel robes and nightgowns. Only wives, with the security of rings, certificates and children, could afford uncombed hair, blouses that might not quite match slacks, underwear that was mainly utilitarian. Only wives could afford to be so careless.

None of that is true, of course, she does know that. It felt true enough, though, that compared with Andrew's wife she had few ways to appeal, and had to stay on her toes.

No doubt his wife would have seen it quite differently.

At any rate, all that was thirty years ago and more. Fashions were different; so was her body. He did enjoy her body. Neither of them was quite young, but that meant neither of them was still inexperienced or clumsy. He traced her bones with his tongue. She tracked with her fingers his skin drawn tight over ribs and spine and cheekbones.

Often they laughed, also. It seemed that in bed they could look at their lives, some events, from different angles that could lead to giggling. Upright in the light, too much – his cases and hers, their situation itself – was serious and weighty, but from a dark and horizontal point of view, there was often a lighter perspective.

This was the sort of recollection that was returning to her, after an absence of so many years, as she fell into her plans to outfit herself properly and to return to his hedge. She did not recall, however, how frequently plans made with a man of varied interests and responsibilities came undone or turned out unexpectedly. This is clearer to her now.

He had graspable buttocks; tense tendons and muscles of thighs; dark hair on calves; long suckable toes; and that glorious penis rising at a touch, reaching up and out to her – oh, she can still shiver at memories; long for reality.

At both ends of lust, perhaps, it goes to waste: at the beginning, for a few years, there's a vague and thwarted longing (until it isn't thwarted any more); and now, apparently, at the end, the longing is even keener and more painful, because it's for something precisely, intimately, deliciously known, and recalled, and finished.

Her mother, other mothers, Claudia too, have spoken of phases: that children are going through some period or other of behaviour as they experiment and form their characters; a method of picking and discarding who they'll turn out to be. Maybe it isn't just children, though. Maybe people never quite finish, and keep trying this and that – who says when a character might be completed? It can hardly be like figuring out when a cake or loaf of bread is done. So this outbreak of curiosity and desire may be only an old-woman phase, and who knows how she'll turn out?

As long as she doesn't turn out to be caught.

No doubt it's funny, but the curiosity and desire don't seem to be for Andrew as, she has been startled to see, he is now. An *old* man, who moves somewhat slowly and has white hair, however luxuriant, doesn't appeal to her. It's a much younger Andrew who intrigues her, and how he got from then to now. Also possibly why.

What kept him there? What still holds him? What grips are in force, behind obscure and innocent blue-painted doors?

"You're the best part of my life," he would tell her. Also, "I can't imagine being without you." Well, he was without her often enough. And shouldn't he have been puzzled, as she was, that he didn't choose to be more often with the best part of his life?

She wouldn't have married him. She wanted him, not a contract. And she wanted him detached from those powerful rivals waiting at home, always, for him.

Such things were more difficult then, she supposes. They might be different now. These days, in the same situation, he might find it possible to make a different decision. Then, he said, "The boys need me. And I love them, you know." He spoke as if, being childless, she might find the love of children less than comprehensible. For a lawyer, he could be awfully tactless and awkward with words. But then, for a social worker perhaps she could be a little frivolous with feelings.

He sometimes bought her black underwear for birthdays, for the Christmases they could not, of course, spend together. They would laugh because after all, it was a joke, black underwear; but still, she would wear it, and he would remove it slowly, with deft fingers, deft tongue, deft teeth.

Oh my.

A few weeks ago, at the dentist's, the hygienist, leaning over her, said, "You have such lovely eyes and cheekbones." Sounding surprised. Presumably Charlotte was supposed to be grateful for the compliment: that despite crumpled skin, her structure is sound. People, the young, fail to see histories in lines, of course; no doubt she did, herself. The capacity for passions of one sort and another become invisible with age.

Claudia confessed – confided – long ago that despite everything, she loved the touch of Bradley's hands, his skin. But who else would know, seeing Claudia or Charlotte now, how their bodies arched with pleasure beneath and over the bodies of lithe men? Would Claudia's daughters imagine, for instance? And if not, could they really know anything at all about her?

Well that's silly, of course they could. Charlotte may have heard Claudia's intimate words, but those girls, women, were observers to her life, day to day, and what could be more intimate than that? Perhaps the touch of skin and hands is nothing, in comparison.

It's true that's what concerned her about Andrew's wife (and

others, for that matter): the day-to-day knowing, compared with mere skin and hands and, yes, even love, on occasion. She might have that, but wives had their husbands' moods in the mornings, their scratchings and snorings, their household repairs, their households themselves. But perhaps wives would have laughed at her jealousy. Perhaps they wakened in the middle of the night and had an urge to shoot their snoring spouses. Perhaps they failed to appreciate, after a time, grumpy men wandering around the house, stupid and melancholy in the early hours of the day.

It seems likely, and ironic.

Would any of Bradley's women have wanted him around all the time? Claudia did, after all. And there was at least one other, the one who came to Claudia's door to announce her existence. How angry Charlotte was, on Claudia's behalf, when she heard!

And in a way she was also angry on her own behalf: on behalf of women who maintain some dignity in these situations. She was astonished at the depths of abasement, incivility and self-certainty involved. Nothing would have impelled Charlotte, on the worst of her unhappy days, to do such a thing. She would like to think she had too much pride and decency; but also she wasn't stupid. She could see that in endings like that, wives do win. Wives like Claudia keep their husbands; women like Charlotte do not. Certainly women who go knocking on doors do not.

It was, as Andrew said, out of the question for him to leave his wife. He said the reason was his children, but Charlotte suspected more, although she could see children would be compelling enough. She thought also habit; contentment, the dailiness of his ordinary life. She wouldn't say he didn't love her; he said he did, and she believed him, as far as it went. And it went pretty far, and pretty long.

But then, and apparently still, Elizabeth (such a dull name, Charlotte couldn't even recall it till she heard it today, had thought it might be Linda, or Susan – or was fooling herself, and knew it perfectly well) went on sharing his bed and raising their children and waking in the middle of the night to his snores, perhaps wanting to shoot him.

It hasn't been possible to tell, really, listening and watching from the hedge, if he's happy these days with his choices. And how about Elizabeth, is she happy with hers?

Claudia has sometimes appeared to regret hers. Once she struck her own forehead with her own fist and cried, "I'm such a *coward*. Why do I put up with it?"

Charlotte had no good answer. Also, they were in a restaurant, and she didn't like people watching her friend punch her own forehead in public. This would have been a quarter-century or so ago. "You have the girls, after all, you'll never have nothing at all."

"Yes, thank God for them. Most of the time, anyway." Claudia became calmer, considering the blessing of her daughters.

Charlotte had been astonished by the speed at which Claudia bore them, so many in so few years. Didn't she ever think, "Without them, I could be free"? Or, "If I stopped now, I could get free more easily"? Did she ever actually want to be free?

Probably not. She has, beyond the ordinary upheavals of raising them, surviving various volatile stages, seemed to love her daughters with a passion Charlotte cannot imagine. (But if she could imagine, she might have had it in her to bear a child.)

There were, however, all those other kids, and all those other tragic families. And then there were also men like Bradley. Or Andrew, and others, for that matter: not criminals, but also not exactly advertisements for family life, or for success, trust or joy. And there were women like herself; like the

ones who caused Claudia such pain (although perhaps, like Charlotte, they caused pain for themselves, as well).

No one gets off free. Well, Bradley, maybe. But even he has died, and in what seems to have been a level of discomfort that might count as some sort of retribution.

Andrew didn't look or sound as if he's actually suffering. Would she like him to? But she hasn't been particularly suffering herself, except perhaps from curiosity. And narrowly averted humiliation. But she doesn't want to think about that right at the moment. She's safer paying attention to her driving, getting safely home from there.

During their ten years together, they managed two actual vacations. Two! At that, the time was available only because Elizabeth (whom he always called her entire formal name, never Liz, or Betty, or Beth, giving her a dignity he didn't give Charlotte, whom he often called Char – how sensitive she was about such small signs of what she took to be degrees of love, respect) had gone off on her own, or at least on her own with the two children, leaving him free.

Otherwise he did not consider himself free. Which of course he wasn't. But he might have put more effort into the comforting pretence. (That was only Charlotte's bitter view, which was by no means her only view.)

For their first vacation, they rented a cabin at a beach they thought would be distant enough that the chance of meeting anyone they knew was slight. They planned, prepared, anticipated and imagined, and eventually drove off, considering themselves luxuriously fortunate and happy to have these days together.

It was strange, getting used to each other. They'd spent so much time in her living-room bent over maps and brochures that the burden of pleasure was huge. Also they were by and large unfamiliar with each other's habits. Andrew was accustomed to his

wife's, not Charlotte's; and Charlotte was accustomed only to her own. Eventually they fought (naturally over the trivial – Charlotte left the top off the jar of peanut butter before heading over the stones for an after-breakfast solitary swim, and Andrew, making his own toast, was enraged, making his stiff-legged, stiff-lipped way down to the beach to confront her, becoming more maddened when, waist-deep in the water, hands on her hips, she tipped her head back and laughed). After the quarrel was out of the way, they relaxed somewhat.

They did not, however, touch what Charlotte suspected the real trouble was. She found him sometimes absent, preoccupied, and assumed he was thinking about his family. She imagined he worried they'd be caught, and also that something would go wrong with his family, someone would be hurt or ill or dying, and Elizabeth would be trying to reach him, futilely. Or that he just plain felt guilty. Charlotte found it sad that he couldn't wholeheartedly enjoy himself with her, out of worry and guilt over those phantom others, those real persons in his real life.

She didn't think she herself was either worried or guilty, except perhaps in her dreams. Sometimes she had quite long and intricate dreams about his wife.

Still, there were pine woods, and a rocky beach, and they went for long walks holding hands and built fires in the evenings. They made vigorous love. Charlotte felt their time together running and racing away, and of course it did run and race away, so that it was no time at all before they were in the car again, headed home.

It was interesting, though. A pleasure, as long as they could manage pleasure in such fits and starts.

Four years later they had their second vacation, flying to Mexico, to a coastal condominium Charlotte rented from the real-estate agent who'd found her her house. The resort was reasonably inexpensive. That was important, because Andrew

had to account for his money; not, he explained, because anyone else controlled it, but because he was responsible to others.

As if she needed reminding.

They were careful to leave no paper trail, or any other sort of trail.

She considered herself responsible and fair. Now, from a distance, it looks like madness, or at least unlike herself: to accept for so long, so responsibly and fairly, such a placement in his life and in her own eyes.

Not much saner, anyway, than today's small madness.

Oh, but he was fun. They did laugh. And were serious, too. There was never enough time for all the talking they wanted to do: about his work, her work, what they wanted, what they did. They had much in common. They agreed that their work involved efforts towards fairness, or justice, a certain upstream swimming involved when it appeared there was little natural fairness or justice, and certainly no guarantees. "We're privileged," he said. That meant they had certain responsibilities towards those who were not. And that might have been merely charitable, patronizing, except that they enjoyed their work; not satisfied, or always successful, but they did find their own pleasures in using their skills well. They were both sceptical of intentional virtue and leery of the motives of those who seemed to court sainthood.

Their conversations were delicate, however; a slightly wrong word could lead anywhere. Andrew, for instance, suffered occasionally from inconsistency (a flaw, Charlotte thought, in a lawyer), and referred once to his wife as a saint. "She's the one who raises the kids," he said. "She puts up with a lot."

He failed to comprehend the fury in Charlotte's "Really?" or in her raised eyebrows. "What do you think she gets out of it, then?" she asked coldly. "Let's see, if she does all the work and endures so much, do you think she's really a saint, or do you

suppose there's power in that kind of righteousness? Do you suppose she might have exactly what she wants, have you thought of that?" Of course she knew she ought to keep silent; that she was damaging herself, and by no means injuring his saintly wife. But really!

He was offended, of course, on his wife's behalf. And no doubt on his own. He called Charlotte cynical, which she understood to be quite the opposite of saintly.

Still. All couples quarrel. People so intensely interested in each other must have disputes and disagreements. So of course they fought. They also laughed, in and out of bed, and talked for hours. They fell into their own patterns of time and resentment and passion and rage and humour and love. She could almost have failed to save herself.

But why should it matter again?

Because, she supposes, if nothing else it's an important part of being human to assess certain important events. Patterns. Ways of being. And because it might be useful to know some things, such as whether love cannot last, or self-destructs, or buckles under its own weight, or if there is some true kind that does go on and on.

Is it possible that Elizabeth loves Andrew?

These are things carved into trees by adolescent penknives, mere romance and sentiment. Surely.

Sometimes she was desperate. But once into it, she could find no good way out. Although perhaps the same applies to marriage, maybe married couples also find themselves staring about frantically on occasion, blinded and surrounded, wondering how they got themselves here and which way they might escape, and finding there really are no hidden tunnels or apparent routes.

So instead they might learn, as she tried to for quite some time, that keeping still could have its pleasures and comforts.

A lesson that recently she seems to have forgotten.

How dull the clothes are that are available to her and suitable for a hedge. It seems to her now, driving home, that she put disproportionate effort and time into finding outfits that today, at least, were useful so briefly.

Elasticized waists are dreadful, but that's how slacks for old women are made, and likely quite properly, shifting bodies being what they are. She found navy blue ones and dark grey ones; and also a deep forest-green blouse, long-sleeved and tailored, and a grey cotton one that doesn't tuck in. Smart enough; nothing to be ashamed of. And comfortable, for spying and driving. She wore the deep green blouse and dark grey pants today.

New shoes, also, because the only flats she had were somewhat stiff leather. These navy sneakers are hardly smart, but she thought them quicker if she had to make a run for it. And then laughed, thinking that if she had to make a run for it, she'd better hope the person chasing her was a decrepit Andrew or a slow Elizabeth. Sneakers were hardly going to make her speedy.

Well, at least she hadn't had to run.

When she woke up this morning, knowing (she thought) exactly what she was going to do, she had to spend a moment thinking out what day it was. Weekends and weekdays have little to distinguish them from each other, so sometimes she has to do that; nor does she worry about it. It only makes sense that someone not working wouldn't have to be concerned very often about specifically what day it is.

She hoped by now Claudia would have her letter, but these things can take unexpectedly long.

She drew her hair back and tied it with yarn. In the full-length mirror on the back of her bedroom door, she saw a reasonably well-turned-out, reasonably distinguished, reasonably respectable-looking woman whom no one would suspect of anything at all.

In the car, driving cautiously but not too slowly, she kept a

city map handy beside her. It's more than half an hour between her house and Andrew's subdivision, and it's easy to get lost in suburban labyrinths.

She drove once past his house and saw no one out in the neighbourhood. It was not quite nine o'clock. The people next door would have gone off to work. Her way was clear.

She parked; walked as if she had a perfectly good reason to be there, around the corner, down the street, to the neighbours' driveway and bordering hedge. She pulled aside branches, getting a few light scratches on her face and her hands, smelling the dark green coolness. It's a sturdy old hedge. Shifting carefully, she found a trunk to lean against, cushioned by branches.

She heard birds, and a couple of cars driving along the next block, but again it was weirdly silent and she wondered how anyone could bear it.

But on such a warm day, the windows were open. She heard what sounded like a pot clattering into a sink behind what must be the kitchen window at the end of the house nearest the hedge. "Andrew?" she heard. "You ready for coffee? You want it here or outside?"

This was exactly the homely sort of conversation she used to imagine, and which made her heart hurt.

"Be right there." That seemed to come from down the hall – a bathroom perhaps? Some time, she thought, she might dare to creep closer; make her way right to the house, where she could crouch beneath an open window and even hear sighs. From this distance, however, she heard nothing for several minutes; then his voice again, nearer: "It's cold. What did you pour it for, when I wasn't ready for it yet?"

"Because you said you'd be right here. If you didn't want it poured, you could have said so. If it's cold, get yourself another one, I don't care."

That was better. Refreshing irritability; even perhaps hostility. Didn't Andrew sound grumpy, though? Charlotte could imagine that, if he were speaking to her the way he just did to his wife, she'd answer just as snappishly. It must be quite a test, the two of them together day after day in this house. No wonder his wife was reluctant to see her son and grandsons leave.

At least if Charlotte's home is silent, it's her own silence. And if there's a bad mood in the air, it's only her mood, not someone else's, and she's the one who has to cure it for herself. Perhaps that's why she has ended up living alone.

But if she lived with someone else – if Andrew, say, had shifted his life differently – that person might help cure her moods, and she his. Friends may undertake that for each other, and lovers certainly should. And after all, any small thing can lift spirits, and re-create hope: a note on a pillow, champagne, an amusing card, a silly gift. Maybe people forget. Get out of the habit. Become weary, even, of pleasure.

"Do you have plans for today?"

"I thought I'd do something about the basement." Could she have told, if she didn't know, how old he is from his voice? Did he sound seventy?

Imagine, Andrew seventy!

"What about it?"

"Well, Christ, have you looked down there lately? It looks to me as if you just put anything down there any old way. I went down yesterday after the rain to check for seepage and couldn't get near the foundation for crap piled up."

Charlotte was reminded of her own basement. He would hate it, too, also heaped with this and that, empty boxes and potentially useful debris she's gathered over the years. Does she have seepage around her own foundation? How useful, someone who thinks about these things, and acts on them.

How discouraging, someone who's so testy about it, though.

"You're going to spend a lovely sunny day in the basement?"

"Well, somebody's got to take care of it sometime. Things don't get done by magic, Elizabeth."

Oh, right about then Charlotte would have turned on him. Not Elizabeth, though. "No, they don't," she said calmly; but was there an edge? "It's a big job, though. I hope you pace yourself and don't try to do it all at once. You know what the doctor said about the way you go to extremes and how hard that can be on your heart. You don't want another attack."

A heart attack? Andrew'd had a heart attack? Had felt that suffocating pain, the terror, the hospital? Was Elizabeth there, and did she call for the ambulance? Charlotte's own heart sped. And she remembered the vision she had years ago, of some devastating illness that took him away from her, kept her away from him. And now, see, she was right! If love hadn't died, and they'd survived all this time, that's exactly what would have happened. He'd have been in the hospital, all tubed and connected to this and that machinery, and she would have had to grieve and worry all alone, out of touch and wondering from moment to moment if he was even alive.

He used to laugh at her. He said, "Good God, Char, that's a bit far-fetched." But it wasn't at all.

"Good God, Elizabeth," she heard, "stop *hovering*. It's my own damn heart, I know when to stop."

Maybe he wonders, too. Maybe he's irritable because his wife isn't Charlotte, and he mourns all those years they might have been together. Maybe he can hardly bear having made the wrong choice.

That wouldn't have made him sound any less unpleasant, though. It was hardly his wife's fault he couldn't bring himself to leave her thirty years ago. Charlotte thought she might enjoy this more if his wife, not Andrew, were the cranky and unreasonable one.

"You?" he asked.

"You mean my plans? Nothing much. I'll do up the dishes when you've finished, and then do a little work in the garden. I wanted to ask you about the front borders, if you have time. And I have a book to finish. It's really too nice a day to spend indoors. You know, we could do the basement together sometime when it's not so lovely out. It doesn't need to be done today."

Charlotte thought that was extremely generous. She could imagine a day in her own basement with him in this mood, him carping about the odd possessions she's kept.

"I won't spend the whole day." His voice had softened. "I'll just make a start for an hour or two."

So. After all, Elizabeth had quietly, calmly brought him around. There'd been no quarrel, no confrontation. Perhaps this was how it's always worked. Maybe it's even how a marriage is supposed to work. At any rate it was certainly clear to Charlotte why it wouldn't have worked for her. She hasn't the temperament.

"But," he went on, "I'll look at the garden with you first, if you want." Charlotte drew back a little in the hedge.

She'd have thought it would be easier to overhear them once they were outdoors, and of course it would have been except that a little warm, opposing breeze sprang up, sending words off in another direction. They stood just outside their front door, Elizabeth bending, touching plants, looking up questioningly. At one point she closed her eyes for a few seconds; perhaps, Charlotte thought, she was praying for patience.

Andrew was standing, hands on hips, regarding and sometimes speaking briefly. The sounds reaching the hedge were all mutter mutter mutter.

Charlotte couldn't get closer. Beyond the hedge, the small lawn was as open as meadow.

Andrew, in shorts, turned out to have sinewy, old-man legs.

Elizabeth's were white, with tracings of puffy, purple veins.

If Elizabeth died, if those veins turned out to be fatal, would Andrew be lonely? Charlotte is somewhat vain about her own legs, which remain shapely even if the skin here and there – on the insides of her thighs, on her calves, for instance – has certain chicken-like qualities.

At any rate, an ordinary old couple they looked, with ordinary old-people bodies, crinkling and bulging here and there, just as she does.

She wished he didn't look ordinary. She wished he looked marked by her, as if she'd left a permanent, visible impression; as if she'd managed to change some small thing about him.

Well, who could tell? Perhaps she had. He was old, and didn't much resemble the man she remembers.

Didn't he used to have a voice that carried? He was accustomed to speaking in courtrooms; accustomed to making himself heard. He was good at using tone to capture emotion. Now Charlotte wanted to call out across the lawn, "Speak up!"

She might as well have done just that. Leaning, leaning towards all that mutter-mutter, trying if nothing else to catch the sentiment, the mood if not the actual words, she was suddenly falling, how peculiar and swift, reaching out, grabbing at a cedar trunk – was it a knee giving way or had she just overbalanced? – at any rate she was toppling forward and caught a branch instead of a trunk and heard it snap, heard the shuffling sound of her feet as they worked to stay under her, heard her own sharp breath (but at least she didn't actually cry out) – and finally, finally (but it could only have been a moment's event, a second, less than a second) she was leaning into one of those sturdy upright trunks, it had caught her, and she was almost through the hedge, but not quite.

She was lucky they're old, and turn slowly.

"What was that?" Elizabeth asked. *Now* she was speaking

up, or the breeze had dropped. *Now* Charlotte could hear her quite plainly.

Both of them were looking in the direction of the hedge. If Charlotte moved at all, they would see her. She wished for the hedge-green track suit. She was afraid to breathe. She was afraid one of them would spot the trembling of the branches and of her own limbs. They felt terribly close to each other, she, and Andrew, and Elizabeth. She could see Andrew's alert eyes so clearly; felt she and he must be staring directly at each other. How could he not see her?

What if he did?

"Sounded like something in the hedge," he said. Indeed it had. Charlotte had a mad impulse to mew like a kitten; wondered for a second what sort of sound a squirrel would make, and if she could make it, too.

But then, Elizabeth was probably the sort of woman who took kittens, or even squirrels, to her bosom. A mew would no doubt bring her running. (Although Charlotte really knew nothing about her. For all she knew, Elizabeth was a woman who puts out poisons for strays, setting fatal dishes on the back step at midnight. There were times years ago when she thought of Elizabeth as witch-like; and not the good kind of witch, either, but the evil mythic sort with irresistible, unaccountable lures.)

And now it's turned out she's just a little old woman with big angry veins in her legs.

There were several moments of absolute stillness. Andrew and Elizabeth looked at the hedge so intently it seemed they must think they could hear with their eyes. How could they not see Charlotte's pale, terrified face through the rough screen of branches? Another couple of inches and she would have fallen right through, that's how close she was to disaster.

What a splash she would have made, toppling and crashing

onto their tidy green lawn. Might even have broken something. Would at any rate have been lying on the ground, looking up helplessly at a horrified Andrew; a bewildered Elizabeth. When Charlotte and Andrew were together, they became gifted at lying. What might they come up with, between them, for this occasion?

Charlotte could have said she was a Jehovah's Witness, perhaps. Taking a short cut. Mutilating her flesh with cedar pricks, with the aim of salvation.

Andrew would speak to her like a stranger. Which, of course, after thirty years, she must be. Still, he might have come to her later, for an explanation. It might be nice to talk to him again; hear from him directly how his life has gone.

Oh really, is that what she's wanted, after all? Is that why she's kept running these risks?

They shrugged at each other finally, turned away, back to their garden. "Some animal," Andrew said. And that Charlotte could hear also. Finally.

And the rest. Apparently what long-married people talk about is very little. They were speaking of this weed and that, the propriety of sprays, whether chicken salad or omelette would be preferable for dinner. Imagine days, Charlotte thought, spent thinking up words to so little purpose! She has never been gifted at small talk – imagine the exhaustion of so many hours of speaking trivia. What luxury, her own life. "Shall we," Elizabeth suggested eventually, "tackle the basement together, just for a little while?"

Didn't she get bored, worn out, accommodating?

Charlotte certainly would have.

She was not able to make out, watching and listening, the ways Andrew may have had to accommodate Elizabeth. Perhaps those ways were more subtle. Or more drastic. Perhaps simply being there was his grand, invisible accommodation.

There wasn't much about the scene that seemed enviable, at any rate. Charlotte didn't think she'd care to feel her own last precious years flying by in drudgery and compromise.

It could hardly be called an improvement, however, that some of the moments of her own last precious years she was apparently spending clinging to a narrow cedar hedge trunk, eavesdropping on the ordinary conversations of an ordinary old couple, and narrowly escaping discovery.

"Yes, go to the basement," she implored silently. "Go now. Please, at least go in the house and let me get out of here." Ah, the powerful and controlling mind of the witch-like ex-mistress – away they went! Not without one last visible gesture that caused a small lurch in Charlotte's heart: Andrew, walking just behind his wife, placing a hand on her back, not to steady her or to hurry her, simply to touch her. So.

Between that pain and the various pains of her body – palms smarting from the rough cedar bark, knees and thighs aching from strain, shoulders tense from leaning – Charlotte felt she did well to pull herself free and walk, with reasonable dignity, back to her car. Still, she hoped nobody was watching, in case she wasn't moving with as much dignity as she imagined.

Now, almost home, she remembers being startled sometimes, in the old days, by how clearly Andrew saw her, plucking true moods and emotions out of air when she could have sworn she had them camouflaged. He made her feel transparent. The truest mood and emotion he plucked, the one she must have failed most often to camouflage, was envy. Terrible, ugly, sunken-pit jealousy.

Yet she had to assume she must have gone about choosing their arrangement, in her way. She didn't think that could be a very pleasant part of herself; or a very normal one, either. What sort of person, man or woman, would choose to love someone occupied mainly elsewhere?

One with no gift for small talk, perhaps. One who could not bear day-to-day life, however she imagined longing for it and resented it elsewhere. Or one who had her own best interests buried somewhere unreachable in her heart.

She wonders what sort of book Elizabeth is planning to sit outside reading today? Knowing the title would tell her something about the woman, likely.

Has Andrew changed so much? She knows he used to have sweetness, but now he sounds quite unpleasant – how would that have happened? Would he find Charlotte much altered?

Turning into her driveway, she finds herself curious again.

With the rest of today, she will make herself a cup of tea and then, like Andrew's wife, sit outside reading for a while. Later, when it's not so nice out, she maybe ought to take a look at the basement. It really is a mess, and who knows if behind it all the foundations may be crumbling, and the thing is, if she doesn't take care of these problems, there isn't anyone else who will.

She can think of that as lonely, or she can think of it as responsible and competent. She thinks she'll think about it later; and meanwhile try to remember gratitude for safety and for the remains of dignity.

eight

THESE DAYS CLAUDIA READS THE newspaper avidly every morning. This is both a luxury and an inclination she hasn't experienced before, but now it is also something like an addiction. What did she do before, without all these words from the outside world?

Well, she was busy. She had her own demanding world.

As Bradley became increasingly unable to do things for himself, he insisted she read the paper to him. She would tell him a headline and he would nod or shake his head: interested or not. Really, that was the first time she paid particular attention to news. He was especially keen on armed conflicts here and there, of which there'd been no shortage. He liked to follow battles and incursions, with a view, perhaps, to tactics. It didn't seem to Claudia that he perceived wounds; and wasn't that odd, from a man who had actually experienced battle?

She read those stories to him and thought of people, mothers and their children mainly, fleeing, hungry, hurt. She imagined herself years ago, with four young daughters, trying to save and protect them, watching them wither, perhaps seeing them die.

She and Bradley did not discuss the news. He made his comments, and she read and kept her thoughts to herself. She didn't think he would be interested in her point of view; but perhaps she misjudged him. He might have enjoyed it. They might have come to some conclusions, merging his views and hers.

Her conclusion was that after all, her troubles were small and unremarkable. Nothing that had ever happened to her would rate even a word in the news. She thought it must be an exceptional blessing, to have survived without any drama so dreadful it rated public attention.

And who would dare measure infidelity against famine? Or hard angry whispers against rape, or any despairing sinking of the spirit against death, slow or quick, from a bullet?

This was good, to have her sorrows in perspective.

And her pleasures, too, of course. Maybe she never won millions in a lottery (although Bradley used to buy tickets, imagining the easy lives of winners), but she had a home and many comforts. Maybe she never did anything spectacularly good or heroic, but she seems to have raised four satisfactory women. It may not have felt like an especially placid life, but it appears, reading the newspaper, to have been one.

She does wonder if that is different now: whether she might rate space, a small headline, a few words.

She looks these days more carefully, with more interest, at the photographs of criminals. Captured, being led into court, they often wear coats over their heads, walk bowed and hunched and handcuffed between burly police. They seem to

be deemed especially dangerous, to warrant these photographs, and they are almost without exception men.

She supposes that, even so, she may have things in common with some of them. She supposes there's a bond of sorts.

But perhaps not. Perhaps she overestimates her secret. It may be like everything else about her, compared with huge and public events: insignificant in the scheme of things. For all she knows, viewed from the perspective of the outside world she may still be perfectly ordinary and indulged and fortunate.

She is fascinated, at this late date, by the variety of lives that can apparently be lived, by the great range of character that is possible, and by the oddities of circumstance. All these seem to merge, at particular moments, to create news of various kinds. Perhaps all three are required: a mode of living, combined with a kind of character, confronted by a demanding event. Perhaps it's only the collision of the three that has eluded her, preventing her appearance in the pages of her newspaper.

After all, what are the odds?

Charlotte, now – she has, in the past, found her name in the papers; although not to do with her own occasions and events, but because she's an expert of sorts on the tragedies and dilemmas of others. She was able to find, it seemed to Claudia, ways and words to spin general meanings from various individual terrors, no doubt a gift. No doubt it's essential for there to be those who can do this; so that, if nothing else, people don't feel surrounded or absorbed by chaos and anarchy, but can see that there may be order and predictability even in horror.

Charlotte's area of expertise has been in certain domestic disasters, a circumstance not without irony in Claudia's view.

No doubt it's that she has a great deal more time on her hands these days that accounts for part of Claudia's absorption in her morning newspaper; just as no doubt it was partly due to lack of time that she had no such relationship with it in earlier

times. And really, she does see this as a relationship: she finds herself waking in the mornings with anticipation, as if an interesting friend is waiting at the door, bringing word of the outside. Nor does she feel, although the newspaper can hardly know this, that the relationship is one-sided. Her own concentration on events, her speculations, her very desire to know, seem a contribution, and her part of the bargain.

It is, she supposes, something like Charlotte: bringing events, occurrences, analyses and passions to her front door; although with Charlotte, of course, there's been also the dimension of human affection.

Surely Charlotte has received Claudia's letter by now. If she's at home, and if she's alive – how have they slipped so out of touch that Claudia doesn't even know? And that for some time Bradley has been dead and Charlotte didn't know?

But their friendship has survived gaps before, there have been long periods when it has been sufficient to know each other exists, carrying their mutual and separate histories.

Even friendship is a great luxury in the world as it's described in Claudia's newspaper. People uproot themselves for sheer survival, wrench themselves from place, family, everything that's known, to set out on perilous, irrevocable journeys. They say final farewells, then just go: across waters that may drown them, across deserts that may starve them; like stepping off the edge of the world, eyes closed, hoping.

By comparison, even the moment that seems to Claudia enormous must be pretty paltry. It is quite possible there are some who would even see it as something to be proud of. She would see it that way herself, if she were less aware of mixed feelings. Of course, mixed motivations, she would judge by her readings of events described as virtuous, are common enough. They are even perhaps especially common with acts of goodness. Claudia does not believe in saints. She does not

believe there is something for nothing. There is always some return on investment.

Well then, what was her return from caring for Bradley? The sense of a job well done? Not, she is fairly sure, repayment for any sort of debt; more a desire for perfect completion.

And perhaps, on the subject of mixed motivations, it was also true that she wouldn't have objected if Bradley felt, in comparison, not only sick to death, but inadequate, unvirtuous, inferior. If he ever once looked at her and thought, "I do not deserve this woman; she is so giving and good and generous, and I've been mean-spirited, certainly less than full-hearted, always keeping something to myself, to offer someone else, holding my reserves – and even now, when I'm crumbling and I even know about that smell of rotting, here she is, at my beck and call, always serving, caring, oh, I do not deserve this woman" – imagine if he ever looked at her and thought any of that! Most unlikely. Unimaginably unlikely! He was demanding to the end.

But perhaps she is unkind. Unfair. Perhaps that is only what she needs to think: the worst of him.

She should now be filled with air of one sort or another – both oxygen and helium, for instance – able to breathe for the first time in years, able to float and to fly. She ought to feel free and daring and ready for anything.

She has made adventures difficult to imagine, has spent too many years training herself not to dream of possibilities. It seemed more important to make herself be reconciled, not bold.

Again, though, she may be revising her own history, in the light of its most recent events. This may be only what is most comforting and necessary to believe right now, not what was or felt true at the time.

It is clear from her newspapers that history can be revised

quite swiftly; almost on the run, as it were. What was a crime yesterday becomes today, on closer examination of the facts, an understandable, even necessary, outcome. Or what seemed a clear act of virtue and necessity yesterday becomes today, with further documentation, a mixture of guile and profit. And after all, politics and wars, depressions and recessions and periods of prosperity, oppressions of one sort and another, violent outbreaks and acts of hope and charity – all these large events can only be the results of individual human impulses colliding and merging in particular ways. It's not, for instance, as if war gets declared in some impersonal way, but from various desires and prides banging into each other. If there were such things as scientists of souls, it might be possible to track these events to the smallest components of the human spirits involved; rather like microbiologists, peering through powerful lenses, trying to make out the most infinitesimal organisms, to discern how small life can become and still be related to enormous effect.

No doubt, Claudia supposes, the reason people don't try to unravel motives or events to their true, tiny sources is because where does it get you? Because for all you know – for all that peering microbiologist can tell – there's something even more infinitesimal, and at the same time more potent, really going on.

And it simply is not possible to live open to every breath and whisper, able to hear and smell each impression floating by. It is necessary to dull some senses in order to survive – otherwise one would be battered and badgered and deafened and nibbled by an intolerable, overwhelming, barrage of sensation.

The closing off and shutting down is growing up, Claudia supposes. And when one has closed off and shut down sufficiently, one is mature. At the same time, there is a tricky line: to become entirely anaesthetized is to become very dangerous.

Well, she's never been that. It wasn't that she didn't, right to the end, cringe when she heard his voice demanding something, even only a drink, or that his fingers, gripping her wrist, didn't cause her nerves to flinch. His words could still hurt; the stories he kept wanting to tell.

Now her heart is larger, and her eyes and ears are able to absorb a larger landscape. Now she can see and hear, rising daily like smoke from the pages of her paper, the wounds and cries of people far more seriously wounded than either she or Bradley ever was.

This may be the sort of thing Charlotte has always known. Certainly she has lived much closer to those wounds and cries. It's that perspective that may have made the injuries she both administered and endured seem trivial, more or less.

The long view must be comforting, as long as it can be maintained. Except it's hardly human, is it? Even Charlotte has shattered into sharply distressing events now and then, so personal (and perhaps predictable) that her view has been entirely filled, and even the most frantically waving battered, beaten child would fail to catch her attention. And Claudia – if one of her daughters was crying for help, she wouldn't want to have such a long view that she couldn't hear, for all the noise of weapons and weeping elsewhere. There is such a thing as too much perspective, that's for sure.

She should have paid more attention, when the girls were here, to what they had to say about their children; Claudia's grandchildren. Who, at this point, she barely knows. In the lives of children, a year is an enormous time; a great fraction of their total time on earth so far. They grow and change in a month, or a moment. She missed so much, caring for Bradley.

So that it seems, now that it's finished, that the will to do her best (or the desire for a cutting and complete revenge) has resulted in other, perhaps more important, losses. She may have

buried her unfaithful, foolish husband, but she also seems to have lost track of the small hopeful humans who succeeded him.

"You must come for a visit, Mother," Sonia said, as she and her sisters gathered their belongings at the end of their weekend, preparing to leave. "We'd love to have you." The others agreed, pitched in with invitations as well (except for Susan, who'd left first thing Sunday morning, with a casual, fond hug and a smile, and a mere "See you, Mum.").

Sandra nodded. "You don't have to stay here all on your own if you don't want to, you know."

And Sharon said, "All our kids would like it. They really miss you, you know."

Well, some of those "kids" are quite old enough to come to see her on their own, if they really wanted to. Sonia's in particular. But perhaps they haven't had an opportunity to get into the habit of visiting grandparents, independently or any other way. In the year of Bradley's illness, they tended to stay away. The few times they did come, they found their grandfather (or his condition) distressing, even frightening. Which of course it was, headed as it was towards death, that state quite properly mysterious and horrifying to the young.

And Bradley, even with them, wasn't quite pleasant company. He could get irritated by their presence, looked on them, occasionally, with resentment. Perhaps he envied their youth. Their whole lives ahead of them. Or perhaps he looked at them and couldn't discern their importance: that they were what came of him and Claudia. That, if they were not exactly his and Claudia's purpose, they were certainly what emerged from them.

Or, he could see but was angry that, after all, he'd be finally forgotten anyway. Those children's children would know little about him, and the generation after that nothing at all. He

made such a little mark, Bradley. Except on Claudia herself. And, for all she knows, a few others.

How many of her lovers does Charlotte remember with any intensity or grief? Until he was dying, Claudia heard only one part of Bradley's side of things: "It didn't matter," "It wasn't important," and "She was nothing to me, truly."

Truly! What a word on his lips!

What was it he cared about so much? Why did he keep trying to keep her, hold her in his house? When he was so willing to stray, in what he claimed were merely curious excursions, what was it that was so important about her? She can't imagine it was what he said: that above all else, anyone else, he loved her. Surely that was simply absurd; a denial of any possible definition of love she can think of.

He must have said, "I love you," to some of those others, at least. They can't all have not cared whether he did or did not. What on earth did he mean by the word?

Claudia meant what she has always meant, and still does mean: sturdiness, care, loyalty, and a thoughtful, anxious empathy. There is no way of viewing love that she can see, that includes impassivity towards the joys, much less the pains, of its object.

She is free enough of his presence now to see that her suffering and the sufferings of various other women of his acquaintance may have much in common. She is not free enough yet to care much about, or be very interested in, their sufferings.

She is even becoming somewhat bored by her own.

Charlotte was better at this sort of thing. She'd generally just shrug, once her first sorrow was done with. "When it's over, it's over," she'd say. "If it doesn't work, what can you do? You just go on to the next thing. Something always happens, after all. Something always turns up." There weren't many times when Charlotte grieved in ways that were recognizable to Claudia;

she was rarely as unstrung as Claudia sometimes felt herself to be.

But then, Claudia didn't have the gift of abandonment. What she seemed to have instead was a gift, if that's what it was, for hanging on, no matter what. And her daughters, if they're to be believed, consider her brave. They say they admire her. They do, however, live quite differently themselves. They don't care to share her attitudes, or her stubbornness, or her devotion – whatever it was that held her to this house and that husband.

It would be easy to say, "I made promises, and I keep my promises." Even Claudia, though, doesn't believe in keeping stupid promises, she doesn't believe there's anything especially sacred about a pledge that becomes manifestly absurd.

"Perhaps," she thinks, "it will come down to only having faith in my own character." Whatever that is. Whatever possibly stupid and absurd thing that is.

A person her age ought to know. She ought to know her own character, not merely her characteristics. She makes herself sound like a horoscope: If your birthday is today, you are loyal, kind, dependable, determined – all that.

She told the girls she'd like to visit them. "We could just keep bouncing you around from one to another and you'd never have to come home again," Sharon said, laughing. Claudia wondered if, when those words were said out loud, turning her into a dependent vagabond, they felt the sort of shiver she did.

She'd laughed too, though. "Oh, you don't need to set up any permanent spare rooms for me. I'll come visit when I get my feet under me again, but I could never be away from home for long."

Why not? She has no idea if it's true. She's never been away for long. And she's never lived here without Bradley, until the

last few weeks. She really has no idea how she'll prefer to live, left to her own devices.

Was there ever a time she's been left to her own devices? She can't think of one. Despite her promise to visit the girls, she may discover a preference for being alone. She may sink into the luxuries of her own rhythms and desires, her own heart.

Or she may, when she has sufficiently absorbed the horrors and terrors of the news that arrives on her doorstep daily, launch herself into action: do something, throw her heart and body into some small act of grander healing. There seems nothing large to be done, but she might still make some difference. Someone, after all, has to fill bags at a food bank; sit on the end of telephone lines, listening to desperate voices; visit the dying; fold arms around survivors of rape. There are people out there, doing these things.

And she has been a mother, she is certainly not without those skills that have to do with providing food, counsel, comfort. A mother's impulse is to act: to do something that will fix or cure. It is not in contemplation; it is hardly in the vague, sorrowful scrutiny of tragedy left, unaltered and unacted on, merely tragic.

Is this her nature, though? And is that a discouraging question, after raising four daughters, to wonder if it is actually her nature to be a mother; maternal?

She nursed Bradley, and she would not say it was her nature. Perhaps she has spent her time simply rising to occasions of one sort or another.

She has been accustomed to small goals: meals made by a certain hour, dishes done, medicines administered, laundries hung out to dry, groceries selected and paid for and put away into cupboards, meals planned. Have those been goals, though, or merely deadlines? Whatever, she is uncomfortable without them: an explorer who has lost sight of a crucial river,

a careless guide who, somewhere along the trail, has dropped the compass.

The choice is between blundering on, hoping to stumble into some safe place; or sitting down right on the spot, hoping either to pick saving clues from the surroundings, or for rescue.

She should perhaps fix her vision on some unaltering symbol, the way a lost explorer might head towards a distant mountain, or orient to a familiar star. Claudia will have her seventieth birthday in just two months. She could set herself to devise a future for herself by then.

Well, any fool can devise a future. The trick is to settle on the right one. She wouldn't want to find herself in an ill-fitting, uncomfortable, unflattering future.

One good thing is, those night visions have receded. Just since the girls were here, she has gone to sleep more easily, and slept more freely. She wonders where they've gone, those creatures that reared up in her mind when it let down its guard just a little. They were there, real enough, and now are they no longer real? Surely things that have existed don't simply cease to exist. They were only parts of herself – one way of looking at them – that were evil or ugly or at very least distressing. But parts of oneself don't simply vanish like amputated limbs, or dead husbands.

Perhaps she's just gotten used to her own evil.

Also lurking, like wickedness, is self-indulgence: all this wallowing in time and questions that don't have answers. She has never had time before. Or it might be more accurate to say she could not have borne it before. Because it's hard to do two things at once, especially when they might easily contradict each other. What if she'd ever had time to think, really think, and had concluded her life didn't suit? What use would that have been, what good could have come of it?

It's not by any means that she now has infinite time – she is

old, after all, and at any age who knows when some terminal lump of internal something is speeding towards the heart, ready to slam into it, stop it right in its tracks? But no one wants anything from her, no one needs anything. It can't be true, but this feels like the first time this has been the case: that she is free of all that.

Charlotte has been just the opposite. Charlotte has lived by her own desires and rhythms; is, in fact, the only person Claudia can think of who has been able to do that. Except perhaps Bradley, who seemed to spot some attraction and simply wander off, like a bird diverted by shiny objects in the grass; but that was just weak-mindedness, merely an inability to concentrate. Charlotte has had quite a different kind of concentration: intent on the rhythms and beats of her own heart. She's had demands and desires, not impulses and whims.

Charlotte's seventieth birthday is also soon. The two of them are very close in age, even the same astrological sign. So that makes nonsense of astrology, doesn't it, seeing how different they are?

Charlotte has tried, it seems to Claudia, always to have done, and to have had, it all. That isn't possible, of course. Charlotte has done a good deal, attempted a lot, headed boldly (to Claudia) into different adventures, but of course she hasn't had it all. She hasn't had, for instance, children, husband, the solidity of that particular configuration of security.

Of course Claudia would like to visit her daughters; watch and listen to her grandchildren, explore what they're like, imagine what they may become; lie back with her eyes closed and listen to the sounds of those four quite different households, try to make out if all their parts are working – like listening to a piece of machinery, a car, say, to see what may be rubbing or grinding, and what is functioning smoothly. Of course she would like that.

But she has now a greater longing to see Charlotte, that oldest of old friends; who knows quite a different Claudia than Claudia's daughters ever can. Or should. Who knows the little scared child as well as the hopeful young woman and the occasionally shattered older one. Who has, perhaps, a sense of Claudia's soul, as well as of her life. She would like them to settle in comfortable chairs, she and Charlotte, drinks in their hands, and trail randomly through events, connecting things up here and there, and tracking differences, as well.

Claudia believes Charlotte has a sense of her soul? Does that mean she has, herself, a sense of Charlotte's? She means, at least, a terrible fondness; something fierce and mysterious. Also something that wouldn't have a hope of existing, no doubt, if they met now for the first time. If there were a circumstance now in which they even could meet. No, their histories are too different. Charlotte would no doubt look at Claudia and think, "How dull. Poor little mud hen, what a tedious, dutiful life." And Claudia – well, how could someone like Claudia look at someone like Charlotte, and not grow fierce? Slut, tramp, home-wrecker (although that wouldn't quite be true, Charlotte never actually wrecked anyone's home), frivolous dilettante, muddling about in the lives of seriously intentioned adults – Claudia would surely despise Charlotte, meeting her now, towards the end of their lives, with all their experiences between them.

Is she angry with Charlotte, then? Even now, are those words she would like to speak to her? Crimes she would like to accuse her of? Perhaps. Claudia wouldn't rule it out.

But of course they're not meeting now, they met more than six decades ago. Their friendship is a spine that has grown with them, and whatever aches and pains and inflexibilities it has developed here and there, now and then, its absence is not imaginable. What would one be without a spine? They might

well not like each other, meeting now. But that has nothing to do with who they are to each other.

And it must be true, there is some magic, or something mysterious, anyway, between them because here, opening her mail, she finds a letter from Charlotte. Finally! It's very light. Claudia fingers the envelope, comparing it to the bulging one she sent off, words and lines that turned into paragraphs, then pages – as if she were sweating onto paper the last year of her life, trying to describe how it felt, how it smelled, how, really, it was; except for the secret. Dodging around facts, words being weapons when they're laid down too bluntly, apt to backfire and blind, staring up from the page. This, though – has Charlotte so little to say?

Ah, Charlotte began reading Claudia with a drink in her hand. A Scotch, she says. That seems the right idea, although Claudia detests Scotch, can't think how Charlotte can drink the stuff. She herself pours a small glass of white wine.

"Love, Charlotte," it ends. So that's all right. Now she can begin properly at the beginning. Sometimes Claudia also peeks at the endings of books; just to be sure, just to relieve the worry and suspense.

Charlotte says she wishes she'd known Bradley was ill. She says she would have come and helped, Claudia if not Bradley. She's quite right, Bradley wouldn't have welcomed her attentions. And that's precisely why (besides exhaustion, and the difficulty of putting into words just what was going on) Claudia did not call or write. She couldn't have managed a single thing more. She couldn't have had Charlotte offering help, Bradley refusing it, herself in the middle, on the telephone or in letters or in this house.

Now, though, now she could use help. And oh, perfect friend – "I wish you were with me," Charlotte writes. "I wish we could help each other."

Yes, they are old, as Charlotte says. People are indeed dying, including themselves. Claudia has a sudden vision of herself at Charlotte's funeral – would she weep, the way Charlotte wept at her wedding?

"Maybe we could sit up late again, like we used to," Charlotte writes, "and tell each other secrets."

If there is anyone Claudia can tell, it will be Charlotte.

Can Charlotte be frightened? So she says. "Fear has some peculiar results, I am finding." Claudia can't remember Charlotte ever speaking of fear before; never her own, at any rate. It's one of the things that amazed Claudia: if she were Charlotte, leading Charlotte's life, she could imagine being in a constant state of terror. Just of the unknown, if nothing else.

"Do come," Charlotte writes. She says her breasts are sagging. Claudia's own nipples, when she sits, can almost touch her belly. And they used to be so upright, she was so proud of her full, large white breasts. It makes sense that Charlotte's would only sag; hers were never as bountiful as Claudia's.

And now no one cares, except perhaps the two of them. Their breasts are of no concern whatever to anyone but themselves, and are certainly of no appeal. How very sad: the delights of breasts and penises, both gone.

Perhaps some people do get wise with age. Perhaps they understand this isn't so important. Perhaps they understand resignation even better than Claudia does. It doesn't sound as if Charlotte does, though, which is a relief, after all.

She and the girls talked a bit about Charlotte on the weekend. "I always wanted a best friend like that, like you guys were," Sandra said. "And wasn't Daddy jealous!"

"I think she scared him," said Sharon. "He'd get a scrunched look when the two of you were on the phone."

Claudia laughed. "He thought she was a bad influence on me. Maybe he was right, in a way."

"Sure," said Susan. "In *his* way. I always thought she was terrific. Such guts she had." No doubt it was wrong for Claudia to feel a clutch of jealousy, just for a moment: that her daughters saw, not her sturdy, stoic self, but the more outrageous, careless Charlotte, as the appropriate example.

Now, though, it seems a good thing they had a choice. It also seems that her least favourite daughter (although of course she loves them all, truly and deeply) is Sonia, the one who may be most like herself; and her most favourite may well be Susan, of whom she knows least, but whom she assumes must be brave, much like Charlotte.

This is a very small world, this house. She can feel, looking around, that the rooms, this living-room for instance, may be unhealthy. If she is looking for some long view, it may not be possible within these narrow walls.

And it would be lovely to see Charlotte. It could be good, too, to look back, from far away, at this place, and this life, and all her events, and see what differences distance may make.

She can imagine finding the words to tell Charlotte. She can imagine Charlotte listening carefully; nodding gravely at the end; holding Claudia's plump hands between her long fingers. She can hear Charlotte saying, "How awful for you. I'm so sorry. But you're a good woman, don't ever doubt it."

Not so the secret would go away, but so that it could make itself a comfortable place in Claudia's memory, turn around once or twice more in her mind, then lie down and be still.

She wonders what Charlotte's up to these days. Some adventure, no doubt; something interesting she was too tactful to mention in her letter of invitation and condolence. How they will talk! What secrets indeed they may tell.

nine

MAYBE CHARLOTTE SHOULD HAVE telephoned Claudia, instead of writing. For one thing if she had, and Claudia agreed, she might even be here now for a visit, a neat diversion from hedges. Claudia could have confided whatever her unmentionable secret might be. Charlotte could have sought her wisdom on the subject of marital maintenance.

All in all, they would have much to discuss.

But Claudia wrote instead of telephoning. And Charlotte does have to pay attention to money. Sometimes she wonders what she worked so hard for all those years – certainly not for security in her old age. But that would have been a poor goal, after all.

Even so, the world is the wrong way around. There she was, day after perilous and tragic (or dull and bureaucratic) day,

doing the job of the circus shit-sweeper: after the glamorous and public events, cleaning up the unpleasant leftovers. When the circus left town, no one would want to see great steaming heaps of elephant crap; nor did they care to be confronted with the horror that may go on behind ordinary doors. Actors and athletes, even accountants or lawyers, made more money, stored larger pensions, than Charlotte ever could.

She imagines Claudia's in much the same position as herself, after a career just as thankless as Charlotte's.

Thankless, at least, from the point of view of the outside world. Maybe less so from inside. Claudia's daughters must be grateful to her; certainly they ought to be. And while Charlotte can't think of anyone who actually ought to be grateful to her, she did, as in other matters, do her best. At least what she thought at the time was best; one risked, of course, being wrong.

It really would be interesting (more interesting than Andrew? Less humiliating, anyway) to find out what happened to Lissa and Tim. If she puts her mind to it she can recall fairly precisely a number of the kids who passed through her life, just as she can precisely recall other lovers than Andrew (remember Paul? Remember Brian? Well, yes; only frankly, they are less to the point). Like Andrew, Lissa and Tim may represent not only greater investments of effort and time, but of summary and hope: lessons of the long run.

They'd be harder to trace, no doubt, than Andrew; far less likely to be listed neatly in the phone book. There were few signs their lives would ever become so tidy they might someday be settled long or sturdily enough to have a listing for a phone.

Where are they now?

Then they were kids on the street. She met them, ran into them, a few months after her ten years with Andrew ended.

They were fifteen, sixteen, then. Now, if they've survived, they'll be middle-aged and surely unrecognizable. Not like Andrew.

The most likely and efficient way to find them might be not with phone books but with prison records. At the time she hoped for better for them, but without much faith, and she doubts she made so much difference that she changed the way their lives were headed. After all, it doesn't look as if she altered Andrew's life much, in the end.

She met them in somewhat similar fashion, too – in physical collision. Well, what happened was that Tim stepped suddenly out of a shop doorway downtown and tried to grab her purse.

Silly boy – far too weedy and malnourished; although desperate, and desperation gives strength to the frailest frame. Charlotte, though, at the time, had some rage and desperation of her own. And was hardly weedy. She turned on the boy, grabbed his wrist, twisted the skin until he let go of her purse, then hung on. His hair was blond, uncut and dirty, and his shirt was torn at the shoulder. She could make out a scrawny hairless chest dimpled with cold. She thought he had mean eyes.

The thing was, she wanted to hurt this kid, had an impulse to strike him until he fell to the ground, and kick him until he curled up into himself, whimpering. She wanted to make him howl.

She was appalled.

"What did you think you were doing?" she asked.

"Let me go." He was no longer looking into her eyes; cast down, his looked less mean.

"No. You wanted my money? You'd have been disappointed, you know." But that wasn't true; she could see he needed whatever he could get. "What did you want it for?"

"Let me go."

"Drugs? Food? Booze? Someplace to crash?"

"You got no right. Let me go."

Charlotte almost did loosen her grip, startled, when the girl stepped out of the doorway. "Tim? Let's go, come on, let's take off, what're you doing?" This could be trouble, two of them. Until now she'd been grateful for the careful disinterest of passers-by, but that wouldn't be to her advantage if these two ganged up on her. The girl was bigger than her friend; slightly taller and more flesh-packed, healthier. More recently on the streets, Charlotte supposed, although equally shabby and dirty. Her dark hair was as lank as his. It wasn't possible to live on the streets hygienically.

"I was asking your friend what he wanted," she said to the girl. "Money, of course, but what for? Are you hungry, or was it for drugs?"

The girl stared at her. "Who cares? Let him go, okay? You got your purse, so who cares?"

"I do." She wasn't angry any longer, now that they weren't quite strangers; now that they were just kids and unsuccessful purse-snatchers. "Because if it's for drugs, I can't do much, but I can if it was food you were after." Once again she tightened her grip on the boy's struggling wrist. "If it's food, I can buy you a meal."

"Are you nuts?" The boy looked up at her, and she saw he really thought she might be; that she was possibly crazy, in some dangerous way. That he and his friend had fallen into the hands of a woman of evil, unpredictable designs.

Charlotte laughed. She rather liked being dangerous. She'd rather enjoyed it sometimes, scaring Andrew, too, although in other ways. "No, I'm not nuts," she said calmly. "But you obviously need something badly or you wouldn't be trying to steal purses. And from the looks of the two of you, you're famished and I could use a meal myself. So let's the three of us go across

the street to that restaurant," gesturing with her free arm to a greasy spoon, "and check it out. Because," she added, "you tried to steal my purse, and you could have knocked me down or hurt me, but since I caught you and it didn't work, I figure you owe me. I can call a cop, or you can eat. Your choice."

She watched them as they looked at each other. They weren't very good at wordless signals. Finally the girl shrugged. "Okay then, food. Now let Tim go, all right? We'll go to the restaurant with you, if that's what you want."

They would, of course, escape at the first possible instant. Charlotte made sure that the boy slid before her across the red-vinyl-covered seat, herself beside him, so that he was blocked by her and the grey table in front of them. The girl sat across from them; if she were going to run without him, she would have already done so.

Charlotte let go of his wrist. "Three milk," she told the waitress. "Three coffees. Five cheeseburgers with everything. Three fries. Then we'll see."

She paid attention to her food. After their first hesitation, they did, too. She thought kids were something like wary animals – once they were captured, you had to treat them with a kind of ignoring, nonchalant kindness, until they relaxed. It just took longer, and was trickier, with kids than with wary animals.

The girl's name was Lissa. "Aw, shit," she said when she asked, and Charlotte told her, what she did for a living. "A social worker. Christ."

"Yes, I know," Charlotte said calmly. "If nothing else, social workers have no money. If you'd managed to get my purse, it'd have been tough luck for you. In any case, today I'm just a shopper. So that's a piece of luck, right?"

They didn't know what to make of her, sitting there grinning at them. They might not trust her, but she confused them and

since, like most people, they were disarmed by a combination of interest and silence, they told her some things about themselves.

Not a whole lot, they'd been around enough to be neither naïve nor trusting, but enough, they may have thought, to earn the meal. Charlotte had also been around enough to be neither naïve nor trusting, and had no particular reason to assume they were telling their true stories.

They were both from suburbs, although from different ends of the city. Tim said he'd left home two years ago, when he was fourteen, because his well-off and charming father came home regularly from the office or the golf course and was transformed. "He beat on me for *anything*," Tim said. "My little brother and my mother, too."

"And is this better?" Charlotte asked.

"Oh yeah. It's too bad for them, though, I guess. Sometimes I think I'll go back and get them out, too. Or kill him." Well, that had a ring of truth. And certainly the story was not unusual. Charlotte heard such tales all the time; which meant it could be either true or so ordinary Tim had simply picked it up from someone else.

Lissa was less forthcoming. Or less imaginative. She shrugged. "My parents were always on my case. So I left."

"How long ago?"

She shrugged again. "I don't know. Couple of months."

"Do you think they're worried about you?"

"Yeah, probably. I hope so."

Interesting, that desire for revenge. For what? More than for parents who were "always on my case." At any rate, she was tougher than Tim, one way and another.

"How do you live? Stealing purses?"

Tim's turn to shrug. "Scrounge. Shoplift. Whatever." Charlotte saw him glance uneasily at Lissa.

Who looked directly at Charlotte and said flatly, "I hook. Twenty bucks a blow job, two or three a day and we're cool, we can live."

"You like that?"

"Of course I fucking don't, they're assholes. Creeps. Old guys."

"So," turning to Tim, "you don't mind that? Living off your friend giving blow jobs to old guys? Like your father? You figure?"

Tim startled to tremble, struck the table with his fist. "Hey, just fuck off, a cheeseburger doesn't give you the right to say shit like that."

"That's true, it doesn't. I wondered, though, if you thought your father was that kind of guy, to be drifting around downtown looking for young girls. How old are you, Lissa?"

"Seventeen."

"No. Fifteen, maybe. Right?"

"Yeah, okay. So what? Just don't bother, okay? We don't need social workers or drop-in centres or clinics or any of that shit, we do fine. We look after each other, me and Tim."

"I guess you do." Charlotte was peering at the bill, getting out money, pulling herself together. "And that's nice, I expect. It's good to have a friend to look after you. You're lucky." In an odd way, that was quite true: they were lucky to have each other. Most kids were out on their own. Charlotte herself felt, more vividly than usual, out on her own these days.

They looked confused. "So," Tim said, "like, what now?"

"What now? I'm going to finish my shopping. And," turning to Lissa, "I'm going to leave thirty dollars with you. It's all the cash I've got. You can pay our bill here and keep the rest. It'll save you part of a blow job." By then she was standing, looking down at them. Two men at the next table looked up sharply, frowning – well, they probably didn't often hear, and no doubt

disapproved of, well-dressed, middle-aged women using the words "blow job." She stared back at them. Lissa laughed. She and Charlotte grinned at each other.

"What if I just keep it all?" Lissa asked. "What if we walk out without paying?"

"Then I'll have made a mistake, I guess." Now Charlotte shrugged. "Good luck. I'll see you around." She took a couple of steps, turned back. "I mean that. I know what it sounds like, but I'd like things to work out for you." Whatever that might mean, to either of them. Mere survival seemed their biggest, most immediate hurdle.

"So, I'll see you around." She did, too – they ran into each other after that more often than could be accounted for just by coincidence – and some things happened. But she'd bet neither one of them has a home she could locate, with a hedge she could lurk in.

There were things it was necessary to be particularly clear about. Definitions and distinctions. Andrew, for instance, had told her that she lacked romance. She told him romance was a luxury; that she preferred love to romance, emotion to sentiment. For a man who used words in his work, he was never very good at definitions. He'd frowned, lightly puzzled, not taking her very seriously.

Well, Charlotte had to know these things. She had to know with fair precision the difference between, for instance, discipline and abuse; discouragement and despair; affection and addiction. All sorts of life-and-death shavings of meaning.

Such judgements were formed not by pure reasoning, but by a sort of informed intuition: a combination of knowledge and experience and some less definable gauging of prospects and likelihoods. Reason only, for instance, would have advised her to be very cautious in her contacts with Tim and Lissa. Experience told her they were in the kinds of trouble that spiralled

into more and worse. The informed intuition, however, caused her, encountering them again downtown, to regard them carefully and closely, and then invite them to her home for dinner. On the face of it, perilous: they'd tried to take her purse in daylight on a busy street; what might they do after nightfall, alone with her behind the doors of her home, where, if nothing else, she had some appealing possessions?

Well, she couldn't live that way. "Dinner at your *house*?" Lissa asked, astonished, as well she might have been. She and Tim had to make their judgements, too. For all they could deduce with reason alone, Charlotte might have dire purposes in mind for them. For all of them, it was a matter of calculation, balance. They stood in their own small circle on the sidewalk and made their silent assessments.

"Okay," Lissa said finally. Certainly a girl who provided blow jobs to strangers would need at least as acute an ability as Charlotte's to make swift judgements of possible perils.

And so the two of them arrived, ill-at-ease, on her doorstep. Charlotte tried not to appear to keep too close an eye on them as they regarded her possessions; and in fact, she realized, there wasn't so much after all that might lure them, or anyone, to theft: the TV, the stereo, that would be about all. The things that were really important would have no value: the small carved or glass figures, the vases, the art – gifts and purchases that had to do with the moves and shifts of her life.

"Nice place," said Tim, nodding.

The houses where they'd grown up, at distant ends of the city, were quite different from hers, they told her over salad and spaghetti, although similar to each other's.

Now that she's seen it, she imagines Andrew's house is the sort of place Tim and Lissa grew up in, but of course she had no real picture of it then.

In her dining-room, the two of them seemed to expand. She

thought how tightly they must hold themselves most of the time.

"If I was home right now," Tim said, "everybody'd be eating. I guess they are anyways. Saturdays we'd get pizza, usually."

"Yeah?" Lissa looked impressed. "We never got anything ordered in. My dad said what the hell else did my mother have to do except cook and why should he spend his money on something somebody else made when that was her job."

"Goodness," Charlotte murmured. "Not much of a man for treats, I guess. Not much of a gift for celebration."

Lissa grinned. "Not much."

"My dad was always bringing presents for my mom," Tim said. "Flowers and chocolates, stuff like that. After he'd beat her up, he'd give her something. Me and my brother, too, I got a shitload of stuff, but it was always because he'd beat us up, so I started putting it away in a box. My mum would eat the chocolates, though. I guess right now they're having pizza, and then there'll be chocolates, likely."

He was just a kid. They both were. That did not, of course, make them undangerous.

"Yeah, and at my house," Lissa said bitterly, "we'd have dinner and then my dad would get drinking more while my mother cleaned up, and then she'd say she was tired and she'd take off to their room with a book, some big romance, and she *knew*. She must have known, and she just didn't care. I'd try to think of ways to leave before she did, but it never worked, he'd tell me to stay and she'd say, 'Yes, you keep your father company, I'm so tired,' and then he'd fuck me on the living-room floor while she was upstairs reading her shitty stupid books."

Tim put an arm around her. There they were, across the table from Charlotte, two kids holding on to each other. "Well, shit," Lissa said, straightening. "Fuck them." Charlotte could quite see her point.

How had they managed to leave those homes, instead of turning knives or guns or fists on guilty, evil parents? Why had they turned themselves onto the streets? But then, she knew it was difficult for any child, however hurt, to turn on a parent. Not only from fear, but because who else was there?

And now they had each other.

Do they still, she wonders? That might have been a happy outcome, but it seems, although neat, somewhat unlikely.

"Thanks," they said awkwardly at the end of the evening. She did not offer them beds, or to drive them downtown. She wanted neither to become responsible for them, nor to frighten them with her attentions. She couldn't save them. Could, however, show some possibilities; ways and rewards for saving themselves.

She didn't particularly encourage them to talk about their histories, although they sometimes did. Nor did she nag them about their futures, did not collect lists of courses they might take, professions they might pursue if they just did this or that. Instead they talked about various current events; and watched television programs, sometimes quite stupid ones, together. But she realized that what she found stupid, they might well see as restful and diverting.

They came to dinner every few weeks. Tim's sorrow was appealing, and Lissa's frank rage sounded hopeful. No one broke into Charlotte's home late at night to make off with her television set, or to club her in her bed. If she did nothing extraordinarily good, she equally did them no extraordinary harm, and certainly suffered no harm at their hands. So her sense, so much more acute than Andrew's, of definitions and distinctions, served her well enough. She wasn't wrong in distinguishing between the dangers of a pair like Tim and Lissa and others she wouldn't have dreamed of having in her home. Although she would have had difficulty putting the difference

into words. And in the end she lost track and has no idea what has become of them.

Just the way she lost track of, had no idea what became of, Andrew.

What if she has made all the wrong choices? What if, after all, she does have things to regret?

What if she comes to hate growing old on her own? What if she would have liked the grown-up Tim and Lissa dropping in on her, perhaps with their own children, seeing how well things turned out? Sitting around in the sunshine with them, talking about their pasts as if all that were now a far-off, foreign country from which they'd made their ways, successful refugees?

Or, what if she would have preferred puttering around a garden with an old familiar man, talking about nothing at all?

Loneliness is reasonably unfamiliar; when it comes on her like this, like a wave over her head, pulling her under, she doesn't know what to do, how to feel, how to make it go away.

She has expected too much, perhaps, and so may simply be doomed to dissatisfaction. She may have aimed for the enormous and impossible, with the cost a failure to be satisfied with everyday achievements. She tried very hard with Andrew, for instance, to be satisfied with what there was – it was a great deal, after all: a lover and friend, all in one – but it wasn't in her nature. And her nature, wanting more, made him angry, and anger made him sad and sorrow made him chilly, which caused her pain, so that she attempted more demands. There were times the two of them must have looked quite unappealing to each other.

Still, they survived for a decade. Longer than many marriages. Perhaps that was because they also shared stubbornness. Then too, their time together was measured in hours, not days, so ten years hardly amounted to a real decade.

It seemed long enough at the time.

She supposes, sipping a restorative and warranted Scotch at the end of the dangerous day of near-discovery, that this may be the point of hiding and eavesdropping, at this far-too-late date: to try to discover the nature of love.

As it applies to herself, of course; she isn't especially interested in the broader question so thoroughly and tediously explored by poets, psychologists, brain-and-heart-pickers of one sort and another. Just, what is her own nature of love? Does it even apply to her? Did she ever have it? Did she have it and then lose it? Is there such a thing, or is it some comforting, or discomfiting, dramatic myth, created like television to entertain, provide a plot, a little surge of interest in the midst of day-to-day survival?

Perhaps she should have had tea. Scotch seems to have an awfully depressing effect.

Because of course there is such a thing as love. She recalls its sturdiness, its heat warm as a blanket, and as comforting. What a foundation of joy it built for each day.

But is that after all merely romantic?

No, because she can remember. "I won't ever forget you," she used to promise Andrew, and that appears to be true.

The nature of reality is something quite different. As she is uninterested in poets' and psychologists' visions of love, equally philosophers' views of the nature of reality do not absorb her. She thinks, rather, that it's like definitions of words: everyone brings shadings of their own histories to words like "happiness," like "love"; and so it is with the experiences and events that shape reality. Because two people can spend a day together and lay their heads down at night with quite different, even conflicting impressions. Should this be as astonishing as it so often turns out to be?

And this must be at the very root of conflict: this is what

happened, but no, not at all because you did that and this is what that meant to me, I heard what you said, I saw what you did, and how could you dream it wouldn't mean this? Are you crazy, that's not what happened at all. And so forth.

Look at Claudia and Bradley: he wandered off, returned to tell her, "But it was nothing, really"; and that may have been, for him, quite true. It may not speak well of Bradley, but it may have been true enough. But for Claudia it was breach of faith and heartbreak. It seemed to Charlotte that at some point the heartbreak was less the actual adultery (what a word!) than that Bradley didn't care enough about Claudia's reality to temper his. And the lies, of course. They added up, as well.

But if Charlotte despised Bradley for his failure to take her friend into account, for what, then, did she despise herself, or Andrew?

Well, "despise" may be too strong a word. But perhaps at the root of their failure was a terminal disrespect for each other: her unwillingness to take Elizabeth into account; his more complicated (from Charlotte's point of view) capacity somehow to take them both into account. Along with himself, of course.

Charlotte wasn't blind to her own cowardice: he was right (although for the wrong reasons) that she should have become acquainted with Elizabeth, at least to the extent that Elizabeth had a shape in her mind, a voice, a character. It was less than brave to maintain her merely as a vague, invisible competitor.

But one must live, somehow.

She heard Claudia saying, "But then he tells me it was nothing, and he loves me." And heard Andrew speaking tenderly to his wife, in much the same tone he used with Charlotte, saying, "I love you, you know. I truly do." And meaning it. Charlotte never thought, when he said that, that he was lying to her, so presumably he would not be lying to Elizabeth.

At least, unlike Bradley, he would not have had to say, "It was nothing." Because of course he was able to sustain a secret.

What secrets did he sustain with Charlotte? Certainly he never told her he discussed love with his wife; she was only sure he must have. And those were the worms of disrespect that finally ruined them.

Even worms have a point of view. People tread blithely and worms, looking up, see only boot soles and narrow escapes, or destruction. A little outing for one is peril and death for another. And that, in Charlotte's view, is the nature of reality.

And what may Elizabeth's view be?

Now there's a question that opens up some possibilities, some prospects for unconsidered actions: like stepping right up that suburban walk, between the oval gardens, and knocking on that blue-painted door.

Charlotte might easily pose as a cosmetics salesperson, a canvasser for votes or money for a worthy cause, a researcher conducting a survey. How clever, that last! And women love surveys; Elizabeth might find it irresistible.

"What are your views," Charlotte might ask, clipboard in hand, pen poised, "about marriage? Your own, specifically, and don't worry, it's all confidential, anonymous, will be stirred into results with thousands of others. But in your case, specifically: how long have you been married? Children? Grandchildren? Do you own your home? What has your career been? And your husband's?"

She knows the answers, of course, but the easy, factual questions would ease Elizabeth into comfort with more difficult and trusting ones. She might pour them each a coffee and settle into a chair opposite Charlotte in that living-room (with fireplace) where Charlotte has never been. She might hold her cup in both hands and look down, into the coffee, putting words together, finding the right ones for her answers. Or she

might look directly into Charlotte's eyes, speaking up confidently, sure of her marriage and certain of her version of it.

Would Charlotte be able to look directly back at that little round face, into those pure, trusting eyes?

Well, she wouldn't have to. She'd be concentrating on her clipboard.

And surely it's contemptuous to give Elizabeth doggy-like qualities: pure trusting eyes, indeed!

"To what do you attribute the length of your marriage?" she might ask. "Please be as detailed as you can." And, "Have you ever been unfaithful? Has your husband, to your knowledge?" (What a surprise, if Elizabeth said, "Oh yes, I had several lovers. It kept our marriage fresh. It was always a choice, you see, I could always feel I had an alternative, so I never was trapped. I do think that's important.")

Just once, Charlotte asked Andrew if he ever imagined that Elizabeth might fall in love with someone he didn't dream of. "Good lord, no." How shocked he looked! "Not Elizabeth."

She didn't venture to ask why he found the idea incomprehensible, or shocking, or outrageous. Nor did she point out how he had, once again, insulted her, a woman without obvious scruples when it came to love, in comparison with the sainted, trusted Elizabeth.

"Did you find having children brought you closer together, or made a wedge between you?" Charlotte might ask, pen busy. "Did you decide to have children, or did they just happen? Did your husband work long hours? Did you ever suspect his absences? Did you actually care where he was, or might be? Do you ever think you deliberately failed to notice things about him? If you trusted him, exactly what measures did he take, what words did he say, to cultivate that trust? Would you say you made love often, not often enough, hardly ever? Exactly how often, would you say? Did it seem like a

habit, or an expectation, or did it really feel like making love? What were your preferred positions? His? Did you make each other happy in your bedroom? Would you mind showing me your bedroom?"

Perhaps by now even Elizabeth would be wondering about this survey. Or this surveyor. "Who *are* you?" she might finally get around to asking. "These are rather odd questions, aren't they?"

"What do you think," Charlotte would like to know, "your husband thought about your marriage? Do you think he was happy (whatever that might mean)? Do you think he was contented? Do you think your existence made him feel safe, or secure, or that he had a place he belonged? Did you ever consider him a coward? Do you feel he took you into account, or did you ever feel taken for granted? Did you have little tender habits to remind yourselves of each other? I mean things like leaving notes pinned to pillows, or touching fingers to neck just briefly, walking by. You must have had signals, codes, ways of speaking that meant something just to the two of you – can you tell me some of those, please?"

Yes indeed, keep that salt pouring, that acid burning.

"Do you think that if, say, he'd ever had an affair, he'd have used similar expressions and codes and signals, just to keep from getting too confused? Do you think he would have done the same things or different things with someone else in bed?

"Did he ever startle you with a position or technique or words that struck you as oddly different or new?

"Can you describe him for me? His character as you see it, I mean. What sort of man would you say he is? If he had ever, say, had an affair, what sort of woman do you think he'd have had it with? Can you describe what you'd think of her? Can you describe what kind of character she might have needed to have? Would you see her as sluttish, or frivolous, or maybe

even as a reasonably good woman not necessarily unlike yourself? How much would you have minded? Or did you know? Did you know and feel grateful that he'd taken his attentions elsewhere? Was it a relief? Did you know and get on with your own, quite interesting life?

"And if so, what's it like now that he's retired and home all the time – was that a big adjustment? He was out for such long hours for so many years, has it come as a shock, living with him so constantly? Has he seemed like a stranger at all? Has his presence had much effect on your routines, or your pleasures?

"Tell me, do you like him? Do you love him? Do you trust him? Do you think he likes, loves and trusts you?

"Tell me, really, what do you think is the secret of marriage? Tell me what you think its true deep nature is."

A survey would really be a good idea because she could write down all the answers and look at them later. Almost like a real surveyor, she could try to correlate responses, make patterns from the answers, even maybe draw graphs and charts to illuminate their meaning.

Or she could just stare and stare at certain passages. Some combinations of words might make everything devastatingly clear.

Why devastating? Elizabeth might well smile and shrug and say, "Oh, we have never been suited, we have never been happy. We almost never made love. It was merely convenient. I never cared much for him or what he did."

She cannot imagine Elizabeth's answers. They might be anything at all. Andrew maintained her privacy severely (maintaining his own, of course, at the same time), and Charlotte never had a clue. Certainly there's no way of knowing from that small round exterior what sort of woman Elizabeth is. Still, unless she was as clever a liar as Andrew, the marriage-of-convenience answer would be most unlikely. If it were only

that, he wouldn't have made such an effort to keep his secret.

Odd, to think of herself as a secret: reducing her merely to words that couldn't be said, and actions that couldn't be revealed.

What if, while she was sitting in that living-room, in that easy chair, with that cup of coffee on an end table beside her, and with that clipboard perched on her lap, pen poised, asking Elizabeth questions, nodding and writing and trying to look unattached, undisturbed – what if Andrew wandered in? Would he recognize her? Would she have known him anywhere? Probably. Although he does move differently; his shape is somewhat altered; and he speaks to his wife in tones unfamiliar to Charlotte.

She didn't want to think he loved his wife, but she also doesn't care to believe that he has always spoken to her so peremptorily.

On the other hand, there was his hand, gentle on Elizabeth's back, as they turned to enter their home.

Every marriage may be different; but even so, surely there's some secret common to all those that survive, and even some that don't? There must be something to be known about how two people go on together, or more particularly, why. Whatever it is, Charlotte hasn't had the gift for it. A talent is missing that is common in the world.

Claudia must know. Of course, people who have talents, and who are in the middle of using them to lead their lives, don't necessarily recognize them as anything very special. They don't necessarily understand that what is evident to them may be quite a mystery to someone else.

So it may well be that Charlotte only needs to ask.

Ah, Scotch, after all, isn't necessarily so depressing. It also opens possibilities, expands imagination. And now she will make herself a pot of tea and soberly realize, and firmly point

out to herself, that she will not, ever, find herself in Elizabeth's living-room (Elizabeth's, not Andrew's also?) conducting an imaginary survey. She must keep strictly aware of the differences between entertaining fantasy and true peril. Not to mention simple bad behaviour. She is not a bad woman.

Although she has, so far, eavesdropped and spied and generally abased herself. Also, of course, she has had Elizabeth's husband's body in and around her own, and they have spoken many tender words to each other. How is that not bad?

Well, it probably is bad. Was. But still, she is not a bad woman.

She'd better, sitting here now with her tea, start thinking of satisfying, satisfactory ways to occupy her life. Useful and enlightening projects – pursuing, perhaps, how events turned out for Tim and Lissa? That would surely be an improvement over outings like this morning's. There can't be a great deal of time to waste before she's old or ill or dotty or dying, and what foolishness to consider spending more of it in Andrew's hedge.

She wonders if anyone will notice the broken branches. They were on the neighbours' side, and who knows, they may have driven in from work and regarded with some puzzlement the signs of – what? – some large animal marauding through the greenery.

Thirty years ago, Andrew's affections were a mystery. What made her think she might unravel them now? Or that knowing would make some difference?

It would be pleasant to learn to be a contented person. She would like to be able to tell herself something like, "Well, I've certainly done some interesting things. I don't think I've missed much, at least in the way of feelings, if not of actual experiences. I don't regret not climbing mountains, or flinging myself out of airplanes, and I don't regret some of the humbler pleasures, either. I've felt all the most powerful passions, I'm

sure – love and hatred, despair and joy, jealousy, rage, tenderness – everything's in there somewhere, in some form. And more to come."

Yes, that would be pleasant. She has never had the gift of contentment, but this may be the time to cultivate it. Only, it seems a pale goal. And a rather small, pathetic and terminal one.

Maybe just one more venture? Oh dear.

But she could promise that whatever happened, or even if she saw no one and heard nothing, it'd be the last time. Or, even if she saw some great domestic drama and heard stirring, significant words, she wouldn't go back. She could give this outrageous, apparently indomitable curiosity of hers a deadline here, and stick to it, and that would be that.

And what if "that" involves discovery? She mustn't forget the terror, when she thought she was going to land on the lawn in front of Andrew and Elizabeth today. It makes her shiver. But still.

Ah, saved. How rarely her telephone rings any more! Quite startling, so her hand jerks and tea slops onto her robe. "Charlotte?" she hears. It takes her a second to identify the voice, which hasn't been heard for so long.

"Claudia! Oh, my dear Claudia, how are you? Did you get my letter? Are you coming? Oh, I would like to see you, please come. Is that why you're calling?"

She hears Claudia's old familiar laugh. "Lovely to hear your voice too, Charlotte, but be quiet now, so I can tell you." And Charlotte leans back into the cushions of her sofa for a discussion of an immediate, preoccupying future that doesn't include a word of Andrew, or marriage, or hedges, but which does have a good deal to do with the nature of love.

ten

CHARLOTTE'S VOICE IS AS CLEAR and vital as Claudia has been imagining and remembering. And fond, too, and excited – she does sound pleased. "I'm taking you at your word," Claudia says. "That I can come visit. I'd love to, if it's still all right."

"How soon?" Charlotte asks. "Tomorrow?"

She sounds very eager. Can something be wrong? "Well, not quite *that* soon, I have a few things to take care of. But maybe the day after? I just wanted to know if it was really okay. I've been thinking about you. I wanted to see you."

"Me too. Oh, Claudia, it's lovely to hear you. I was thinking I should have called instead of writing, but then I thought maybe you were tired of the telephone. I'm so glad you've called now. I can't wait to see you."

"Me neither. But don't go to any trouble, okay?"

"What trouble? How long can you stay? You're welcome, you know, for as long as you want."

Claudia feels stupid. She hasn't thought about the length of her visit. She has imagined its beginning, when she and Charlotte see each other for the first time in what, five years, but not its ending, when they will hug and say goodbye again. "I don't know exactly."

"Doesn't matter. Will you be taking the train? I can meet you if you let me know when."

"I'll call. I'll let you know as soon as I find out."

"God, this is exciting! It's been ages, and I've been dying to see you. Oh dear. Sorry." They both giggle. That's better.

"Are *you* all right, Charlotte?"

"Don't I sound it?" Actually, no. She sounds speeded-up, as if her speech is losing its brakes. "I'm just so happy you're coming."

"But you're well?"

"Quite. Peculiar, but well."

"What do you mean, peculiar?"

"Oh, not senile, don't worry. But you tell me your secrets, I'll tell you mine. We'll eat and drink and tell secrets, okay?" Her voice turns serious, and with that her pace slows. "But listen. You can do whatever you feel like. Just as if you're in your own place. If you need time on your own, we don't even have to be in the same room. You can do whatever pops into your head. But when you want company, I'll be here. And there'll be food, and booze, and whatever you want."

"Thanks, Char. Please don't go to any trouble, though. I just want to see you."

"No trouble. You're a friend, not a guest, so don't worry."

Claudia laughs. "I didn't mean you shouldn't go to *any* trouble. Please don't ignore me entirely."

Charlotte laughs, too. "I see you remember what it's like not

being treated like a guest here. But I'll look after you."

"Listen, Char, I don't know how it'll feel, being away from here. I haven't been, before. So if I get homesick or something, please don't mind if I come back all of a sudden, it won't have anything to do with you. I just never know these days what's going to happen or how I'm going to feel or how I'll deal with things. So much keeps taking me by surprise. Everything keeps changing, or I keep seeing things differently every time I look at them. Or think about them. So I just can't tell you. Is that all right?"

And did it make any sense? How incoherent she sounded. It seems she is almost relearning the language of feeling; or is learning so many new feelings she hasn't had words for before. She tells that to Charlotte.

"Claudie, you can do anything you please. Come and go, rest and nap or eat and drink or talk or just sit. Feel your heart out. Okay?"

"Bless you."

Besides Claudia's father, and Bradley, Charlotte is the only person who has called her Claudie.

"And Char? Don't get in a lot of food. We can go shopping together when I get there. I know I told you I'm eating too much, and heaven knows I am, but I promise not to eat you out of house and home, and I'll pay for my cravings. And yours, too, if you have some. But you have to promise me something, too."

"What's that?"

"Remind me if I forget to stop eating? I don't want to embarrass myself, bloating up in your living-room. Sometimes I do, you know. Forget to stop eating, I mean."

"You're coming to the wrong person if you expect help with self-discipline, remember?" She's right: no expert on restraint, Charlotte.

"I'll call you when I know what train. I shouldn't stay on the

phone too long now. The bills – this is the first long-distance call I've made except to the girls since I had to let people know Bradley'd died. I looked at that phone bill and thought I'd never just be able to pick up the receiver and dial, ever again." Claudia laughs. "On the other hand, if I didn't eat so much I could probably afford to make calls around the world, twenty-four hours a day."

"But you're okay?"

"For money? Enough. I just have to be careful."

"Okay, we'll get off the line now, and when you call back, just tell me where and when, and I'll see you in a couple of days. Oh, Claudie, I can't wait!"

"Me neither. Thanks, Char."

"I love you."

"Me too."

How long has it been since someone's told Claudia they love her? Or, how long since she's felt this grateful swelling of affection? Well, the girls of course. Them in their nightgowns, on the living-room floor. Voices like music. She remembers.

But a grown-up. Of course they're grown-ups, but she means someone – equal to her. Equivalently adult.

How many times did Bradley tell her he loved her when the words didn't form part of some kind of apology? "I'm sorry," he would be saying. "I love you." There may have been times he said it with joy and on impulse. She just doesn't remember them now.

He came home from the doctor's and sat down heavily on a kitchen chair. She was standing at the sink, washing dishes, not thinking. "I got the results," he said.

"Oh yes?" She still wasn't thinking.

"It's malignant. It's cancer."

The word "malignant" didn't stop her. The word "cancer" did.

"What?" She turned to face him, the dishcloth dripping soapy water on the floor.

"Cancer."

So. Surgery, which failed to reach the extent of the corruption. Then the kinds of therapy that made him throw up violently, over and over; and all his wavy hair fell out. Who would have dreamed he had such lumps on his head? She considered that old business of phrenology: what might she learn from tracing his skull with her hands? She hated the new hospital; realizing she wouldn't have liked an old shabby one, either. But she disliked this one's brisk entrance, the clean-painted corridors with their cheerful posters, the odd absence of smell. She would have expected at least antiseptic smells. This place, though, seemed designed to avoid as much as possible any aura of illness. The patients, sitting in wheelchairs, groping along corridors, were incongruous. Suffering, or distorted, or mutilated in various ways, they ruined its clean new lines.

Of course Bradley hated it; why wouldn't he? Who wouldn't? He said, finally, "I want to go home. I want to be in my own room again. Would you look after me, Claudie?"

This was almost the moment she dreamed of once: him ill, looking up at her, helpless and in her power. *Needing* her. What was it she'd dreamed of doing then? Looking down coolly? Vengefully? She said, "If you're sure. What does the doctor say?"

Bradley snorted. "He says I'm going to die, except he won't come right out with it. But here or there, I'm going to die. I want to be home."

She thought he might have wanted to be home some years ago. Apparently he hadn't looked around all those other rooms, from the other beds he lay in, and been overcome with any irresistible desire to be home.

Or maybe he had. Maybe that's why he'd always returned in the end.

He'd been more and more careless. He couldn't have imagined when he came in at dawn, telling her he'd been up playing poker with buddies all night, that she believed him. She just rarely bothered discussing disbelief any more.

She thought, "It's only my pride that's hurt, not me. And pride isn't good. If I can defeat my pride, that makes me a better person anyway." Wasn't that right?

The doctor said, "It's going to be hard on you. You'll need help. I'll arrange to have people come in. We'll work out a schedule. And when you can't manage, or he changes his mind, we'll get him back in here. This isn't a good idea. I hope you know what you're getting into. You can make yourself ill, taking this on. People do."

How could she have known what she was getting into? How could she have possibly imagined? She had no idea he would grasp her wrists in his bony harsh hands and drone on and on with his secrets. Watching her. "Why on earth are you telling me?" she asked once. He couldn't seem to help himself. He seemed to have become addicted to revelation.

Perhaps he thought her pain would drown out his.

Women's names rolled off his tongue. The favourite parts of women's bodies, their favourite parts of his. "She liked me licking her," he said. "She'd come and come, that way."

"She'd take me in her mouth, you see," he said. "Warm and wet and dangerous. I came so hard she'd choke. Oh, that was something, coming in her throat, her choking."

She stared at him as if he was a stranger. Which he was. As a stranger, as just words, she could think sometimes, "I wish we'd done that. I wonder what that felt like?" She felt, sometimes, her body growing warm.

Perhaps he wasn't trying to be cruel. Perhaps this was only a perverse sort of courtship: trying to win her, tantalize her, seduce her.

His watchful eyes were cruel, and so were the bones of his hands, gripping her wrists.

He spoke names like rhymes. Could so many be true? She laughed once, said, "My goodness, Bradley, you *have* been a virile fellow, haven't you?" His eyes narrowed. If he'd been strong and well, she might have been frightened. But he wasn't. Even so, she drew back a little.

All this might have been a kind of charity; his last gift to her the freedom from having to care about him. He still required her to look after him, but he certainly put an effort into making her care less and less about him.

But then, just sometimes, just on the very odd occasion, he'd hold her hand differently, not gripping, and say something gentle. Once it was, "Thank you, Claudie. I know what you've done." She didn't know what he meant, exactly, but it sounded kind. "I'd have been less of a man if I'd never met you, Claudie." Again she couldn't tell quite what he meant.

And once, in a spasm of gratitude, he said, "I know this is hard for you. But it won't be forever. I couldn't bear to be away from you now. You're all I have left." It made her feel like debris from a wreck or a fire, but she supposed he meant well.

Towards the end, he began to say now and then, "I hope you understand I've always loved you."

She didn't understand at all, why would she?

And later he would grip her wrists again and resume the litanies of his very private history. Did he think she was his personal priest, to whom he was required to confess before he could achieve a peaceful death? Or that he required some kind of blessing from her?

She read him stories from the newspapers, and fed him drugs at precisely correct times, and turned his body in the bed, trying not to breathe. She watched him carefully, trying to discern the changes from day to day. But the two of them were

so perpetually together – changes blurred and became difficult always to identify. She wondered, in the few evening moments she had to herself before she got ready for bed, went to sleep, exhausted – she wondered if there was any kind of pleasure coming out of all this, into her. And if so, if that was very evil of her, or only human. It got more and more difficult, living so entirely within this house and within her own life, to recall what exactly might be evil, or human, or good. The nurse who came to the house three mornings a week told her, "You're awfully good about all this. Most people can't take it, no matter how much they love the person. It's just too hard."

Claudia didn't feel good. Mainly she felt puzzled.

She stared at him and thought, "Forty-seven years!" She thought she ought to be able to remember more than it seemed she did. "And how about you?" the doctor asked. "Are you managing?"

Of course she was managing. She always managed. She hadn't the faintest idea how to go about not managing. She wished sometimes she did. Some people got along quite nicely not managing – look at Bradley.

She wondered how she would die. Certainly she would have no one caring for her this way. On the other hand, there was no one she would want to punish this way.

After a while she forgot to be lonely. She almost forgot to be tired. It was almost comforting, to know exactly what had to be done, to have such a precise routine so uninterrupted by normal events. She vaguely recalled that ordinary life was often and easily interrupted, thrown into unusual rhythms.

And then, of course, came the terminal interruption, that most drastic of unusual rhythms. And now, here she is.

Here she is in this home-of-many-years, in this small city where they moved almost two decades ago – why did they leave the city where they'd started out, where Claudia and

Charlotte had been in easy reach of each other, where Claudia and Bradley were coming to the end of raising their children, where a strange woman had knocked on the front door, where Claudia and Bradley had wrestled furiously in the hallway, and had touched skin to skin upstairs in their blue-papered bedroom? Bradley came home one day and said, "I've been thinking, this city's getting too big. I could get a job in a place a bit smaller than this, and it'd be cheaper to live. I'm tired of going so far to work. We could get a nicer house, too. And it'd just be a couple of hours away, if we wanted to come into the city sometimes. There's an opening, anyway. I can have it if I want it. What do you think?"

Leave her life?

But then, her life was beginning to leave her, the girls one by one stepping away into their own careers and marriages and plots. There was Charlotte, of course, but they could still see each other, it would only be a couple of hours, just as he said.

The thing was, she felt such a surge of hope. She heard his words as if he were respeaking some form of marriage vow. What was this suggestion, if not a pledge of beginning again, fresh, open, in a new place neither of them knew, where they were unknown, where they would be just the two of them together? Well, with the younger two girls still, of course, but really a family.

Then she wondered why. What brought this on, why was Bradley abruptly keen to begin again, what had happened in that other part of his life? Of course it would be pointless to ask.

There were times, looking at him, when Claudia wanted to take a sharp knife, or her own sharp hands, and carve into his head, open it up, dissect its contents, display on a table or the kitchen counter the secret scenes it contained, reveal its pictures to her scrutiny.

Other times she held her eyes tightly closed, unwilling to imagine. If she could really see, how could she ever go on?

At any rate, they moved. She and Charlotte embraced and pledged to be in constant touch. Which they more or less have been, barring this past year and the inevitable differences it makes when people can't take seeing each other easily for granted. Whatever (or whoever) Bradley was leaving, he kept to himself. The girls finished their growing up. Claudia made a new home, which now is an old home. And Bradley – Bradley found himself new secret events, and then he retired, and then he got sick, and finally died. And that's all.

All that's visible.

Now what? What does this house, or this small city, or any of her life for the past couple of decades, mean to her now? What holds her and what fails entirely to touch her?

She tried to make this house pretty and welcoming when they came here; perhaps trying to tempt him with comfort and appealing colours, graceful shapes. She was very busy, anyway, with her painting and wallpapering, arranging of furniture, pinning and sewing and hemming of curtains and drapes. It reminded her of just being married, moving into their first house; except that this time they had more money, since as he'd said, living really was cheaper here, and they'd made a nice profit on their house.

"Do you like it?" she'd ask when he came home from work, or wherever. He seemed to be making new friends.

"Yeah, nice. It's pretty, yeah."

So she could tell it wasn't going to work, this effort to draw him back home. But then, it was going to be her home, far more than his.

Now she sees that since then she's made hardly any changes or improvements. That first effort seems to have been all that interested her. So the wallpaper is seriously faded, the paint

that was so fresh and shining now is dull, the furniture is old, not in a fashionable, antique way but simply shabby and worn out. Why has she never noticed before? It must be years since she's taken a proper look at the place. She seems to have had peculiar and protective blind spots, doesn't she?

Haven't the girls noticed? They're not here so often they'd be simply accustomed to how the place looks; they would surely have perceived encroaching shabbiness.

Oh dear, what did the nurse think, coming here three mornings a week?

Not that it's grimy, it doesn't look poor in that way. Only too lived in. Once it became clear it wasn't going to contain fresh beginnings, a new run at love or many other of her hopes, something must have gone out of it: some steam, some breath.

After he retired, Bradley went off every morning to meet friends in a restaurant. They drank coffee, chewed over world events, he said. Sometimes he came home for lunch, sometimes not. Sometimes, after the restaurant, they adjourned to a bar for the afternoon. He was old then; he wasn't likely up to much else, except perhaps patting waitresses. Although these days that sort of thing is frowned on; waitresses don't see being patted as part of their jobs, the way they maybe used to have to.

All in all, Bradley's life no doubt became much less entertaining. Despite his outings, he was around the house more; but this turn of events came too late for Claudia. It wasn't as if he'd chosen it, the way he could have at any younger time. It was forced on him, by retirement, by age, by his necessarily dwindling resources – at least she supposed they had dwindled, because any more when he reached for her it was only for comfort, for someone to hold his arms around.

If, when she visits Charlotte, she feels homesick as she suggested she might, what exactly would she be homesick for?

Looking around, she can't imagine. But that's partly the point of going away: the long, dispassionate, unattached view that makes things come clear. And if it doesn't? If, as when she and Bradley moved here, she's hoping for too much from a mere change of place?

Just the day after tomorrow! Her first journey in so long, and then Charlotte at the end of it – she can just see Charlotte in that glorious, booming, rushing, enormous train station, standing at the top of the concourse, smiling, arms open.

Claudia must hurry. She has things to do. First she calls the train station and reserves herself a ticket. "Club?" It's tempting; but no, too great an extravagance for just a couple of hours. She really doesn't have money to spare.

She calls to cancel her newspaper. "No, I can't give you a date to start up again. I'll call when I want it." She feels a small grief at this loss; but Charlotte no doubt gets a paper.

She goes to the bank. "Are you sure you want this much cash? It isn't a good idea to carry a lot," the young teller advises, looking concerned. Claudia knows what he means – she could be knocked down or hurt for her money – but is offended. Would he take it upon himself to warn someone young?

"Quite sure," she snaps. She pauses to let that tone echo in her head; it emerged so naturally, and yet sounds entirely unfamiliar. Some new peremptoriness? Rather appealing, and possibly worth cultivating. She could become crisp and stern enough to warn off anyone contemplating snatching her purse, for instance. Or any patronizing young man in a bank.

She phones the teenager down the block who mows her lawn and keeps the hedges trimmed around the small backyard. "I'm not sure how long I'll be gone. If you come by, I'll give you post-dated cheques and a key to the house. I'll be paying you to check on it, as well as keep up the yard. I'll leave you

the phone number where I'll be, in case anything goes wrong. I don't know how long I'll be gone. Likely not long. But I want someone to take in the mail and make sure the place doesn't blow up or burn down." It does occur to her to wonder how well she knows this boy. He might take it into his head to use her house for huge parties, raucous teenagers drinking and smoking, throwing up and making illicit love, blaring music through the windows, spilling onto the lawn, annoying the neighbours, breaking the furniture, writing obscenities on the walls – who knows what else? She reads of these sorts of things in her newspaper.

He seems a nice, solid, respectful young man, but she can remember a little how tempting freedom can be. And not comprehending, or caring, what its limits are.

But her own freedom is due, too, and she is beginning to gauge it. She shouldn't begrudge a young man his, and certainly not at the cost of her own. Isn't that what she's already done too much of: restraining her desires in the cause of someone else's greater good, her daughters', or even Bradley's?

That smacks of unpleasing martyrdom, though.

She phones the girls to let them all know where she'll be. It's not that she wants to be disconnected, floating off somewhere unknown. She has her roots.

She whirls through the house doing a hasty housecleaning. Just enough to make it respectable (what, for teenagers holding parties?). She just doesn't want to leave any loose ends, anything major undone. "I don't know when I'll be back," she again tells the boy who'll look after her house, when he comes by to pick up the cheques and the key. "But I'll phone first. I'll let you know. Please, just take care of it."

He's a good kid. "My mother said you should borrow this if you're going away," holding out a light timer. "I can hook it up to your living-room lamp so it'll come on at dark, and then the

place won't look empty, okay? If I set it for seven, it'll switch off in the morning. She says I should open the drapes in the morning, too, and close them at night. That okay?" If he is going to hold parties here, apparently he hasn't formulated the plans yet. His voice, and his eyes, seem utterly guileless and trustworthy; Claudia is ashamed of her doubts. But she's heard guileless voices before, and looked into trustworthy eyes.

"Believe me," Bradley used to plead, sounding desperate for her to believe. He learned to stop saying "Trust me."

Quickly she picks up the phone to call Charlotte. "I get in at 11:07," she says. "Or thereabouts. Isn't it wonderful, how precise they think they can be?"

"I'll be there. Is there anything in particular you want to do? Shopping? The zoo? The museum? Go sailing? Take in a men's strip show? Have a full-body massage?"

Claudia giggles. "All that and more."

"Good. I'll see you at 11:07 tomorrow, then."

"Or thereabouts. Charlotte?"

"Yes?"

"Thank you. I love you."

"I love you too, Claudie. I can't wait to see you."

A strip show! A massage! Of course they won't, Charlotte was kidding (Claudia thinks), but imagine! There are adventures just ahead, just a day or two away. Entirely new events.

How long has it been since she's seen fresh pictures in her mind? Since she's looked at a single unfamiliar thing?

She might yet see another yearning penis. Although it wouldn't be yearning for her. And she couldn't afford, like other women, to tuck money into whatever clothing male strippers do keep on.

Did Bradley go to strip shows? Perhaps. She wouldn't have thought he'd need to, but who knows what he imagined his needs were? They were apparently extensive.

At any rate, from what she's read it seems that women go to these things in a different spirit from men. More for salacious amusement than salacious longing. And maybe that's why so many men seem to wander off from promises, Bradley included. Maybe they have to keep proving to themselves that no one will laugh.

But then they must have doubts, later: was there laughter?

Bradley hated how much time she spent with Charlotte. "What the hell do you find to talk about?" he used to ask.

"Oh, anything that pops into our heads," she answered carelessly. Perhaps he thought that included his penis.

Well, in some ways it did. Its vagaries were sometimes included in their conversations, it's true. But hardly for purposes of laughter.

Perhaps they should have laughed. Maybe she and Charlotte between them could have made not only Bradley's penis, but Bradley himself, into a huge, undignified, hardly-worth-the-anger joke.

Was Charlotte serious, suggesting massage? Is that the sort of thing she does these days? Oh my – Claudia isn't sure at all it would appeal to her. A strange person's hands on her body? A strange person *seeing* her body, crumpled and wrinkled, rippling here and there – hardly fit. Hardly attractive. All very well for the angular Charlotte: however wrinkled, she's at least likely lean. But the waking Claudia sometimes finds her hands cupped around her soft and overflowing belly as if it were a child she loved and comforted in the night but which, awake, feels repulsive and odd.

Not the sort of thing she'd want someone else to feel.

If she did try it, though, how would she describe where she hurts, where the muscles are tightest and tense, where clever hands might relieve? That's probably the sort of thing a person who gives massages knows with a glance, or with a running of

fingers over the body. But where in the body does grief gather in knots? Where does guilt turn for a hiding place?

Charlotte was just making jokes, of course. More likely she's in the midst of a circle of menacing adolescents, popping in for dinner and a spot of old-lady mayhem.

Her own girls were so peaceful, compared with the youngsters Charlotte dealt with, or the ones Claudia skirted today on her trip to the bank. Even here, on the downtown streets of her own small city, the peculiar young lurk. There was a moment when she worried she ought to have paid attention to the young teller's advice, instead of taking offence. Just down the block and across the street from the bank, two teenaged boys barrelled out of a doorway – an arcade, she saw. Their hair was greased and oddly spiked and one of them brushed into her shoulder, not knocking her off her feet or spinning her around, but dislodging her a little, startling and scaring her. "Geez, Grandma, watch out." She hates being made aware of her fragility.

"I'm not your grandma." The words were out, in that new sharp tone, before she thought. But the boys were gone, they had their own concerns and headed off laughing down the street.

They were just boys. And, she saw, peering into the darkness beyond the arcade doorway, girls as well. What would happen if she went in? Surely, underneath the camouflage, they were just ordinary kids, not so unlike her daughters at that age. What if she struck up a conversation? She might learn just ordinary things: like that they're scared of getting pregnant, or failing school, or never having much of a life. Her own girls didn't talk to her much about such matters, but of course those are perpetual, and normal fears, no different then and now or, for that matter, in her own day. One of the girls was laughing. Her lips were purple, her teeth nearly black. Oh dear.

Charlotte might have gone in; not Claudia.

It doesn't do to forget, though, that Claudia's girls were not exactly unblemished. That time Sharon got caught shoplifting, for instance – how swiftly Claudia was on the phone to Charlotte! "I know it was only a lipstick and a pair of stockings, but I can't understand *why* she'd do such a thing. She gets an allowance, she doesn't need to steal. So why would she, Charlotte? I thought I'd taught them right from wrong. Now what should I do? Where did I go wrong?"

And there was Char's calm voice, as if this was the smallest, least significant misdemeanour she'd ever encountered, asking, "So did the store charge her?"

"Oh no! Nothing like that. They know me. They just called me to come and get her."

"Where is she now?"

"Up in her room."

"Did she look scared? Did she apologize?"

"Well, of course. And she cried – she's still crying – and promised she'd never do it again. But what should I do to be sure? What can I say to her?"

Sharon was fifteen. Charlotte said, "Maybe you don't need to say anything. I bet just getting caught and having you know is punishment enough for somebody like her. I mean, she's a good kid, not some criminal. She hardly ranks with the kids I deal with. I bet anything she won't do it again. Of course if she does, then we have to think of something. Have you told Bradley?"

"Oh no. I don't want to get him stirred up. I thought I wouldn't. He'd be so angry and just make things worse. But maybe I should, after all. Maybe he could do something with her. I seem to have gone wrong somewhere, or this wouldn't have happened."

Charlotte snorted. "Honestly, Claudia, I could just shake

you, the way you think everything's your fault. You're so self-important."

Well, Claudia had to laugh, after all.

And Charlotte was right, it didn't happen again.

But was she too careless with her advice? As it turns out, the girls knew things she hadn't realized. Sharon might have been trying to say something about that, with her shoplifted lipstick and stockings. She might, if she were trying to get their serious attention, have moved on to injuring animals or slitting her wrists. There might have been disastrous consequences to Charlotte's light advice. And of course Claudia's relieved acceptance of it.

But there weren't disastrous consequences, Charlotte was right, it didn't happen again.

Claudia does seem to have been under the impression that Charlotte is wiser and more alert and more experienced than she. That Charlotte's advice will be more accurate than any instincts of her own.

Is that true?

Actually, she's rarely asked for Charlotte's advice, and Charlotte has never offered it unsought. It might have been good if she had. If she'd ever rolled her eyes, thrown up her hands, said, "Look, you absolutely must do this, or that, it's impossible to go on this way, for heaven's sake take care of your own life and if you do, I promise you, it'll all work out" – but she didn't. Friends don't do that kind of thing.

And now of course it's far too late for advice anyway. On a drastic, unconsidered whim, Claudia has created her great secret, and there wasn't a second for considering if she should pause, call Charlotte (or the girls, anyone) and inquire, "So what do you think? Is this the right thing, or wrong?" Words didn't come into it. Words still don't come into it. She can't bear to think them. Perhaps Charlotte will help her.

eleven

THERE'S A GOOD DEAL TO BE DONE before Claudia gets here tomorrow; so much that Charlotte, when everything is finally in place, succumbs to an afternoon nap.

This is rare for her. For one thing it seems a wasteful, indulgent misuse of remaining time. Also it disrupts patterns, making the true, late-night sleeping hours restless and fretful.

Mainly, though, the trouble with afternoon naps is the likelihood of troubled dreams. Not nasty ones, exactly, not nightmares, more just erratic, jumpy images. Today, now: here's a gaunt, grim Bradley for goodness' sake, striding through a factory (a factory?) pushing a wheelbarrow loaded with bricks (bricks?). Charlotte's mind surfaces briefly, wondering, then sinks back.

And now he's gone but here's Claudia, in a nursery with

rows of cribs – dozens, hundreds, an infinity of cribs – and she's moving from one to the next, bending, doing something with her hands. Charlotte moves up behind her, bends also and sees – nothing: Claudia's hands patting and smoothing nothing at all, then on to the next crib, whatever it holds. How Charlotte wants to see what Claudia does – it isn't fair. In her dream she is frustrated, irritable, and again almost wakens.

But now she's outdoors, with rocks and sand – a beach somewhere? Off in the distance a figure is walking, a man, but in which direction? Charlotte begins walking towards him, needing to join him, but it's hard, she keeps slipping on rocks and the sand holds her back. They seem closer, though, and now she can see the man is coming towards her, slipping himself sometimes, so their progress is slow. She feels desperate to get to him quickly, before something happens, although whatever the danger is, it's unclear, invisible. She will not stop, however hard this slippery trudging, until she can touch him; or feel him touch her. Gradually, slowly, she begins to see him more clearly. He even waves, or at least makes a small flick with one hand, a greeting of sorts. They must know each other, then? She strains to make out his features and it's – can it be? – Andrew. No wonder they've been trying to reach each other.

How beautiful he is, how firm and well-formed, the blue eyes she remembers so clearly, his hair perfectly shaped and perfectly brown – but that's it, he's still young! She feels her hands fly over her face, because he mustn't see her. It's awful that he's going to find her old, these wrinkles, this hair, the pluckings of skin where her neck, and then her breasts, have shifted and sunk. She tries, or thinks she tries, to turn away, but finds herself still moving forward. And it's too late anyway, here he is, here are his fingertips drawing her hands from her face, holding them, eyes shifting from feature to feature, a grave regard, and then slowly, like a sunrise, his narrow,

familiar lips turn upward and he's smiling, he is looking at her with such love! It reminds her of something. But what is he seeing?

She looks down at her hands. They're still crumpled and lined. So she's old and he's young, and still he's looking at her this way. So it's all right, and she begins to smile back, her fingers press his and abruptly he's frowning. He steps back, he's hurrying backward, away. She moves forward, but his horror stops her. And then he's gone, and this time she's truly awake.

For a moment she misses him as badly as she used to, when he looked as he did in the dream. She is hot, and her chest hurts.

She thinks, "Oh God, what if I'm having a heart attack?" Because sometime she will, after all; or something else just as terminal. Why not now?

It might not be so bad. She thinks she wouldn't necessarily mind, if it didn't take too long. But poor Claudia. What a shock for her!

Well, no, she'd only be puzzled: by Charlotte's absence at the station; by getting no answer when she gave up waiting and came here and rang the bell. Likely she'd get help. Perhaps the police would break in, or a neighbour. But Claudia wouldn't have to be an actual witness.

All Charlotte's shopping would go to waste, though. And the planning and anticipation.

Anyway, she's not having a heart attack, or anything else. Her pulse is slowing, and the perspiration is drying on her skin. She'll just have a bath, and then she'll be fine.

In her bath, she considers the dreams. How odd to remember them – that only happens, really, with that surfacey, slippery sort of afternoon dream. The only one that particularly interests her is the one with Andrew. Bradley, of course, is as insignificant as ever, except as he affected Claudia; although what could that factory and those bricks have been about – some late and

pointless recognition of the tedious load for which he was responsible? No more than one part of his bargain, the rest of which he failed to keep. And in fact drudgery seems a slight punishment for a man who failed the important parts.

The one with the cribs and Claudia is obvious and boring, its point, at this stage, so irrelevant and unchangeable it hardly warrants any thought, either. Charlotte is a little disappointed, that this is the sort of dream her mind takes it upon itself to throw up at her.

But Andrew. Well, here there might be some point, she does seem to have dragged him into the present. She can still see hovering in her vision that appalled expression on his youthful face. The truth may be that he didn't entirely like her; that there were aspects of her he didn't care to recognize. There were times when she was truthful (when he asked her to be truthful) and then found he didn't particularly like what she had to say. He didn't like to hear that she felt some pain when he left her to go home; that she had pictures of his other life that were sharp as broken glass. His view of love was more specific and defined than hers, and so, apparently, was his view of hardship. It seemed to her that some unattainable levels of both silence and devotion came to be required, and that finally, silence and devotion got tangled and came increasingly to mean the same thing, or to demonstrate each other. He was sometimes angry with her failure to love him as dumbly and blindly as he thought, in their circumstances, it was necessary to love. It was peculiar and disheartening to find herself in her thirties, no naïve, longing girl, nevertheless too often cautious; to hear certain of her own words and rages in her head, feel them on her tongue, and bite them back for fear of – what? Of something irretrievable, she supposed. Of making him feel so burdened he would leave, with his own final, infinitely reverberating word.

So there were aspects of her (admittedly unpleasant aspects

but surely love must encompass them also, it can't be only attached to the cheerful, entertaining, bright and intelligent bits) he couldn't bear, apparently. And that came to feel too exhausting for her to bear. So perhaps all he means in the dream is the death of desire.

Maybe that's all.

So at least she can laugh out loud, and pull herself out of the tub, and reach for the towel, and apply make-up with care (although with whatever care, it tends to cake in the creases, looking slightly garish) and step into fresh underwear and into black pants and navy blouse. This may be her last chance. She and Claudia can hardly both go lurking in his hedge, even if Claudia were inclined to.

To tell the truth, when she hung up from talking with Claudia, Charlotte almost regretted the invitation. Who knew what this visit might alter, what disruptions it might cause? Because, however odd, she has been having such interesting, if perilous, times. And she is accustomed to her solitude. She even felt a faint, almost-forgotten tug of resentment, almost anger. Because Claudia has always had such *large* troubles. And such justified ones. Beside them, Charlotte's have sounded, if not exactly trivial, at least not so life-threatening. Claudia's troubles have been pure; Charlotte's somewhat shady.

What have they been in, then, some competition of catastrophe?

Like her troubles, Claudia's secret, apparently, is more profound than Charlotte's.

Charlotte may have imagined she could get free of this latest adventure by putting words to it with Claudia. The loss of this particular curiosity, though, might be cause not only for relief, but also for at least a minor grief.

Well. Suppose they told their secrets, explaining and complaining, and wound up looking at each other with despair.

Suppose they decided there was no further point. They could leave notes explaining they just couldn't be bothered any more. Or that events were too strange to bother untangling. They could write, "We don't want to live, now that the prospect of further penises (or love) is gone." And then wouldn't they howl! Wouldn't they sit back and just laugh and laugh, like kids again, clutching their ribs, gasping with pain and delight.

Then they'd have another drink and talk some more. This picture, of course, quite restored Charlotte's enthusiasm for Claudia's visit.

She must be terribly greedy, or arrogant, wanting so much, wanting more than is possible, the advantage of knowing. People actually dying – the ones who know they're dying, and roughly when, people maybe like Bradley – don't they get frantic? Don't they get desperate? Don't they cry at the end, "Just another few minutes, just a little more time," hoping finally to know?

Scientists learn more every day. One of these times, maybe they'll discern genes for emotion and character, genes that have been harder to spot than the ones that cause blue eyes or brown. It doesn't seem impossible. Knowledge accumulates quickly, discoveries arise every day, and there's not enough time in the universe to keep up. People may know one set of things but be utterly ignorant of another, and what's missing may set their whole lives off-kilter. Charlotte herself: soon she'll be seventy and it's possible, even likely, that her whole life rests on wrong assumptions, faulty ways of seeing, gaps of knowing.

They do love each other, she and Claudia, in that unblinking way of people who've been friends their whole lives. Is it sad to be old and to love only one person, and that person a woman? Claudia has so many people to love – her daughters,

their children, Charlotte of course. Who knows who else? It must be something to have borne and raised four daughters who talk and plan and organize themselves so they can turn up at the same time to comfort their mother in her recent widowhood.

After all, she could hardly wait for Claudia. The visit would be an occasion, something like a holiday, for which she should be a little spendthrift, investing in pleasure. She could cut back, after all, when Claudia left. In this mood for pampering, she decided against supermarket line-ups and carting heavy bags about, and in favour of spending a little extra to have her groceries delivered. She found this agreeable; a person could get used to this sort of luxury, and since Claudia likes wine, Charlotte also ordered a case of white (although she wouldn't have asked for so much if the young man on the phone hadn't told her a minimum order was required for delivery). It didn't matter, it wouldn't go to waste.

It was just a lot of money all at once; and since banks don't deliver, she did have to rouse herself to go out.

Charlotte refuses to use cash machines, insists on humans. A little of that may have to do with mistrust of machinery, but mainly it's because she believes that without people like her, where would all those jobs go? She regards this as a small, right act. Of course it's always been easier to do small right things than large ones; such as staying clear of married men.

These days it's simple to stay clear of men of any sort. Like bank tellers, they are unaware of her solicitous attentions; so eventually virtue can come to anyone, just by the elimination of alternatives. Which struck her as a pretty good joke.

While she was out and amusing herself so nicely, she dropped into a chocolate shop for a couple of decadent truffles and, up the street, into a florist's, tucked in a renovated Victorian house, for a package of pot-pourri, four sachets, one for

each of the spare room's bureau drawers, and two bunches of flowers. She looked with some longing at the yellow roses, but they cost the earth and really, perhaps she was getting carried away; the lilies and mums and irises were quite nice, too.

Quite an armload, in the end. Thinking of everything, taking care of the details, felt more wearing than it used to. She used to be better at comforting touches.

She set out the flowers in vases, one for the dining-room table, the other on the end table in the living-room. In the spare room she placed the pot-pourri in a blue-grey pottery bowl on the bedside table, and tucked the scented sachets in the bureau drawers. Recalling Claudia's fondness for the appearance of purity, she made up the bed not only with crisp white sheets, but with her best duvet, a rarely used, startling white one, with eyelet lacing all around. How virginal!

Has Claudia had trouble learning to sleep by herself? Charlotte, even now, sleeps on one side of her own bed, as if she still assumes some other body will turn up.

Both the spare room and her own contain double beds, narrow, she supposes, compared with enormous modern ones. But how, in them, do people find each other? People already lose each other too easily, without help from vast tundra-like beds.

She seems to have lost track of so many people, one way and another. After a decade with Andrew, she sent him away, which was deliberate and painful, and no doubt wise. Not long after that she ran into Tim and Lissa, or they ran into her in their aborted purse-snatching, and that small, brief connection began. They came to her home and she watched them unwind: lounging in her living-room, feet on her furniture, warm and maybe, almost, trusting. Downtown, she watched for them, and presumably they were alert for her, since they encountered each other more often than could be accounted for by coincidence. She would gather them up, take them, as on that first

day except no longer by force, to a restaurant, or home. She was fond of them in a way that did not imply she should or could save them, and she was also interested in them, in ways that were not so detached. They rarely talked of futures or, very often, pasts; in both directions their lives were too perilous. Charlotte sometimes found her hands clenched into fists with the desire to punish their parents, who it seemed to her had stolen their children's pasts and futures.

They were tough, but were they tough enough, and in ways that would help them survive? "I'd rather give blow jobs to strangers for the rest of my life than let my father fuck me one more time," Lissa said bitterly. But bitterness was by no means as useful in the long run as strength.

On Lissa's sixteenth birthday, Charlotte bought a small cake for the three of them, lit a candle on it and said, without thinking, "Make a wish." She realized instantly how unforgivably stupid that was. Obediently, Lissa blew out the candle.

What on earth did she wish for? To be able to stop giving blow jobs to strangers? For her father to die? For a safe place to live, for food, for a warm winter coat? Charlotte gave her that, at least: a heavy green coat, with removable lining, was her birthday gift to Lissa.

"It's great," Lissa said. "Thanks a lot." There were no embraces. Touching, it seemed to Charlotte, and maybe to them, would have too many unpleasant reverberations. If she reached out, she wouldn't want to see them flinch.

Tim was looking slightly healthier by then: a little more filled out, less pale and weedy, although hardly pink or robust. Charlotte didn't think her own attentions and the odd good meal accounted for this, but didn't care to ask what might. "I know it's not your birthday, but I got you something, too," she told him: also a winter-weight coat, his from an army surplus store, khaki and heavily lined.

"Cool," he said. "Hey, thanks."

And for Lissa, because it *was* her birthday, which warranted something extra and frivolous and unnecessary, a red rosebud, just ready to unfurl, in a small glass bud vase. "See I've packed this wet moss stuff around the stem," Charlotte explained. "If you keep it damp, the flower should last a few days." She didn't ask why Lissa got tears in her eyes, or why she held the flower for the rest of their visit.

"I got her the sweater," Tim said proudly. "The one she's wearing." It was pink, almost wool, with long sleeves and a wavy design picked out in silvery sequiny slivers.

"It's a perfect colour," Charlotte said, and he looked pleased. She certainly wasn't going to ask how he'd "got" it.

These were all small steps; but they were steps. She was attempting mere comfort, nothing ambitious like trust or salvation. She thought she would like to like them, and thought it possible that slowly, they might like her. Any passionate attachment was unlikely; well, they weren't puppies, and were, realistically, far beyond any tail-wagging enthusiasm for passionate attachment themselves. Except perhaps with each other.

And then they disappeared. She walked the usual downtown streets, but no longer saw them rounding a corner towards her or waving from down the block, or leaning together against the walls of stores or restaurants. What could have happened? Well, anything really: they might be dead, jailed, hitchhiking towards a west-coast sunset. She was familiar with all those possibilities. She missed them, although was by no means wounded by the idea they might have disappeared voluntarily. But she was worried, if more like a benevolent aunt than a frantic parent. For a time she walked their streets every day, and stopped in at restaurants and missions and arcades to ask about them. She enquired of police and hospitals if anything were known.

Had Tim or Lissa's parents ever searched for them like this? And if so, for what reasons?

"We have no record," said the police. "Are you a relative?"

"Dunno, man," said a dreadlocked youth, shaking his head so his hair flew around him. "Likely split. Spare some change?"

"Who?" asked a group in an arcade. "Oh yeah, them. No, haven't seen them, not for a while. They're always together, right? Yeah, we know who you mean."

People appeared and vanished and didn't leave much behind, it seemed, in the way of either impact or concern. She was more or less used to that herself; how much more accustomed these people must be to vague and drifting entrances and exits.

By the time she was finished with the police and hospitals, she was pretty sure that at least they weren't dead. But beyond that their lives were so entirely open and unfocused that anything at all might have become of them, then or by now. There's no way to guess where they went, or what has unfolded, or been cut short, for them. They could even be prosperous. They could even be that couple living next door to Andrew, who leave for work so punctually, and are so inadvertently generous with their hedge.

At least with their coats, they'd have been fairly warm.

She did miss them. Sometimes, remembering, she watched some stupid TV program they'd enjoyed, and was sad. Sometimes she lay awake worrying if they were warm, fed, most of all, safe.

She continued to keep an eye out for them on the streets.

It's one thing to know there are rarely conclusions, and events seldom come to tidy, known ends. Their disappearance from her life was simply the end of their connection with her. But it wasn't the end of them, they would have gone on with their own

events, and what, happy or sorrowful, might those have been?

Just as Andrew, having vanished from her life, has gone on with his own events, happy or sorrowful. And here she is in her black pants and navy blouse, setting out, perhaps for the last time, to try to make out the ending of at least one very old plot. Maybe others will follow: she might undertake investigations of other attachments and events, who knows? It must, anyway, all have to do with love; with the nature of love.

"But I love you," he said, as if that was all that needed saying. She thought love required more maintenance, a more constant attention, more feeding and care. He said love was love. She couldn't seem to find a way to say it wasn't quite so pure, in her view. And so they wore each other out. Like a long highway journey they drove on for years, rising and dipping and turning and shifting until they hit a steep slope and the brakes failed and down they went.

Andrew said, "It seems to me you're making this happen. You're doing it on purpose." She admitted that was possible, that maybe she just got in a hurry to bring on an ending that was going to come anyway. Or perhaps he was right, that she should and could have had faith. That she should have tried harder. And that this might apply to far more than just Andrew.

He seemed unable to perceive the grit it required to go as far and as long as she did. She couldn't imagine that being gritty was any way to conduct a whole life.

That helpless grief of watching desire slip, is it anything like what Claudia felt, watching Bradley? Is there anything equivalent between the painful disintegration of a human body and the painful disintegration of some powerful emotion? Claudia wrote of determination and will, and Andrew used to speak of attachment and love. Charlotte remains in the grip of solitude, but will of course go on, amusing herself with outings of one sort or another. Curiosity is no small passion: the desire to

poke under surfaces and see how things work (and fail to work) may not be comfortable or comforting, but it's surely interesting. If she got to have last words, she would like them to be something like, "Boy, I sure learned a few things, I'm glad I was alive to notice all that."

Women in her family tend to live to a great age. She has perhaps another twenty years.

This time she'll be at Andrew's after nightfall. Imagine if he'd had a similar impulse, to hunch outside her windows, listening for clues – the silence he would hear! She laughs aloud in the car. But such a lot occurs in silence, within the mute mind.

She turns into his subdivision, onto the curving, confusing, dark and quiet streets, parks in her usual spot around the corner and down the block, and sets off slowly on foot, alert for other watchers and listeners. There is, at the house next door to Andrew's, a car in the drive, although no people are visible, and there may be no reason not to scoot up the lawn alongside the hedge, dipping into the cool dark interior when she reaches the spot she has made, her small broken place.

She moves on, though, to Andrew's, standing on the sidewalk, regarding his house. His home.

It's so ordinary – she can't get over that. Some lights are on. There's no car in the driveway. A flickering from what must be the living-room is no doubt the television set. After dinner, perhaps Andrew and Elizabeth settle down to watch together. Do they share a sofa, or have separate chairs? What do they watch, and do their tastes agree? Andrew, as Charlotte recalls, preferred music to television, but that may have been because their time was so short. He must have had little time for watching television anywhere, during those years of running from his office to her house to his home.

His and Elizabeth's home.

It's no great distance across the lawn; she's under the living-

room window before she's really considered that that's where she's going.

She steps swiftly, carefully, through what she can see of Andrew's flowers, although she may crush some she can't make out in the darkness. In the light from the living-room, she can see shapes in the garden, and shadows; in just three steps she has reached the sheltering shrubs at the back, by the window. What on earth is she doing?

She is making her way around and behind a bush, and crouching into a huddle between it and the wall of Andrew's house. She can't believe she's done this. And now what? This is far worse, far more dangerous than ringing the doorbell, clipboard in hand, conducting a false, phantom survey. There isn't an excuse or a lie in the world to cover this.

What if Andrew decides on a late watering of his garden? He would come out that front door and gather the hose, turn on the tap and drench the flowers and the shrubs and Charlotte in bone-chilling water. And that's just one possibility, although one that would kill her, no doubt.

She'd rather die than be caught. Why can't she remember this when she's not in a position to be caught? If he came out to water the garden she would let the water pour over her without protest or sound. When it was over she would just lie down, blue and shivering, until the lights of his house went out and he slept. Then, if she had any strength at all, she would try to crawl away, to the hedge, to her car, to anywhere away from Andrew. And then she'd let pneumonia kill her.

Do he and Elizabeth still share a bedroom? They did when she knew him; but after all this time it shouldn't be too painful, should it, to hear them heading down the hall together, entering the same room, even chatting in their bed?

She remembers wondering what they talked about in bed. Wishing they had nothing to say (although of course they did,

their sons, if nothing else) and wishing talking was all they did (although she couldn't reasonably hope for that, either; familiar limbs would reach for each other, if nothing else).

Those pictures gave her nightmares and made her angry in the morning. Poor man, he must have wondered what he'd done to make her angry, when he wasn't even with her. They might embrace at her door when he left her at night, and the next day she'd be furious; how could he be expected to account for that?

She did learn some self-control during those years; but obviously if she'd learned enough, she'd hardly find herself at almost seventy hunched under his living-room window, fitted between a wall and a shrub, on a dark late-summer night.

Claudia, and Claudia coming to visit tomorrow, seem very far away at the moment. Her own home seems very far away. The flowers, the sachets, the truffles, the wine, are tucked away in some entirely distant and separate world. All that's real is this awkward position of limbs, this dark night, those living-room lights and the peculiar state of her mind.

On the other hand. On the other hand, listen.

"No, Elizabeth," she hears, "because I want to do this now. We have to take care of it. For God's sake, I'm a lawyer, I've seen the kind of messes that happen when everything isn't kept up to date. You're just being superstitious, it has nothing to do with dying. Why do we have to go through this every time? Neither of us died the other times, right?"

"I know, you're right," Elizabeth is saying. "But I can't help the feeling. Why can't you just take care of it? It doesn't bother you, and then I'll just sign whatever it is."

"Because it's not just my responsibility, Elizabeth, it's ours. The property's ours, the kids are ours, the decisions are ours." (Oh dear, so much "ours" going on – but what did she expect?) "I don't *want* to decide on my own. It's not right, and it's not

fair, either. I'm not going to do it all and then have you turn around someday and tell me I screwed something up. We're going to do it together, and if we disagree we'll work it out and when it's finished there'll be no complaints."

My, he sounds impatient. Does he really believe he makes decisions unwillingly? As Charlotte recalls, he rather enjoyed being in charge, and in the early days she occasionally had to point out to him how automatically he took over. She taught him to consult; it sounds as if he learned well.

"Well, I don't see why we have to go through *everything* again. We've done it twice before. Surely it's just a matter of a little updating, not starting again."

"Exactly. So it won't take that long. But we do have to make sure any changes we make are consistent and that we don't want to make any others."

"Oh, Andrew, are we going to have to go through this *every* time we get a new grandchild?"

Charlotte's heart hurts. Why is she doing this, if it only makes her heart hurt? Well, why did she stay with him for a decade, when her heart hurt so much of that time?

Another grandchild. They'll have stood at a hospital nursery window, with tears in their eyes, looking together at a new creature who exists because they did, overcome no doubt with sentiment and awe at the tiny achievement. Their arms would be around each other.

There isn't a mistress alive who could compete with a moment, a potential moment, like that.

"So we'll leave it," he is saying, "that when we're both gone, the house gets sold?" Elizabeth must just shrug; Charlotte doesn't hear her speak. She wonders, if she very carefully raised herself, whether she could just peek through the window to see them? But she mustn't make a noise; remember the last time, in the hedge.

Elizabeth is sitting alone on the sofa – a pastel-patterned upholstery, not bad, not unattractive, Charlotte has to admit – with her head back, eyes closed. She looks weary. Andrew is in a matching armchair, a document in his lap, looking – oh, the way he used to, when he was concentrating: a small set of frown lines, eyes paying attention to the papers. But he has glasses now; half-glasses that hang low on his nose. He glances over them, at Elizabeth. Charlotte wonders how visible she is, if either of them looks her way. But she wants to see. Also, standing straight is much easier than crouching.

"Do we still want each of the boys to get a third? Or should we cut that back so the grandchildren will still each get a decent amount?"

"Andrew, I don't *know*." Poor Elizabeth; now her hands are rubbing her closed eyes. Perhaps she has a headache – why doesn't Andrew ask? There might be a better time for doing this.

His voice remains firm. "Okay, we'll leave it. The grandkids should make it up with the bank accounts, anyway, if we keep managing the way we have been."

"Fine."

"See? It's not so difficult, is it?"

"No, I suppose not."

"Does your head hurt?"

There. Now this is exactly why poor Andrew could never win: Charlotte, unhappy with his unconcern about Elizabeth, now is pained that he apparently does notice and care. Charlotte shakes her own head, then abruptly stops herself: what if the movement caught their attention?

"No, I'm all right. Are we done?"

"Not quite yet. There's the specific things. Young Andrew would still get the piano?" Of course, she'd forgotten: he used to speak of his wife playing the piano, the boys singing around her. Cozy family evenings. And where was Andrew? Sitting in

a chair listening, nodding fondly, smiling proudly.

"Andrew, honestly! We decided that years ago." Elizabeth's eyes are open now, and she's sitting up straight. She no longer sounds frail.

"And Jon can have the dining-room suite. I don't know what any of this stuff's worth any more, do you? Will it still come out even?" He doesn't listen very well to Elizabeth, does he? Why is that, when he used to? It used to seem to Charlotte that Elizabeth was the one with his ear. He never said to Charlotte, "What's your schedule like, so we can plan around it?" He said, instead, "Here's what I'm doing, are you free when I am?" Certainly he never said, "You pick any time, any weekend, any night you want, and we'll do whatever you like." Besides work, his life would be dotted with dinners, movies, home and school meetings. Weekends. Holidays.

"Near enough. We'll be dead anyway, what do we care? I don't think they'll fight over things, and if they do, it's surely their problem, not ours."

Good for Elizabeth.

Charlotte wonders if, discounting the pleasures of conversation with Andrew, shared interests, warmth, heat, affection and embraces, she mightn't have preferred Elizabeth.

"We'll still leave Jon and young Andrew as executors?"

"Sure." Elizabeth's eyes have closed again, and her head has sunk back on the sofa. Don't they find it annoying that the television is on, although soundless? People are laughing on the screen, a father tousles the hair of a boy. For a long time, Charlotte was unable to watch shows about families, fathers at breakfast, at dinner, chatting with wives, dispensing advice and affection to youngsters.

"Now there's three grandkids, it's more complicated again. Should we leave them specific things from the house, or let them choose for themselves?"

"How about both? Surely it depends when we die, what they want. If we died tonight, what on earth would the baby choose? And the boys, they'd probably grab the tools and the TV. But if we don't die till they're older, they'd probably pick other things entirely. So let's just leave them the largest part of the money split three ways, and say they can each pick two things instead of one to remember us by, and then, oh, I don't know, just take a guess. Leave one the silverware and another the good china and the third one the bedroom furniture. How about that? Then there's something specific and something left open and everybody should be happy. Except for us being dead, of course, let's hope they're not happy about that." Elizabeth's voice has a nice sardonic edge – she makes Charlotte smile.

Charlotte's will is quite simple: everything is to be sold. The money will go to the shelter for street kids downtown. It might even be possible, depending on the real-estate market at the time, for the shelter to buy the small building it occupies; at least her bequest should cover the rent. In her opinion, it's unlikely there will ever not be a need for such a shelter, so it doesn't particularly matter when she dies, from that perspective. Whatever day or year, the money will be handy.

Is it necessarily wise to leave estates to family? Andrew had to start from scratch, why shouldn't his sons, not to mention his grandchildren? Parents either make things too easy or far too hard for their children, in Charlotte's experience.

"Finished?" Elizabeth asks.

"I guess so. I think we've done well for them, you know. We've done pretty well as a family."

Really, does he think so? Has he forgotten?

On the other hand, here they are. Charlotte's fingers grip the windowsill. "That's why you like doing this, isn't it?" Elizabeth's voice is soft now, amused. "You like going over what we can leave them, so we can say how well we've done. You're very

sweet, Andrew. And you're right, but you know, it doesn't take making a will to realize that. We just have to look at the boys."

"I know." He has set down the papers and is regarding Elizabeth. Smiling. Charlotte remembers precisely that smile: a kind of affectionate pride. It was one of her favourite expressions, it seemed so trustworthy and safe.

So this is how it's turned out.

She really must go.

She makes her fingers loosen on the windowsill, and dips her head. She turns very slowly, tracing first with her eyes, in the light from their living-room, the path she will take. Edging carefully sideways, she frees herself from the small space between the wall and the shrub, and tries not to crush any more flowers on her way back through the small garden.

Has she left footprints? Will they be puzzled, or frightened, when they look outside in the morning and see signs of sneakers under the window?

Now she is a dignified, elderly woman walking, as if she belongs, down Andrew's street and around the corner. She forgets to look back, although realizes when she reaches her car that an earlier, more sentimental Charlotte likely would have.

She is behind the wheel of the car, winding her way back out of the subdivision, when she thinks, "I won't be driving these streets again." Then she thinks what she really means: "I won't ever see Andrew again." Right at the moment she feels nothing in particular: not curiosity or satisfaction or sorrow. Just perfectly sure.

She's in a bit of a hurry, now that it's finished. This time spent driving from his place to hers is now a waste, an irritation. But tomorrow Claudia's coming. Her foot presses harder on the accelerator, and after all she's home before she knows it. With the help of two Scotches, she sleeps like a log.

twelve

THIS TRAIN STATION IS UTTERLY glorious: great carved, curved faraway ceilings, frescoes and gargoyles, echoes and rumblings, fogged loudspeaker voices – and the people! Old women with shopping bags and young ones with briefcases, patient mothers gripping excited, slippery children, men standing silent, or sitting hunched – Charlotte, too excited to wait, is here early, but delighted now with so much to see. The commuters, the men and women with briefcases and suits, all of them in such a hurry, look the least interesting, but even they must have interesting lives, or interesting events. Except rushing so much, when would they notice?

She recalls the days of hurrying, herself. What luxury, to be able to sit here and watch – if she's looking for fresh adventures and outings, here's an obvious place. There's no particular

reason to spy only on people she knows, or once loved. Perfect strangers could be just as revealing.

Whatever it says in the newspapers or on TV, this remains a polite city. When Claudia's train is announced, Charlotte makes her way to the arrival hall less briskly than the surging crowds around her, but nobody jostles, nobody touches. There are some odd-looking people, yes, but none, she thinks, who require actual wariness. On TV and in the papers it sounds quite different: as if danger is random, with violence in the mildest locations. They make it sound as if this is something new. Perhaps it is worse than it used to be. She understands there are reasons it ought to be worse: a much greater despair abroad in the world than she was ever accustomed to, too much awareness of tragedy, the simple avalanche of evil news. In a world in which so much horror is known, horror may come to seem simply the nature of being human.

Will she and Claudia recognize each other?

Of course they will. They're just older, more extreme versions of the women they were five years ago. Five years is a long time; the longest they've ever gone between visits. A great deal (although, after all, perhaps less than in earlier decades) has happened. Will they see each other and be instantly at home, or will there have to be some cautious, polite time first?

Last night, sitting in bed with her Scotch, she felt in the middle of things: between her last night with Andrew and her first day with Claudia. All betwixt and between, as her mother would have said.

Charlotte's mother died only four years ago, and was more or less healthy until the last year. Her grandmother died at ninety-three. Charlotte had better be ready for a lot more time. Well, she feels more prepared than that day in the supermarket when fear and age assaulted her. She may not be able to define

her repairs, but however foolishly she has obviously behaved, something is firmer.

. . . .

Claudia, feeling like herself camouflaged behind the face and body of an old woman, watches the city as the train draws through the last track-riddled blocks towards the station. So much is new! What are these buildings? What are they for? She feels herself craning and gaping, and smiles: the country mouse comes to town.

She knows she looks like an old woman because she has caught herself sitting exactly like her own vision of one: knees and ankles pressed together, purse firmly on her lap, her two hands folded on top of it. What a prim and nervous picture she must have made for the past two hours for the gum-snapping teenage girls opposite, who have spent much of the journey looking at a fashion magazine and talking, mainly about boys. How much changes? She would have smiled at them benevolently, if they'd paid her any attention and if she didn't realize that benevolent smiles from old women can look somewhat crazed. She would have liked, though, to lean forward and tap them on the knees and say, "You know, I'm just off to visit my friend and we'll be doing exactly what you are, giggling and gossiping and talking about ourselves and the world and people with penises. Isn't it fun?"

She wonders if they also have unhappy secrets they divulge only to each other.

She began to feel lighter and more distant the moment the train pulled out of her own town's small station. They have ticked through other towns and past farms, and she's looked out into backyards and gardens and junk yards and factories, and bits of history and past have dropped away like dreams. Now she almost hates to arrive. If she could only keep going,

riding on and on with her purse tucked tidily on her lap, leaving her whole life behind, it seems she could only get freer and freer, until she had no history at all, becoming entirely fresh and forgetful.

Now, with the train slowing, the past seems far away, but the future is immediate and demanding: in a very few minutes she'll see Charlotte again, and what will she tell her? What will they say?

The gum-snapping girls are already standing, wrestling their luggage from the overhead compartment. "Get yours?" asks the one with spiky silvered hair, looking down at Claudia.

"Thank you." Claudia is surprised, then ashamed of being surprised. She ought to know better than to assume she was invisible, or that they might be entirely self-absorbed. "Thank you very much, dear."

"No prob." No prob indeed, for their strong young arms, but thoughtful and kind. The girls head for the exit, kicking their cases ahead of them, although the train is still moving. People are lining up, eager to leave. Claudia thinks she won't join the crush. She doesn't care to be hurried or pushed, and as the train comes to its brake-squealing halt, she sits waiting patiently.

. . . .

At first a few and then a horde of people begin pouring off Claudia's train. Charlotte watches carefully, but doesn't expect to see Claudia for a few minutes. She'll have luggage, and she's old, and she's also the kind of person who stands back because she won't want to be knocked off her feet, and anyway, except that she has a friend waiting, she has all the time in the world, while everyone else is evidently in a rush. Charlotte, as the waiting friend, isn't entirely patient with that point of view.

It's not just age, though: if Claudia were twenty, she'd still be

standing back, ushering some old woman ahead of her, making sure no one rushed or pushed her. Charlotte smiles.

And smiles more broadly, because here, finally, comes Claudia: staggering a bit under the weight of her suitcases, looking around anxiously, peering for Charlotte, brave Claudia (because all this noise and light, so many people, may be dazzling and disorienting) is making her way along the platform. She was right, she is plumper. But still pretty and sweet-looking. Her hair has gone purely and absolutely white – she never mentioned that – and she's had it cut short. Maybe it was easier to keep that way, nursing Bradley. Charlotte's hand goes to her own long, merely grey hair, tied loosely back.

She waves; Claudia spots her and grins. They head towards each other and it's like Charlotte's dream of Andrew, except the other person is an old woman, not a young man, and when they do reach each other there's not much surprise, and of course no distaste.

. . . .

Claudia sets down her cases. Charlotte, at last! Should she be so thin? Is she less elegant than gaunt? Oh, look at that smile. She didn't realize until they smiled and headed for each other that she was frightened something essential might have changed. "Oh, Char, I'm so *happy* to see you." She feels herself almost dancing. They stand at arms' length. Claudia sees tears in Charlotte's eyes, and feels them also in her own. They hug. People skirt them, and some smile.

Charlotte, with her arms around Claudia, Claudia's arms around her, remembers Andrew saying, "Bodies talk, they have their own language, a lot better than words for some things." In this as in many other matters, he was of course right.

"You've cut your hair," she says. "And it's all gone white."

"I dye it, you know," as if this is a mischievous secret. "It

wasn't turning as fast as I wanted. It wasn't a nice grey, like yours is, so I speeded things up."

"Remember when I dyed yours that awful red?" They were sixteen. The shade turned out to be unexpectedly, vividly, orange. Claudia was heartbroken. It was also one of the few times Charlotte remembers Claudia angry with her.

"Oh God, do I ever." Their mothers were furious, also.

"Come on, let me take one of your bags."

"Subway?"

"No chance. I'm treating us to a taxi." Charlotte puts her free arm around Claudia's shoulders. "I thought you told me you were getting fat. You're not fat." Claudia's chin and breasts and body and legs are just more roly-poly than they used to be.

"Getting fat, I said. Just working on it. Lord, I'm hungry right now. Can I treat you to lunch? Is it too early for lunch? What time do you eat?" Claudia's laughter is a silver ripple. A few people smile at them, touched by the contagion of pleasure. Or, Charlotte thinks, because they look like a pair of old goofs.

Nothing wrong with that.

"No, let's get you settled, and I'll whip us up something. We can eat out tomorrow, if you like. We can do whatever we feel like. Whatever appeals."

Claudia remains astonished at the city, and peers out the taxi windows like a tourist. "What's that?" she asks. "Oh, look at that." There are whole new canyons of buildings. "But you know," she says, "when we lived here I used to think everything was moving too fast. Now it looks too slow. It looks almost paralysed. Look at all those cars, and nothing's moving. And people dodging each other on the sidewalk – it'd drive me crazy now, moving so slowly."

It's a perspective Charlotte hasn't considered, but she sees what Claudia means. "I don't come right downtown so much

any more. But you're right, it does look a bit mad. Maddening. Have you stopped missing it, then?"

For years after she and Bradley moved away, Claudia spoke of homesickness. "I like this well enough," she used to say, "but oh, I miss being there." Charlotte was never sure why; it wasn't as if Claudia ever got out much. Unless she and Charlotte went, Claudia didn't get to the theatre, or concerts, or dances, or bars. Whatever Bradley did by way of a social life, and Charlotte was sure it didn't include theatre or concerts or dance performances, Claudia was rarely invited along. "Actually," she told Charlotte just a few years ago, "I guess it wasn't really the place I missed, it's you. I've always been homesick for you."

Absence does alter, of course it does. Taken-for-granted presence is a luxury, whether it applies to a lover like Andrew with obligations (and desires) elsewhere, or to Claudia. Too much has to be contained within too little time, when absence consumes far more hours than presence. "I hope you're planning to stay for a good long visit," Charlotte tells Claudia. "We have a lot of catching up to do."

What would she and Andrew talk about if they met now? Besides, of course, what they've been up to for the past three decades. Once they got beyond that, would they have much to say?

Unlocking her front door, setting down Claudia's bags, steering her into the living-room, Charlotte feels, as she always does, the arms of her home folding around her again. "I love your house," Claudia says, as if she feels a similar embrace. "It's always felt so much like a real home. And so much like you, too."

Except having this pointed out makes Charlotte wonder for a moment how it might have been to have someone else's life reflected here as well. Some mixture of tastes. Might that have made the place richer, or just less Charlotte's own? Even Claudia's luggage, even Claudia's figure now standing in the middle of the living-room, looking around, shifts the balance of the

house, tilting it slightly away from Charlotte. Which actually is rather nice; puts things at a somewhat different angle, for a fresh view.

She likes her house as much through Claudia's eyes as she does through her own.

"This is so strange," Claudia says. "This is the first place I've been – I mean actually gone to and been – in more than a year. All that time – I might have been on Mars for all the difference the rest of the world made. Oh, Charlotte," and the lines around her mouth, her eyes, are crinkling upward like a happy child's, "it is so good to be here. And away from there. I feel so *far* away from there. Thank you."

"I'm glad. And you're welcome." In the face of Claudia's delight, Charlotte feels a little clumsy; a little overwhelmed, to be honest. "If you want to unpack, I'll get lunch. We can take your bags up. I've made up the spare room." Is she fussing? She hopes not. "How about a drink?"

"A reward for unpacking. Then food. Then tea and talk? And maybe a snack and then some more talk and maybe more food – I did warn you, didn't I?"

Charlotte thinks that for two old women, they manage the stairs, lugging Claudia's bags, quite spryly. "This is lovely," Claudia says, looking around the room that will be hers while she's here. "Absolutely peaceful and pure."

In Claudia's plump and beaming face, Charlotte can make out all the ages of her friend. And does Claudia see all the Charlottes she has known, rolling back to childhood? She puts an arm around Claudia. "This is grand, Claudie. I'm so pleased."

Downstairs in the kitchen, Charlotte hears Claudia's footsteps crossing back and forth over her head, drawers opening and closing. It's odd, hearing sounds of another human. If Claudia gets up in the night, will Charlotte be wakened, startled by thoughts of intruders?

All the senses, it seems, have to adjust even to small changes.

Charlotte opens the first bottle from the case of white wine. When Claudia gets down to the kitchen, her glass is waiting for her and lunch is almost ready. She perches on a kitchen chair, leaning forward with her elbows on the table, watching Charlotte tear up spinach for the salad.

"Settled okay?"

"Perfectly. I feel right at home. No, better than that – I feel a long way from home, and lighter already."

"Lighter?"

Claudia laughs. "Not literally. Obviously. But, oh, I don't know – lighter in spirit? When you're just in one place, it's easy to think that's the whole world. And it's all weighing down on you, and everything that happens gets magnified when you're only thinking about your own circumstances. You lose perspective. You forget. And now I'm already looking back as if all that was a million miles and a million years away. It's odd."

Charlotte nods. It seems they're still clicking along nicely together. All the ages they have been, together and apart – this is just the latest one. "Now tell me," Claudia says, smiling, "everything that's happened to you in the past five years."

Where to begin? They have hours, and days, to catch up. A great many details will be required to fill in their pictures. At some point she will tell Claudia about the dreams, for instance, and those awful moments in the supermarket. Claudia will talk about her daughters, how they're doing, and about her days during the last year of Bradley's life. They'll talk about shopping, and clothing, and flaws in their characters, and purposes and getting old. There are days and days for all that.

What she wants to tell now is about crouching in Andrew's hedge and under his living-room window. "Do you remember Andrew?"

"Andrew." Claudia frowns. "He was years ago, wasn't he? Lawyer? Good-looking? Mar . . ." She breaks off. Charlotte laughs.

"Married, yes."

"You don't mean you see him, do you?"

"Good heavens no, not that way. But I have seen him. He just, thank God, hasn't seen me. Let me tell you."

She does begin, after all, with the supermarket. It does still seem to her to have been the cause. "I have trouble," Claudia says, shaking her head, "imagining you being afraid."

"I did, too. It was the oddest, most awful feeling. It terrified me, being frightened like that. So of course I had to do something, I couldn't go on being scared of fear."

"So what did you do? What does Andrew have to do with it?"

Charlotte holds up her hand. "Patience, Claudie." They've finished their first course and she's cutting chocolate cake. "Ice cream?"

"Oh, please, yes."

"Let's have dessert in the living-room."

When they've settled, plates on their laps, in chairs facing each other, Charlotte resumes. She has eaten too much; her stomach feels stretched and unhealthy. Later, the chocolate will keep her awake. She watches Claudia's face as she talks, seeing it shift from amazement to fear to shock to amusement and back again. Charlotte supposes Claudia's expression reflects her own; or the various tones she chooses for the telling.

She talks of: looking up Andrew in the telephone book; scouting his neighbourhood; her first view of his home, its normalcy compared with its power; the prickliness of the cedar hedge. The first sounds of voices.

"Good lord, Charlotte," Claudia breathes.

"Well, yes. I don't know what possessed me."

So she must circle back to her decade with Andrew. "So much happened, you see. It was a kind of decision decade, although I guess I didn't know that then. But by the end of it, certain avenues were closed. A lot got lost and a lot of things were gained, but at the end I wasn't the same person any more, and some things simply were no longer possible. Trust, I suppose. Belief. Maybe even love. At very least I understood nothing lasts, and I was alone."

"But there were others, I remember."

"Oh yes, I don't mean Andrew was the end of that, only, I saw things differently. I understood endings better, and beginnings for that matter. Tell me, how did you forgive me?"

"For what?"

"For men like Andrew."

"Because of Bradley?" Claudia shrugs. "I don't know. I guess, to tell the truth, I was upset for a while. I don't know if you realized." Charlotte shakes her head. She hadn't known. "But you were my friend. You were different. I knew you so well, and I knew you weren't bad. You were my friend." She shrugs again. "I know that doesn't make sense. You were just different, that's all. And I guess I didn't think you were fooling around. I think I understood you were serious."

"That's true. Although there were some frivolities, too, Andrew just wasn't one of them. Anyway, thanks. I don't know what I'd have done without you."

"I think we tried to look after each other. I think that's what friends do."

The first bottle is almost finished. At this rate, a case may not be enough. Charlotte uncorks a second.

"So anyway, there I was in his hedge. I did find myself hard to believe. And if I thought the supermarket was a scary moment, it was nothing to hunching there wondering what on earth would happen if somebody spotted me."

"But nobody did?"

Charlotte spreads her hands. "Here I am, unarrested. And, I hope, unaddicted."

"Satisfied?"

"Oh, never that. But I learned some things, although not necessarily what I had in mind."

She recounts conversations, tones of voice, the small events witnessed. Describes Andrew, Elizabeth, the house, the son she saw, the grandsons. "So what is it," Claudia asks, "you wanted to find out, exactly? What *did* you find out?"

"You'll think I'm crazy. Maybe I was. But I wanted to find out what happened, and if he made the right choice, and if I made the right decision. I just wanted to know the end of the story. Dumb, eh? But you know what's really dumb?"

Claudia shakes her head.

"What's really dumb is what I truly wanted to know. Which is, really, what's the secret of domestic life? How do people go along, how does daily life work? It's as if practically everybody else speaks a language I simply do not understand. It's not that I necessarily wanted to speak it; just, it's maddening not even to know how."

"Oh, Charlotte. You should have asked." Claudia is laughing. "You'll be furious if I tell you now."

"No I won't. Go ahead. I should have asked you in the first place and saved myself all this trouble. Although it's been *interesting* trouble."

"See, that's it exactly." They are both grinning. "You don't get to know the secret of ordinary getting along because you keep wanting things to be interesting. You don't get to have both, by and large. So you chose interesting, and lost out on ordinary. Me, I chose ordinary, so I couldn't have thrills and change. But now I can finally tell you: the secret is, it's just one damn thing after another. A step and a step and a step and finally there you

are. Just plunk, plunk, plunk, that's the big secret. It's bloody dull most of the time, and it sure isn't often romantic. It's not necessarily grim or tragic, either, it's just getting along. Now tell me you envy that. And tell me if that isn't what you saw and heard at Andrew's: just people getting along. And tell me you ever wished for it, even for a second."

Somewhere in there, they both stopped smiling.

"For a second, yes. For several seconds, now and then."

"Truly?"

Charlotte considers. "Truly. But you're right, of course. I got what I wanted. Had what I needed. And that's a good thing to be sure of. Heavens, doesn't that sound like dying words? Actually, I don't suppose they'd be bad dying words. Do you ever think about that, Claudie? What you'd like to say right at the end? That last minute, what you'd like to be remembered for?"

"Not really. I guess it'd depend who was there at the time. I'd likely say something different to the girls than to you."

Charlotte laughs. "Considering the audience? Thoughtful right to the finish. But I can imagine rehearsing something eloquent and sweeping and then when the time comes, what'll come out will be something like, 'Oh shit, not yet.' Or I'll be all alone and won't have any audience at all. Wasted last words – that'd be really annoying." This, it occurs to her too late, is more than tactless. She is making jokes about last words to a woman who just recently lost her husband. What were Bradley's last words, then? "Sorry, Claudie. You probably don't find the subject very funny. I didn't think."

"Because of Bradley? No, it's okay. You know more about me and Bradley than just about anybody else. Except for the girls, it turns out."

"What turns out? Tell me. And how are they, the girls?"

Claudia smiles. "They're fine. They're lovely. Their visit was

a little difficult in spots, a little more revealing than I'd expected, but I'm so proud of them. I'm so pleased with the women they've turned out to be. It was surprising, though. I hadn't realized how much they knew, growing up. It made me think I worried too much. Or worried about the wrong things. I was trying to protect them, and as it happens, they knew all along. I guess they were trying to protect me. Maybe it's all for the best, I don't know. It's good to have it out in the open, anyway. At least that's good."

"Claudia, what are you talking about? You and Bradley? Is that what they knew about all along?"

"Yes. Sorry. That's what I meant."

"So tell me."

"Can we eat first?"

It seems they (or Charlotte) have talked their way to late-afternoon-snack time. "You know, I was wondering if we'd have to make small talk until we were comfortable again, and here I've bent your ear all afternoon about my little hedge adventures, and that's exactly what my secret was and what I was embarrassed about, and now I've spit it out the second you walked in the door! Five whole years, and the moment I see you I tell you my deepest, darkest foolishness."

Claudia squeezes Charlotte's shoulder. But does not tell her own secret.

Charlotte sets out cheese and crackers to nibble while they peel potatoes and carrots to go around a small roast. "This way we'll hardly have any dishes to do. A meal in a pot. And more chocolate cake for dessert?"

"Grand. But tomorrow it's my turn, I don't want you taking care of me. Or subsidizing me, especially when I'm so hungry all the time."

"Oh well," Charlotte shrugs, "I'm not quite poor."

They do talk seriously, though, for a time, of budgeting and

finances and taking care. "Of course," Claudia says, "I've always had to budget fairly carefully. I don't find it totally strange."

"I don't exactly find it strange, but I guess I would have liked more freedom. I don't like having to watch where every dollar goes. And I don't like wondering if I live as long as my mother, or my grandmother for that matter, whether I'll have enough at the end. I don't want to be out on the street when I'm ninety. I won't be, of course, I don't mean that. I just resent having to be so careful. I'd like to be, oh, unburdened by practical matters. I'd like," Charlotte grins, "to have my mind free for finer, more meaningful questions."

"Like Andrew, and hedges?" Claudia digs an elbow into Charlotte's ribs.

"Yeah," Charlotte giggles. "Finer, more meaningful stuff like that. Coffee? Tea? A little sobering up before we pour the next round?"

"We'll be up all night."

"And who would care?"

They sit across from each other at the kitchen table, darkness creeping up outside, smells of dinner growing rich around them. "I didn't tell you," Claudia says, "about Bradley's funeral, did I?"

"No. What about it?"

So Claudia tells the story of the anguished woman at the back of the room. And Susan's furious defence. And the conversations last weekend with the girls. She tries to tell it wryly, with an amused tinge of metal in her tone.

But "What a nightmare," Charlotte exclaims. "How ghastly for you." And for that woman, she is thinking. And wonders if Claudia also absorbs their conversations on two levels, hearing not only each other, but the absent figures: wives and other women.

Apparently so. "I must tell you," Claudia says, "although

maybe I wouldn't if I hadn't had all this wine: when you were talking about listening in on Andrew's life, I couldn't help picturing somebody listening in on me and Bradley. That woman from the funeral, maybe. Trying to figure out our lives. How we got on."

"Me too. I mean, I picture things from two or three points of view, too."

"I bet we both always have, we just never discussed it."

This is true. Now they can look at each other with comprehension, and also amusement. They eat dinner in thoughtful, companionable, near-total silence.

"You must," Charlotte says, clearing the table, "do whatever you feel like, you know. If you want to go to bed, or read, or watch TV, whatever you're inclined to do, please feel free. I want you to be at home."

"I should sleep, probably, it's been a long day, but I don't feel like it yet. You're right, it's kind of a miracle, falling back into friendship this way. I'd forgotten how good it feels to have a friend. I never had another one like you. Well, of course I didn't. But it's so long since I've had a real friend of any kind, I guess. I knew I was isolated the last year or so, but I didn't realize until today how glorious it is not to be isolated. You know what it is, really?"

"What?"

"I forgot what it's like to be truthful. It's such a luxury, not to have to *be* somebody. Be whatever Claudia somebody's expecting, a nurse or a wife or a mother or just a set of ears. I can be the Claudia I am to me here. Does that make sense?"

"Of course." Charlotte smiles. "That's why I could tell you about the Andrew business. That's me."

"And a very silly you it is, too. Will you go back?"

"Oh God, I hope not. I just need to find another hobby now. I thought when I was waiting at the station today, maybe I'll

start eavesdropping on strangers. Roam around park benches or courtrooms. Or the train station, for that matter."

"But did you learn what you wanted to?"

"In a way. It was a bit painful, and after all I couldn't make it end, I couldn't make it tidy. But I expect I'll get used to that. It's nice he's still alive. He didn't seem exactly happy, but I do hope he's content. He wouldn't have been content with me, and I wouldn't have been, I think, with him. But that wasn't the point, after all."

"What was?"

"Oh, maybe I have a better sense of magic now. That I guess I wound up with more or less the right kind of life, and he probably did, too. Pretty lucky, really. Pretty magic."

"We are lucky, aren't we? I've gotten the habit of reading the news every day, and that's what I see: how fortunate I am, compared. And then I feel a bit guilty: no civil wars, no dead children, no starvation. A little turmoil now and then is nothing; and I wonder, how have we escaped? In the scheme of things, I've had a charmed life. I wonder if I should have known that better at the time. If I would have been less upset if I'd had the sense to think, 'But at least the fridge is full and the girls are healthy. At least I *have* a fridge. And girls. At least nobody is actively trying to hurt me.'"

Charlotte shrugs. In her opinion, Bradley was rather active in his efforts to hurt Claudia. "Maybe. But I don't think it makes much difference. Pain is pain. You're right, some is horrendous, but somebody else's doesn't make yours less. A lot of the families I used to see – I could hardly believe what people did to each other. But that didn't make my events small, by any means. Maybe it should have, but it never did."

They pick up their glasses and the bottle, head back to the living-room once more. "I hope I don't get sick." Claudia giggles. "I'm not used to this."

"I hope we both don't get sick. I only have one bathroom. I still feel okay, though, do you?"

"Only a bit tipsy. And full – that was a grand dinner, thank you, Char. But really, my turn tomorrow."

"Have you thought how long you can stay?" Charlotte hopes that didn't sound as if she's keen now for Claudia to leave. "On and on, I hope."

"I don't know. Do you mind? Right now I feel as if I could be here forever, but I've also gotten used to random feelings popping out of nowhere, so I can never be sure of anything any more. I think it's because for such a long time, I just set myself to enduring. And now all that's finished, my own feelings poke out here and there and they're so new and inexperienced, they aren't very tempered. They just happen, and I don't quite know what to do with them. I don't seem to have much control. I just watch and see what they do. So right this minute, sitting here with you feels like eternity, but I can't predict the next second. I guess what I'm learning is unpredictability. Or maybe," she laughs, "instability. Maybe I'm just entirely off the leash."

Charlotte smiles. "I doubt it."

"Or maybe," and now Claudia looks very serious, "I'm working my way back from madness. I did something enormous, you know. I went over a terrible edge." She looks frightened. And also a little frightening. Charlotte has never thought of Claudia as someone who steps over edges; but she doesn't seem to be exaggerating.

"Do you want to tell me?"

Claudia looks hard at Charlotte. "I do, you know. But I'm scared what you'll think. And as long as I don't say it out loud, I can almost believe it's all right. Or, not all right, but not quite real."

"Claudia, you don't have to tell anything, obviously, but maybe if you don't, it'll get too big in your mind. Like me hiding

in Andrew's hedge: that's not something I could tell anybody else, and it was pretty huge, and now it's just something that was a bit foolish, but still makes sense. It's slipped into place. I hope."

Claudia sighs. "I don't even have the words. I haven't thought out the words to use, all I have is the picture."

"Then you can describe the picture to me. If you want."

"Oh, I do!" Claudia cries, then looks startled by her own volume and vehemence. "I have to! I just don't know *how*."

"Just start. It's okay." Charlotte makes her voice soothing; but is a little unnerved. She may be farther over her head than she realized. She sees she has failed to take Claudia entirely seriously; has believed that whatever it is, the secret will be Claudia-sized: will fit within the frame of what she understands of Claudia. Now she wonders if that may not be the case.

On the other hand, she has listened to true tales of horror, in her time. And Claudia, whatever she may think, does not contain horror; nothing comparable at all to children held screaming on the burning elements of stoves.

Claudia, pale, takes a deep breath.

"You know my house, you remember what it's like. It hasn't changed since you were last there. Remember?" Charlotte nods.

"So I was in the kitchen, getting a meal ready, when Bradley came in and told me he had cancer. I didn't take it in right away, but I guess that's normal. He didn't, either. Neither of us had any idea what it was going to mean. Actually, the first thing I remember about it is being annoyed, that I finally had a peaceful kind of life and now Bradley was going to turn everything upside down again. I was *irritated*. I thought, 'Because of this man, I am never going to have any peace at all. He ruins everything.' Awful, eh?"

"You're being hard on yourself again, Claudia."

"Ah, but wait. Anyway, he had treatments. He had surgery. He was desperate to live, you know. He couldn't bear the idea of not existing. Well, I don't suppose I'll be much better. It was touching, in a way, how hard he wanted to live, though. Being in hospital put him in an awful rage. He couldn't get around what was happening to him, as long as he was there. He said he wanted to go home because he wanted me to look after him, he trusted me, not strangers, but I think it was more that we were so used to lying to each other, and making the lies true enough that we could survive, he thought he could do it again, about death. Or no, he didn't *think* that, exactly, he wouldn't have reasoned it through, he just felt it."

"So you took him home."

"I did. It's better these days than it used to be, there are agencies that help, but still. Bradley didn't like the visiting nurses, or the homemakers, he didn't even seem to like it much when the girls came and took over for a few hours. He kept saying he just wanted me." She laughs. "That's what I thought of, when I imagined somebody hanging around outside *our* windows listening to our lives and trying to figure out what they meant. What impression would she have had? Maybe even some kind of devotion. She might have decided we were absolutely welded.

"You remember the kitchen, and our bedroom, and the stairs. That was my world, for months and months. And the laundry room behind the kitchen, of course. And sometimes in the evening, for a little while I'd get to watch TV in the living-room, or sit and read. But not for long. He got very restless. Well, he was in a lot of pain fairly often. He'd want something and I'd be running up and down those stairs. Or even if he was quiet, I was always listening. In the worst and best moments of our marriage, I was never so *alert* to him as I was then. Every second, whether I was with him or not, and

whether he was quiet or not, I was *aware* of him. It was exhausting."

"But you didn't stop."

"No. Because you know why? It wasn't devotion, or love. I think it was that I didn't want to leave anything undone. I wanted to feel pure at the end – that I'd done my very, absolute best." Claudia shakes her head. "You'll see the irony." Charlotte leans forward, pours them each more wine, settles back.

"Sometimes we were close, though. He'd talk about our lives and tell me how important I was to him. He said whatever'd happened, I should know he'd always loved me. And it's funny, but maybe it was true, in his terms, by his standards. It was just, he'd never learned to take my terms and standards into account. He'd never bothered to adjust to me. I think it didn't even occur to him that he ought to; that that was part of the deal. But anyway, it's too late now. It was too late then, for that matter. What I'm saying is, there were some nice moments while he was ill. If nothing else, we'd had all those years, and all those events just between the two of us, nobody else, happy or not, they were ours. Do you see?"

Charlotte nods. She does see. She also sees that this, not the dull plodding Claudia spoke of before, is likely the true secret of domestic life: shared, unspoken, private events. Regardless of quality, or passions aroused, it must simply be the accumulation of enclosed, two-person pictures. Well, she already knew that. It's the difference between knowing and understanding, though. It's what she knew she was missing, and it's exactly what used to put her in a rage, and what also made her very sad.

This is not her story, though, it's Claudia's.

"I think it must be like being a firefighter, something like that: long periods of tedium, or drudgery, and then these awful crises. We'd almost adjust and then suddenly his disease

would take a leap and he'd be in some new, terrible pain, or lose some ability or function, and there we'd be, in yet another world of difficulty. Well, I guess I told you some of it in the letter. How bad things got. So there was all that.

"But also, maybe because of the pain, maybe because he lost control of himself, or maybe he was angry to have to depend on me so much, even though that was what he insisted on – anyway, I don't know why, but he started telling me all these things. Details, I mean. What he and other women had done. Ways they'd been together. Things he and I had never dreamed of. Or I hadn't, anyway. This one and that one – oh, it was dreadful." Claudia's hands go over her ears, as if she can still hear his voice. "He made me listen. He had a kind of death grip on my wrists, and he'd hold on and make me listen."

"Oh, Claudia." Charlotte can hardly breathe. She would kill Bradley, if he weren't dead.

What if Andrew were inclined to do such a thing? What would poor Elizabeth hear?

"Anyway," Claudia smiles, a little shakily, her hands once more reaching for her glass, "you can see why I didn't call you, or write. I had no energy left. It was the strangest world all those months, just the two of us. Even with other people going in and out, it was really just the two of us. Years ago I longed for that. It's funny, how wishes can turn out, if you're unlucky enough to have them come true." She sips, sets the glass down.

"I got to be a pretty good nurse, in a limited way. I learned about tubes and different kinds of machines and veins and medication schedules, and what different kinds of medication did and how they balanced with each other. I did my absolute, very best to keep him as comfortable as I could. I cooked my heart out, trying to tempt him. I bathed him and cleaned him and turned him; sometimes I even sang to him, if he was drifting and I could remember some old song that might draw him

back. That was tricky, though; I never knew when I might stumble into one that would bring someone else back to him, and there we'd go again, off into another one of those nightmare sessions."

Another secret of domestic life: that this is how it may end up. And by then people are tied together so tightly, by love or memory or experience or simple circumstance, they can't get loose. They are beyond any point of abandonment. Charlotte wouldn't have done well in this situation, either.

"Can you see it, Charlotte? Can you begin to imagine?"

"Yes, I can. I don't see how you managed, but I can see the ways you had to, yes."

"Good. Because you need that picture in order to see what happened. I don't understand, myself, but I can see." At times while she's been speaking, Claudia has frowned, or smiled, or her lips have trembled or the skin around her mouth and eyes has tightened. Now Charlotte is startled to see an expression that is entirely unfamiliar: an astounding coldness. Real ruthlessness.

"So here it is, here's the point." Claudia's expression changes again, becoming flat and direct.

"It was one of his good days. Although you understand that was just relative; none of his days were actually good. But he started off in less pain than the day before, and he was pretty alert. And so he was being reasonably cheerful and kind. At that point I was grateful for such little blessings, Char – just to have some small space of time that wasn't profoundly dreadful was enough to make me glad. So I was especially gentle when I turned him, and gave him the first morphine of the day, and it was nice, almost restful, when he asked me to sit down beside the bed. He took hold of my hand. He was smiling at me – I can't tell you how rare it was by then, him smiling. Well, he didn't have much to smile about, I suppose, and not much strength.

"So he was kind of stroking my fingers – his hands were so thin it was like being touched by a skeleton, but that was all right. Because there are times and ways it's nice to be touched, as long as it's with fondness. His voice never lasted long, but he told me how nice it was to open his eyes in the morning and see me. He said I was pretty. He said I had the loveliest eyes he'd ever seen. And that I was the nicest, sweetest, gentlest person he'd ever known. He said he was grateful to me, and he'd always loved me. He even said he was sorry. For everything. He said he wished he could undo every hurtful thing he'd ever done. If he could live his life over again, he said, he'd do it entirely differently; he'd dedicate his life to loving me.

"He was so frail, Charlotte. And the curtains were open, so there was this splash of sunshine falling across him. His fingers were just bones touching mine. How can I say this? – it was almost as if he made his life true, just speaking those words. As if all the things he'd actually done were undone, because he said he wished it had been different." She shrugs. "I can't explain, exactly, but for a few minutes he made my whole life – our whole lives – feel right. As if it had been all right.

"And then he fell asleep, and I sat there for a little while because he was still holding my hand, but there was always so much to do, so finally I slipped away and went off to do a laundry, oh, a bunch of chores, I'm not sure what all I did. Until I heard him calling me again. So I went back upstairs. He never slept for very long.

"So I walked into the bedroom and – I don't quite know how to describe it – he seemed to be *glittering*. His eyes, for one thing, but it was more than that. It was as if every nerve was right at the surface of his skin, and his skin had little sparkles of broken glass all over. He seemed *aimed* at me, all his energy and strength, all those sparkling bits of glass. He said to me, 'You bitch. You ruinous, stinking, frigid bitch, I can't stand the

sight of you, you're disgusting, you bitch.' He used another word, too, but I can't say it. He was alive with hatred, Charlotte. A while before, he'd been so tender, and I'd believed him, and now this. And I believed this, too; the hatred was true. Truer than anything. But he didn't say *why*.

"He started with the names. He went on about how they'd pleased him. And then he said that any one of them would have made him happier than I could have dreamed of doing, because they understood what he liked, and they'd do anything to please – I know he was crazy, I know that, but right then it felt like the hugest, blackest betrayal of my life, because of what he'd said just a little while before. I was still standing just inside the doorway, kind of frozen. I couldn't even not look at him.

"Then he said, 'I'm hurting. Give me my shot now.' As if I was a servant. Not even a 'please.' And I didn't move. I don't know if I could have; I just didn't. He said, 'Hurry up, it's time, you don't know what this is like.'

"And I thought, '*You* don't know what it's like.' I just stared at him, and he was right, you could see the pain growing. I thought of it as sharp, like a knife slicing away inside him. He said, 'For God's sake, help me here,' and I didn't. All those times I was so angry. He hurt me like a knife, and I could never make him feel it, there was nothing I could say or do that made him feel it, and stop. But now he was feeling something like it. And I could make it stop for him. And I didn't. Wouldn't. Just like he wouldn't, for me."

Charlotte feels breathless.

"He started crying. Just little dry cries, because he wasn't strong enough for the kind of weeping I'd done over the years. I stood there in the doorway and I thought, 'If I'm very still, I can enter his pain, I can feel how sharp and vicious it is,' and I think it's true, I could. I could feel it coming closer and closer

to my suffering. It didn't take very long. That didn't seem fair, in a way, that he could achieve anguish in just a few minutes, and I'd gone on for years and years and years.

"But he got there. I felt him get there. And he was saying, well, whispering really, a kind of rattle, 'Please, please,' and I used to say please, too, and he'd promise and then pay no attention. I let him say it quite a few times, but nothing close to the number of times I had.

"And then it was enough. I thought we both knew enough. So I finally moved. I went to the dresser where all his drugs and medicines were lined up. I filled a syringe and went over to him and took his arm and pumped it in, and his eyes rolled up with relief.

"I went back to the dresser and filled up the syringe again. Of course he knew that was wrong and tried to pull his arm away, but I kept a grip and I pumped it in again. And then I did it again. He kept trying to pull away, and he was saying, 'No, no, no,' but that's all, he didn't say a reason. Do you see Charlotte? He didn't say why I should stop, or that he saw now, it was just, 'No, no, no.' I wish he'd said something else. Still, it pleased me, how terrified he was.

"I didn't know how much it would take. I think I did it five or six times, and then I sat down and watched him. All he said was 'Why?' He said that several times. It didn't seem worth answering at that point, if he didn't know, so I didn't."

She smiles, in a way that chills Charlotte. "As last words go, his weren't very eloquent, were they? Yours and mine will be better, I'm sure. But then, we'll have had time to put some thought into it. Of course he had the time, too – he had almost a year – but I guess it didn't occur to him."

"And then?"

"And then he died, of course. I watched him. I've never seen such a thing. It's very odd – a kind of creeping absence. Little

by little he just glazed over, and then he left. I could see the moment he left." She shakes her head.

"I sat on there for quite a while. Just looking at him. Trying to see what it was all about. Everything we'd been through, all those years. He looked very small and harmless. It was hard to recall how huge and harmful he'd been, just a little time before.

"But finally I thought, 'I killed him. I did that. I made him suffer, and then I made him dead.' And then I thought, 'I'd better call somebody.' So I phoned the doctor and said he was dead, and the doctor called an ambulance and people were in and out for a while. But nobody wondered. It was no surprise. The doctor said it could have come anytime. He was very kind. He said I'd done the very best anybody could. I called the girls while I was still strong enough to talk to them. And I haven't told a soul. How could I?"

She lifts her head and looks directly into Charlotte's eyes. "So you see, you're sitting here with a torturer and a killer. It wasn't a mercy killing, there was nothing kind about it. I just did it." Charlotte isn't sure what Claudia sees in her face – perhaps only shock – but abruptly Claudia slumps, and finally cries.

Well. Friends perform certain acts, no matter what. Charlotte stands, crosses the room, sits down on the arm of Claudia's chair, puts her arms around Claudia's shoulders, holding her and stroking her hair. They sit like this for quite a long time, until Charlotte's neck and shoulders begin to ache and Claudia's weeping subsides. Charlotte stands, refills their glasses and returns to her own chair. She can't think of a word to say. She can't remember a time with Claudia when she hasn't had a word to say.

Claudia blows her nose, picks up her glass with a hand that's still shaking. "I didn't realize," she says in a strange, soft voice,

"I hadn't really cried before. I kind of did, but not like that. Thank you."

For what? Charlotte's own secret, her spying in the hedge, is now very small, and even more absurd than it was. Looking at Claudia she sees her friend's sweet surface overlaid with a sheen of menace, like theatrical make-up. This cannot be true. "I'm sorry," she says. "It must have been awful for you."

Claudia suddenly laughs. Is she mad? But says, "That must be why you're my dear friend, Charlotte: that you can listen to that and then talk about how awful it must have been for me. I caused terrible suffering and I took a *life* – that's so hard to understand. I took *his* life, and what does that say? It happened. I thought I was almost used to things just happening and then dealing with them, but I don't seem to have much experience with being the one that makes them happen. I guess I got off to a late start that way. And then I had to go to extremes, and now I have to get used to that somehow. When I think about what kind of person I am, I guess from now on I have to think, 'I'm a torturer and a murderer.' I look in the mirror and can't see it, but I am. Charlotte, how can that be? Help me. I don't know how that can be."

What help is there? Charlotte can hardly heal this. She can't say, "Oh, Claudia, you're not those things," because she is. She can't say, "He would have died anyway, he was about to, the doctor said so," because that's not relevant. She can't say, "He deserved it," because that wouldn't be relevant, either.

She takes a deep breath. "I can't make it not be true, Claudia. But I can *see* it. I can understand it." This, she suddenly sees, is the case. For a few moments there, she must have been trying to make a judgement; people are expected to make judgements about this sort of thing. It's supposed to be obvious, but after all, it doesn't actually seem to be. "All I can say is what you just said: it's something that happened, it's an event. I can't make

out right or wrong, or good or bad. It's just something," she shrugs, "that happened."

"That I made happen."

"Yes. But there it is: done. And it's not as if you plotted it or planned it. That might be different, I don't know. But you just simply did it, and now it's part of your life, like a lot of other things. Bigger than other things, of course, but still," again she shrugs, "a single event."

"But wrong. Wicked. Evil. And cruel. That's the hardest part, that I was cruel."

"Cruel, yes, I suppose. Briefly, after all, for just a few minutes, surely, and you understand why. But wicked? Evil? I can't tell. I can't make words like that apply. Maybe because I know *you're* not wicked or evil. You do understand that, I hope? I certainly do." All this is true. She regards Claudia anxiously. "Do you see?"

"No. I don't know. I wish you were right, but it sounds too easy. Too light. It's appealing, I'd like to believe you, but it's so hard to tell. It *feels* all right, what you say, but my brain isn't easy about it. Or it's too tired to think it through some new way. I'm so tired, Char. I'm just exhausted. Would you mind if I went to bed now?"

"Of course not." But has Charlotte failed her?

Well, what could either of them expect? A story like that, right out of the blue – how could she come up with some conclusion that made it all go away, especially on the spur of the moment? At least her own secret had its funny aspects, at least they could make a mild joke of it. At her most amusing and brittle, Charlotte can't think of a way to make light of Claudia's tale.

But after all, Claudia appears to know; when they stand, she says, again, "Thank you," and Charlotte assumes the gratitude is for her effort, at least.

Anyway, this evening, this entire day, is merely another event; like Bradley's death. This could be quite a relaxing way to come to view many circumstances.

Claudia may sleep (how could she?), but Charlotte lies awake. It may be just something that happened, but Bradley's last moments of life replay over and over, vivid in her mind. If she has pity for so much terror, what does Claudia feel and see, having been there? Having been the instrument of terror?

But surely motives do matter. Vengeance, yes, but also just a matter of last straws: that Claudia, who had borne a great deal in the way of betrayals and lies, could simply not bear any more.

How *should* Charlotte see it? Shouldn't she be horrified? Shocked? Well, yes, but also she does seem to have convinced herself, if not necessarily Claudia, that it's a circumstance, admittedly a large one, among a great many years of circumstances, large and small, for both of them. A life ought to be sacred if anything is, but Charlotte has little feeling for Bradley himself; only for human fear. She spent her professional life making judgements about terror and cruelty, weighing the finest distinctions, but now it seems judgement may not always count. But if this were true, would anarchy not be the rule?

If no one knows, perhaps there is no rule. Only she and Claudia know. Only she and Claudia know a great many things. This one may be enormous, but the two of them hold their secrets well.

If it goes no farther, does it matter? It can hardly shatter a whole social order if nobody knows but the two of them. If, for that matter, only the two of them know about Charlotte and her spying, eavesdropping indulgences, her behaviour also has no larger, anarchic effect.

She finds this unconvincing. On the other hand, she finds she doesn't care, particularly.

She cares that she and Claudia know each other's goodnesses, and foolishnesses, and wickednesses. All of it. They are entirely safe, it seems to her, only with each other now.

. . . .

Claudia also lies awake for a while, replaying the ways Charlotte's expressions shifted. Claudia kept her eyes down as she told parts of her story, watching it happen again, so she could tell it properly, without lies or deflections. So she may have missed some reactions, but she does think that if judgement appeared on Charlotte's face, it must have been only briefly.

She finds she is angry with Bradley; in much the way she was annoyed when he came home and told her he had cancer. She is angry that the rest of her life, the entire span of her old age, will be tainted by that ending. That she is not ever going to be free of it. That it will always be with her, what she did. What he required her to do.

Did he? Was that last taunting really his bid for death? Did she end up carrying out more or less his true wish?

If he'd just asked her, said, "Please Claudia, I can't bear this, please put me out of my misery" – would she have?

She would have thought the burden too great, the risk of sin enormous. She didn't care for him enough to do so large a favour, if he'd asked. She would have thought, "No, I couldn't do such a thing and then have to think about it for the rest of my life."

The result, however, turns out to be much the same.

And after all, she does not believe it was some twisted, final wish of his. She believes he did not, ever, want to die. And he certainly wouldn't have wished such suffering on himself.

Well, then, she will have to live with that scene. She will also have to learn not to think of it in this movie-like way, as a scene. She will have to absorb it as her own true action.

Over the years, she has learned to absorb a good many drastic events. This is only different because it was her own drastic event, and not his.

Well, his too, of course, in a way. But it was her action, and that's quite a difference.

Telling it finally didn't make it smaller or less real. It may have made it easier, however. She won't ever tell another soul; won't spill it on her deathbed, wherever and whenever that might be, no matter how dazed or uncontrolled she is by then. She won't do to anyone else what Bradley did to her, telling distressing, evil secrets at the end.

No doubt she and Charlotte will speak of it again, though.

It may be that Charlotte's right: that once done, it's no longer a matter of decision or judgement, but simply an action; bigger and more drastic than Charlotte's secret, but not odder, necessarily. They have both, in their ways, been learning things about love of one sort and another, and it would be foolish for either of them to wonder if they should have done what they have done; any more than it would make sense to see once again the tall lean man standing against the sun at the bottom of her beach towel, so she couldn't see him clearly, and wonder if she should just have looked away.

Her home seems far away, both in time and space. Regarding it from this distance, and from the perspective of this soft, white-linened bed, it feels small and dark. That's not true – she did not feel cramped living there – but its spirit now seems, from this distance, small and dark.

Imagine going back! Stepping on the train; passing again through all those towns, past all those miles; taking a taxi back to that house; going up the walk, stepping up to the door, unlocking it and entering the hall, looking around at the rooms, the stairs – the darkness closes around her heart so it feels squeezed and hurt.

This house, Charlotte's, contains good sense and affection. When Claudia sleeps, there are no night visions, or nightmares. When she wakens, she doesn't remember even dreams. It does take her a moment to work out where she is, lying here under a white duvet in sunshine.

How will they look at each other, now that they know?

. . . .

Charlotte is already up, sitting at her kitchen table in a green plaid robe that falls around her ankles, her hands around a coffee mug, her hair dishevelled and uncombed. She looks, Claudia thinks, something like a witch. A good witch: one powerful enough to put evil in its place.

"Coffee?" Charlotte asks.

"Yes, please. You been up long?"

"A little while. I've been thinking." She sounds very serious. Claudia's hands, lifting her own coffee cup, tremble slightly: what if, after all, Charlotte has thought, "I don't want a torturer, a killer in my home"? Claudia thinks how strange it is, that she could bear a dead husband, but not a lost friend.

But. "I was wondering," Charlotte is saying, "how you're going to feel going back. I was wondering if you'd rather not. So I was thinking, what would you say to moving here?"

"What?" Claudia is sure she has heard wrong, or is making words up. Charlotte couldn't have said that.

Or perhaps she did. She looks quite hurt – Claudia may have answered too sharply. And quickly. "To this house, you mean?" she asks. "With you?" She still doesn't have the tone right. Charlotte shakes her head.

"Never mind. Sorry. I expect it was a stupid idea."

"No, please, are you serious? Come on, Charlotte, tell me."

"Well. It's only, I thought it would be cheaper for both of us, for one thing. But also it might keep us from driving ourselves

crazy. You wouldn't have to be off brooding in that house on your own, and I wouldn't get frightened or tempted by foolishness. I can see getting brave again, instead of ridiculous. I can see us *doing* things."

Claudia feels vaguely that if she did this, she would be avoiding the punishment that going back would involve. She would find herself back there watching that last scene with Bradley over and over, making herself suffer to suit her crime. In her mind, Bradley, who was so little in that house until the last year, now fills it up accusingly.

Imagine not having to go back!

Could she? Could she avoid even going back to sell and pack? She could ask the girls to do that for her, couldn't she? Is there anything she wouldn't want them to see, sorting through all those years of possessions? But the only secret isn't written down, and doesn't show up anywhere.

"Claudia? Is it such a bad idea? Do you think we wouldn't get along? Would it be too hard to give up your home? Was I being stupid?" Charlotte is looking at her anxiously.

Claudia smiles. "That wasn't what I was thinking at all. I was thinking, what a relief. What a blessing, to have such a hope." She could just weep with hope.

Charlotte leans forward, hands around her coffee cup. "We could share. I mean, you could have anything here that you like. I'd get rid of some of my stuff to make room for some of yours."

"I can't think of anything. Although maybe I will. But nothing big. Everything I own feels past. That isn't possible, is it? I won't get rid of it all that easily?"

"No, likely not." Charlotte smiles.

"You thought all this out this morning?"

"Do you know, I didn't, really. I woke up with it, I woke up thinking everything was solved, this was what we must do.

And now that I'm really awake, and I've had my coffee, it still seems right. But I realize I've just thrown it at you."

Claudia looks at Charlotte intently. "There is one thing, though."

"What?"

"Do you think you can trust me? Do you think there might be times when you'd look at me and wonder what I might do? You know what I've already done. Will you be able not to worry?"

Charlotte's expression gets quite peculiar. Claudia can't define it, except it looks as if Charlotte is struggling for control. And then suddenly she gives up, leans back, her head tilts back, her mouth opens, and she is laughing. Peels and hoots of laughter. Claudia is shocked. "What's so funny? Charlotte, what are you laughing at?"

"Oh, Claudie. You and I skulking around this house, kind of sidling around each other. Me wary all the time in case you try to sneak up on me with a needle. In case you decide I need to be put out of my misery. Oh, Claudie!" and she howls again.

Claudia can't help it – Charlotte's right, it's such a picture! She giggles herself, and then starts to laugh, and finally the two of them are rocking, tears rolling down their faces, and except that those faces are lined now, and their hair has changed colours and their bodies are differently shaped, it's just like children, little girls again, laughing helplessly for reasons they can't quite identify. "Oh my," Charlotte gasps, hands on her heart, "that's hard on the system. I hurt!" Her eyes narrow. "But don't be thinking I hurt *too* much. I don't want to be put down yet." And off they go again, until they're breathless.

"I'll have to phone the girls," Claudia says finally. "Make arrangements. They'll think I've gone crazy."

"Will they?"

Perhaps not. They know more than Claudia previously gave them credit for.

"Are you sure about this, Charlotte? This is your home, after all. You're used to being on your own."

Charlotte shrugs. "I seem to be sure. The way I see it, it'll be sort of like a marriage, only without the sex."

"Without some of the troubles, too," Claudia says crisply.

"Although I'm sure we'll have troubles, we'll have to expect that. Only we're friends, so we should be able to iron them out."

"I wish I'd married a friend." Did that sound bitter? Claudia doesn't want to start hearing bitterness in her own voice.

"Some people do, I guess. Get both, I mean. We just didn't happen to, that's all. Still, I wouldn't have missed any of it for the world. I still miss love – is that strange? I miss making love, and those beautiful bodies. Foreign parts."

"Me, too. But."

"But, indeed."

"Charlotte!"

"What?"

"Thank you. It's nice anyway, ending up with a friend." She pauses. "And Charlotte?"

"What?"

"I'm ravenous. Famished. Is there something to eat? And then I'll take you out for lunch. Do you get a newspaper? You'll have to show me where you shop, so I can do my share. Were you doing anything in particular today? Maybe we could see what's on at the movies. I haven't been to one for ages. I miss movie popcorn, too. I wonder if I should call the girls?"

Well. It's going to take some getting used to. "This feels a bit like the first day of school," Charlotte says. "When we met." She means, it seems to have no end in sight.

Arlene Blanchard and Tony Wells are the parents of two grown children. They collect antique toys and children's books and write books for children as a team.

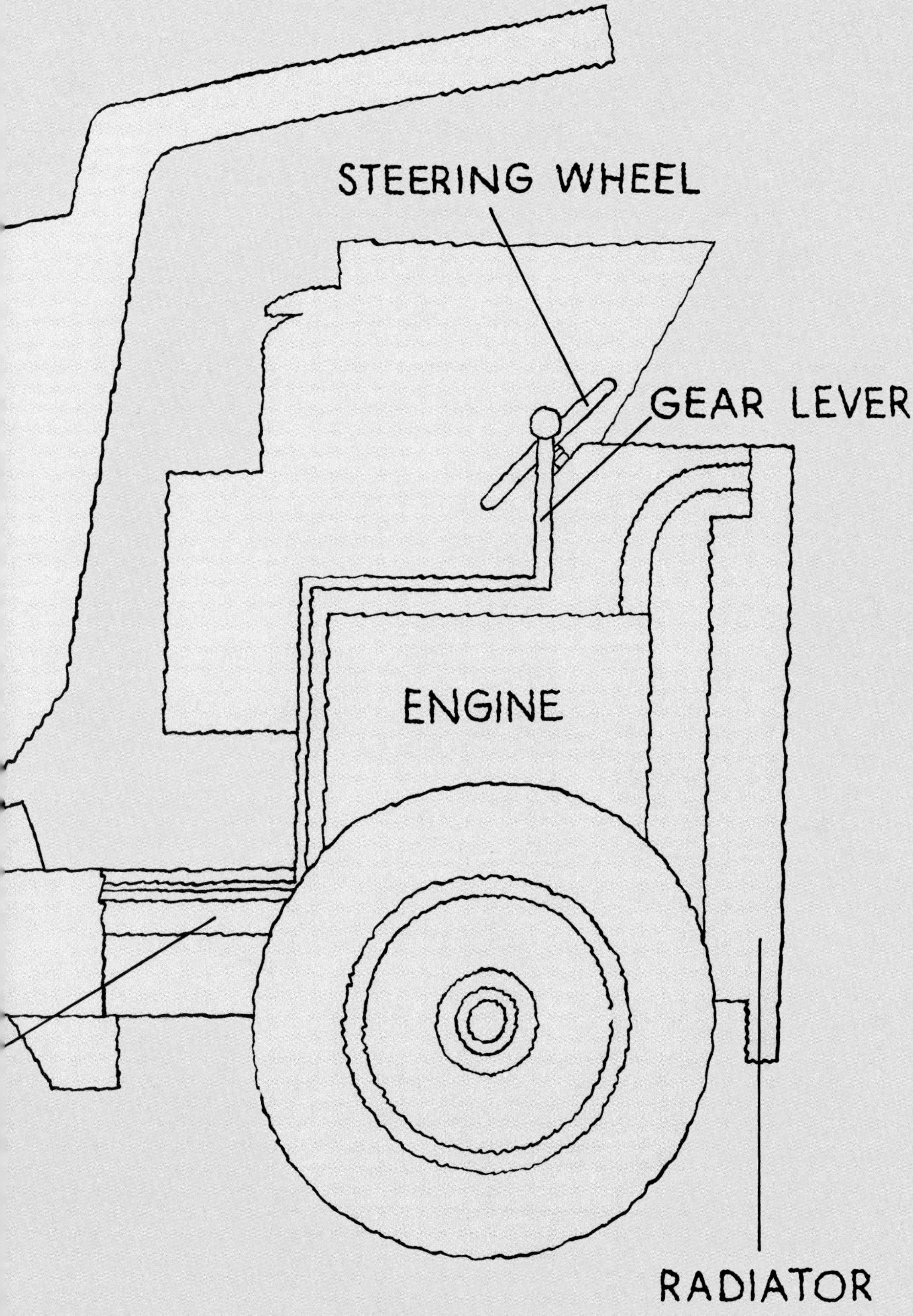
STEERING WHEEL
GEAR LEVER
ENGINE
RADIATOR

DUMP TRUCK

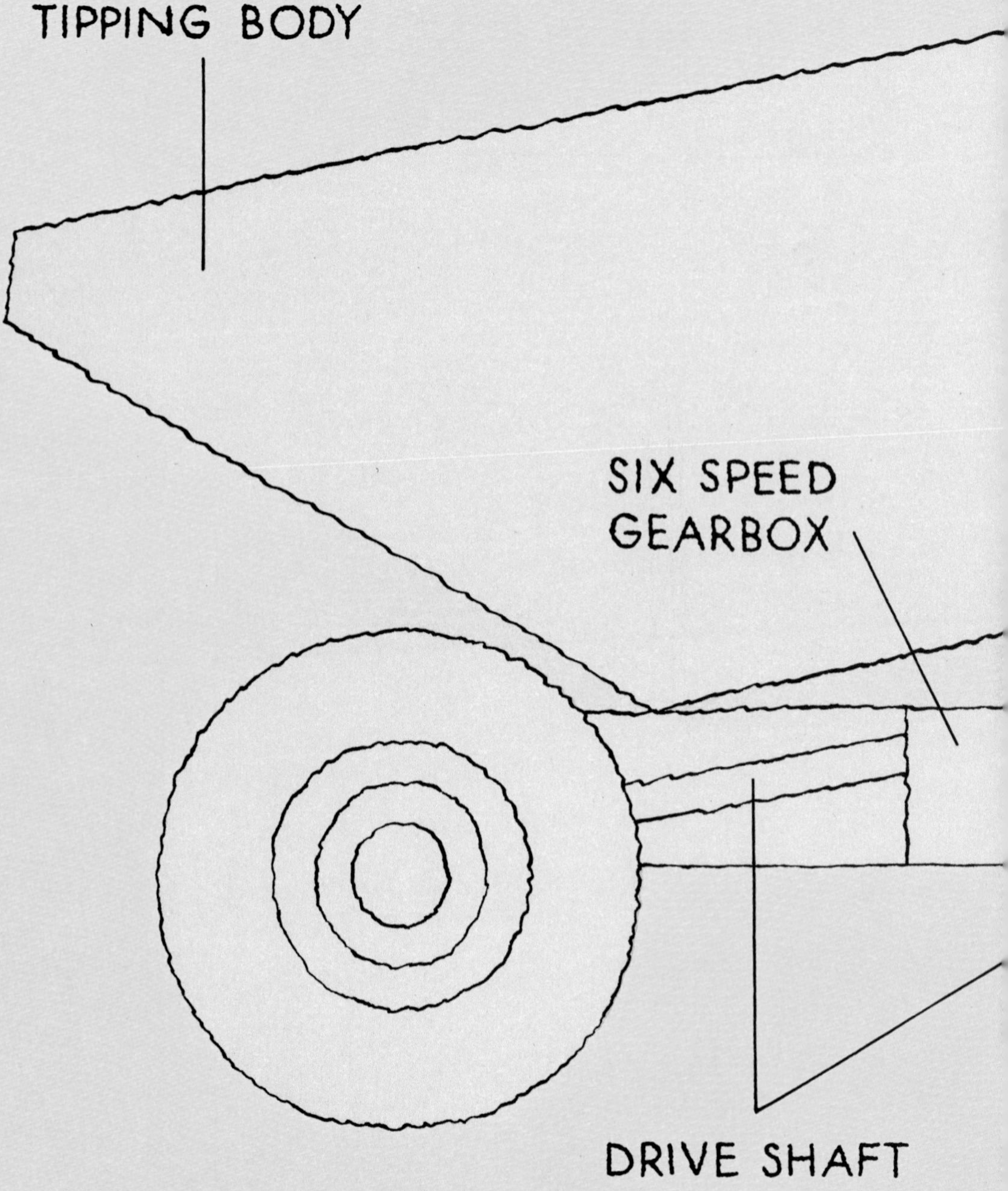
TIPPING BODY
SIX SPEED GEARBOX
DRIVE SHAFT

"Fine," says Ben. "With a dump truck like this one to drive, I feel on top of the world!"

Fred comes to tell Ben it is time for a break. “Come and eat,” he says. “How do you like the job?”

The smaller dump trucks are loaded one by one. They drive away, taking the stones to people who need them.

Inside the cab Ben pulls a lever.
The back of the truck tilts up.
The stones pour out.

Now Ben drives to another part of the quarry where smaller dump trucks wait to load.

Ben drives his dump truck underneath the hopper. *Whoosh!* The back fills up with stones.

Swoosh! Rattle! Crash! Into the chute! *Rumble! Clatter! Grind!* The crusher's jaws chomp the rocks into little stones.

When the truck is full, Ben drives back across the quarry. He backs up and empties his load into the crusher.

Fred mops his brow with a polka-dotted handkerchief. “That was a close call,” he says. “Good job, Ben!”

Bit by bit the huge wheels start to grip.
Ben sighs with relief. The dump truck
is crawling up the slope.

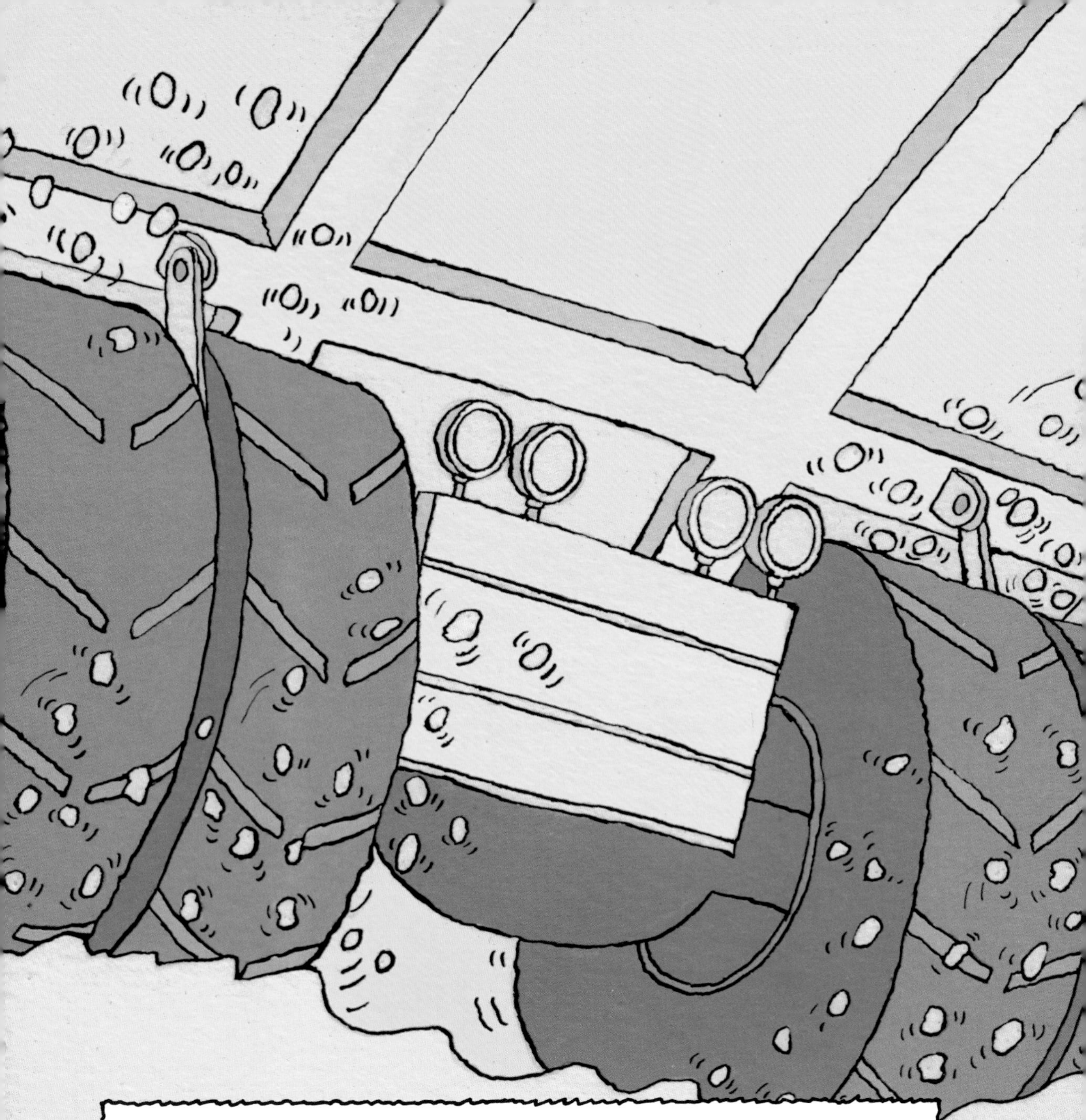

Ben feels the dump truck slide.
“Easy does it,” he says, and he slips
the engine into the lowest gear.

Ben drives slowly—oh, so slowly! The slope goes up and up. The ground is very loose. The wheels begin to spin.

Ben looks at the slope. It is very steep.
“Okay,” says Ben. He hopes he can.

"The next pile is up that slope," says Fred. "Can you take your truck up there?"

The arm swings up and over.
Crash! Clatter! Bang! go the rocks
into the metal back of the dump truck.

The big power shovel's bucket scoops into a pile of rock. *Brrrm!* goes the engine. *Screech!* goes the arm.

Ben leans out of the cab. “Hi!” he calls back. “I’m Ben.” They have to shout above the noise of the machines.

Ben stops by the big red power shovel.
"Hi!" calls the man in the power shovel.
"I'm Fred. We work together."

Ben drives carefully across the quarry. The ground is rough and stony, but the big dump truck doesn't mind.

In the cab Ben feels as tall as a giant.
He starts the engine. It roars strongly.
But in the cab, it is quiet.

I've never driven one as big as this before, Ben thinks. *Well, here goes!*

Ben looks at the huge machine.
The wheels are as high as his head.

He tells Ben, "This is our new dump truck, and you are going to drive it."

It is Ben's first day at his new job.
"Welcome to the quarry," says Jim,
the foreman in charge.

The Dump Truck

Arlene Blanchard
illustrated by Tony Wells

CANDLEWICK PRESS
CAMBRIDGE, MASSACHUSETTS

First U.S. edition 1995

Library of Congress Cataloging-in-Publication Data

Blanchard, Arlene.
The dump truck / Arlene Blanchard ;
illustrated by Tony Wells.—1st U.S. ed.
Summary: Ben learns to operate a new dump truck
on the first day of his new job at the quarry.
ISBN 1-56402-506-3
[1. Dump trucks—Fiction. 2. Trucks—Fiction.]
I. Wells, Tony, ill. II. Title.
PZ7.B592Du 1995
[E]—dc20 94-25704

2 4 6 8 10 9 7 5 3 1

Printed in Hong Kong

The pictures in this book were done in gouache and ink.

Candlewick Press
2067 Massachusetts Avenue
Cambridge, Massachusetts 02140

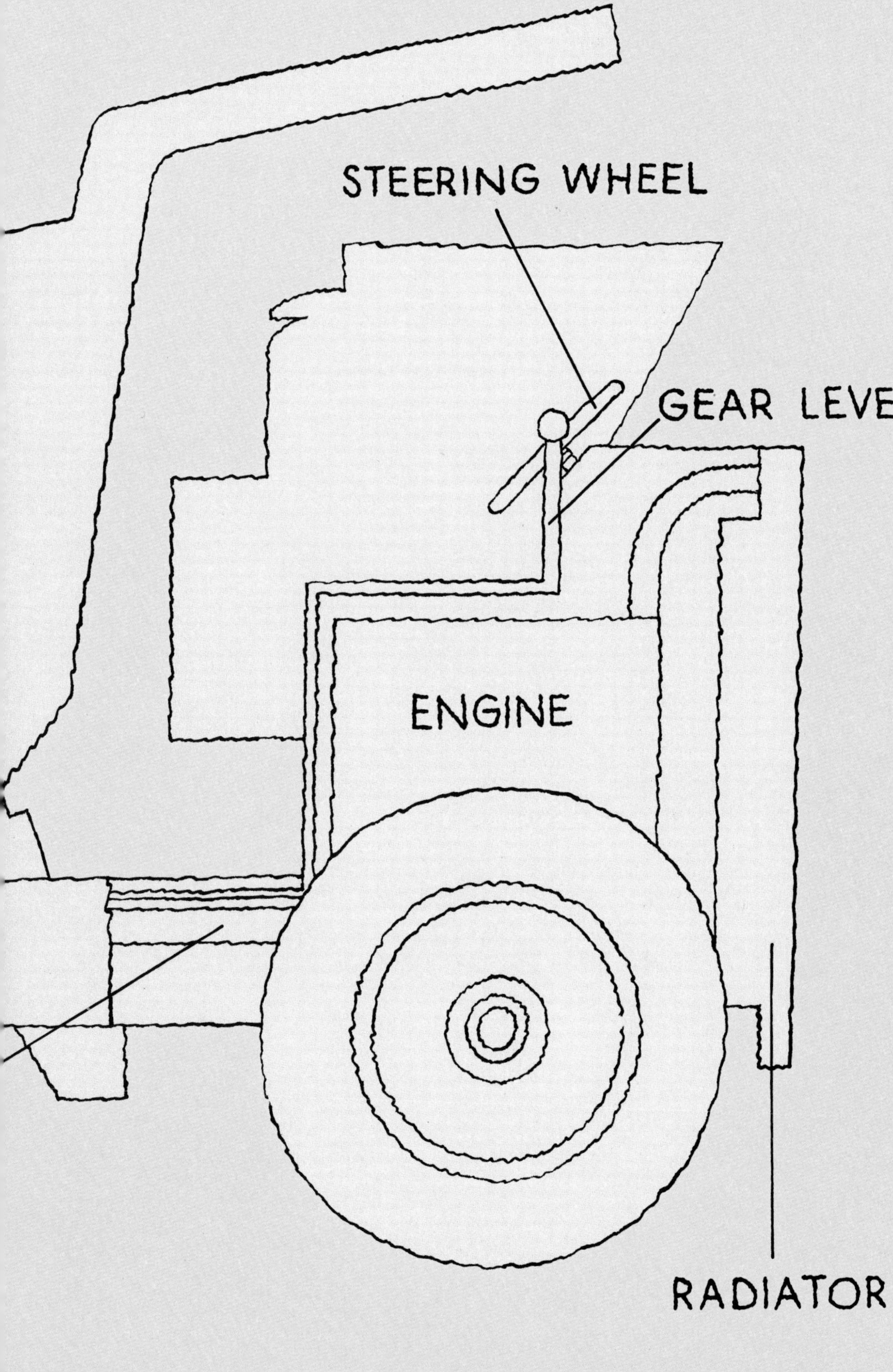
STEERING WHEEL
GEAR LEVER
ENGINE
RADIATOR

DUMP TRUCK

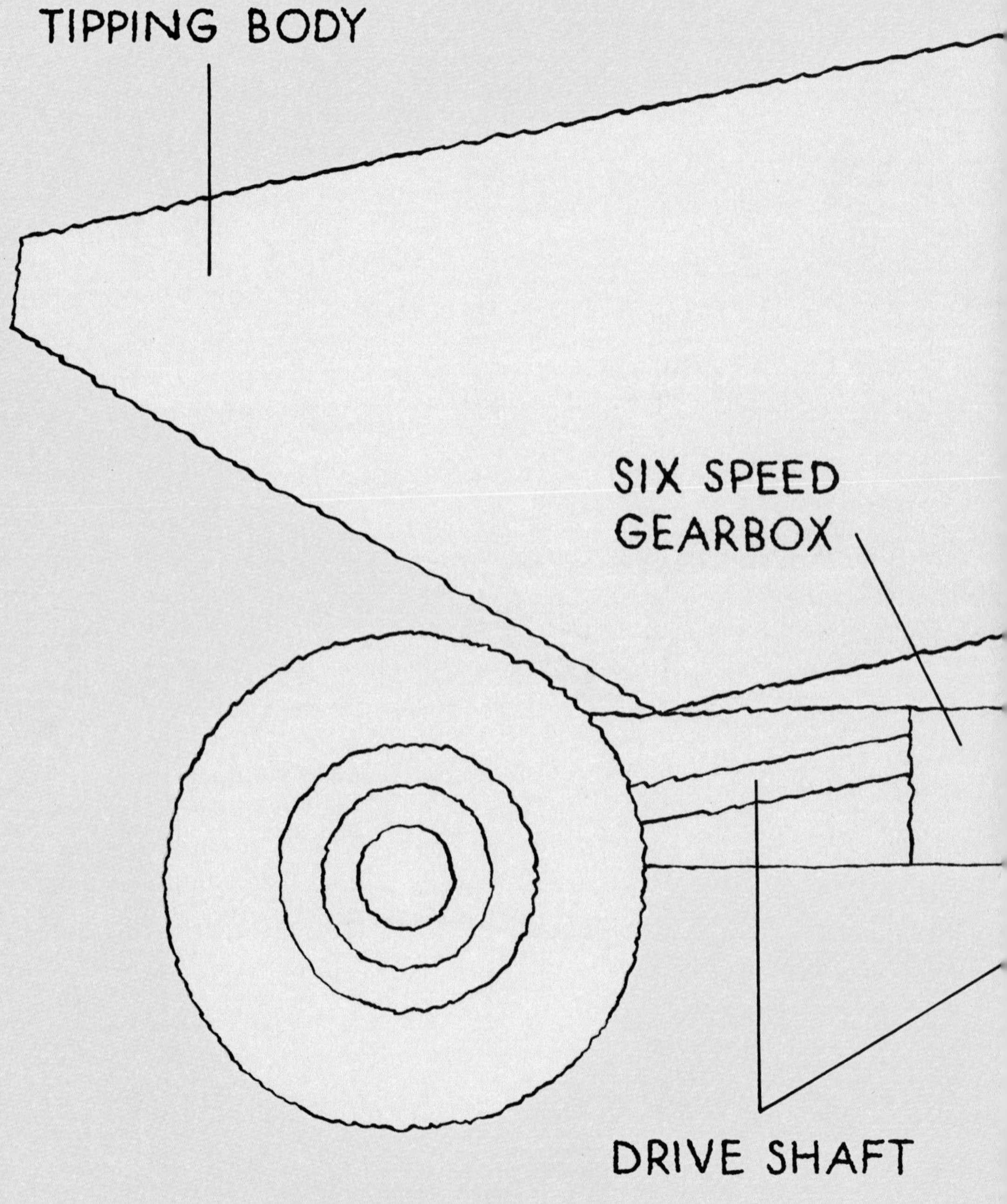

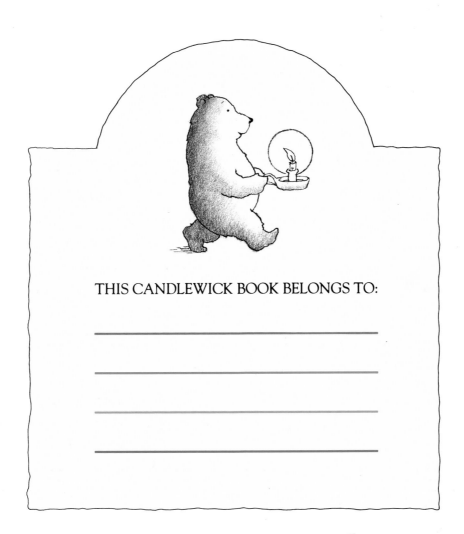

THIS CANDLEWICK BOOK BELONGS TO: